Under Pressure

Redwood Ridge 5

Kelly Moran

To Jim,
Thank you for protecting
& serving your wonderful
county, and for being such
a loyal friend to Bradly.
He's watching over you &
smiling.
Kelly
Moran
xo

Cover Art Design by: Kelly Moran
Photo Credit: Adobe Images

ISBN: 9780463933077
Smashwords eBook Edition
Published in the United States of America

Praise for Kelly Moran's Books:

"Breathes life into an appealing story."
Publishers Weekly

"Readers will fall in love."
Romantic Times

"Great escape reading."
Library Journal

"Touching & gratifying."
Kirkus Reviews

"Sexy, heart-tugging fun."
USA Today HEA

"Emotional & totally engaging."
Carla Neggers

"A gem of a writer."
Sharon Sala

"I read in one sitting."
Carly Phillips

"Compelling characters."
Roxanne St. Claire

"A sexy, emotional romance."
Kim Karr

"An emotionally raw story. A compelling read."
Katie Ashley

"I devoured the book!"
Laura Kaye

Dedicated with love and remembrance to:
Brady "BK" Keith Davis
1957-2019
Devoted husband, loving father, loyal friend, cherished brother, and dedicated police officer. He spent his entire career protecting and serving his community in various forms of law enforcement before passing away from ALS. He was loved and respected by many, and will be greatly missed by all.

And for Jacki, who's been one of my closest, dearest friends for twenty years. She makes me laugh and lets me cry and never, ever allows me think I can't do something. She is one gorgeous, kind, smart, amazing person. The world needs more people like her. Until this year, she's been too afraid to read one of my books in case she didn't like them, despite me telling her I wouldn't be hurt. She finally lost her "book virginity" to my Redwood Ridge series. Now she demands I write more. Go figure. (Sigh of relief). Jacki, I'm so glad you took the plunge and cracked the binding. Love you to the moon and back.

Chapter 1

Parker Maloney tilted his head back and glared at the cobalt sky, so bright, it seared his retinas. Not a cloud in sight.

Leaves on the maples and oaks lining the private suburban street were changing to red and orange, marking a beautiful transition. Some already littered the road and sidewalks, despite the Indian Summer that blasted their small postage stamp of a town. The early morning fog that often plagued their little pocket between the Klamath Mountains and the Pacific had dissipated by afternoon, leaving nothing but the scent of brine for its trouble. A morning dove cooed and crickets chirped and a soft breeze stirred the grass.

This day was turning to shit. Literally.

"Her mutt poo-pooed in my yard, Parker. Do something."

Case in point. Literal shit.

What he should do was arrest the thirty-three year old housewife for saying the word "poo-poo" as if he was supposed to take her seriously after that. Mrs. Granger had been a few years ahead of him in school and a pretentious snob even back then. Some things never changed, he supposed. Her strawberry blonde mane was neatly coifed, her makeup reminiscent of Pennywise, and her red fingernails were just shy of Krueger. She was also glaring at him as if he were a peon.

"Don't you dare call my baby a mutt. Cersei is a pure bred Springer Spaniel, thank you very much." This from Mrs. Edgewater, who was more his speed wearing her messy brown hair up in a clip, sweats, and a tee with a coffee cup on it. She and her husband were recent transplants from Seattle.

"Whatever. You named her after the most hated character in *Game of Thrones*. That says it all."

Score one for Mrs. Granger.

"At least my dog doesn't look like something a cat coughed up."

And Mrs. Edgewater for the knock-out blow.

While the two women bickered, Parker sighed. He glanced from the accused canine in question, sitting next to her owner, calm as you please, not a strand of black and white fur ruffling, to the brown Chihuahua in the other owner's arms, growling and snarling and wiggling like it was actually a threat, not the size of a walnut.

Some days it just didn't pay to get out of bed. He'd gotten a lot of mundane, ridiculous calls in the three years he'd been Redwood Ridge's sheriff, not accounting for the seven prior as an officer, but this dispatch came close to taking the cake. Then again, a sleepy ideal town with eighteen-hundred residents didn't have much crime. Dog poop aside, of course.

This matter was obviously very important to the two parties involved, which meant it had to become important to him. It was his job and he took it seriously, even if he was the only one sometimes.

"Ladies," he said calmly, holding up his hands for peace. Blessedly, they quit sparring. "Why don't you show me the evidence in question and we can talk this out."

And there went any signs of salvaging his self respect on this call. Bye-bye. Adios. Carried off by one of the frenetic squirrels foraging in preparation for winter.

Chihuahua Owner nodded emphatically. "Yes, please. Come see for yourself."

He couldn't wait.

Following the women between their small white ranch homes, he kept his gaze on the pristinely cut lawn so he wouldn't step in future evidence. They came to a stop in the backyard on what had to be the exact marker for property lines.

"See? I left the proof."

He glanced where she pointed at pile of...well, shit. It was shit all right. A *small* pile. In fact, it appeared too small to have come from the Springer Spaniel. He had a rescued Dalmatian at home, his loyal bud for three years now, who was about the same size as the accused. Domino's dumps were twice this size.

Unable to believe he was examining the measurements of canine feces, he looked at the Spaniel's owner. "You don't happen to have an example in your backyard of..." He waved his hand at the poop.

"Sure. I didn't scoop this morning yet." She moved a few steps away and gestured at the grass to a much larger dump.

That's what he thought. He faced the Chihuahua owner and cleared his throat. "Her dog's..." Hesitating, he rolled his head on his neck. "*Poo-poo* is more sizable than the pile you showed me."

Such a great detective he was. Someone issue him a medal. Stat.

"That's it? You're not going to do anything?"

"I'm afraid there's nothing to do. May I suggest putting up a fence between the properties or a row of bushes? Maybe it'll resolve the conflict of whose dog is where." Separation of church and state. Thus, no more *shitty* calls to his station.

"Unbelievable!"

He agreed, and turned to leave with a respectful wave.

"I'm gonna complain to the mayor about this." She stomped her foot, causing the dog in her arms to mimic something close to a seizure. "She'll hear all about it from me."

He nodded, doing his level best to tame an impending grin. Marie, mayor of Redwood Ridge, was one of three women often referred to as The Battleaxes. Her and her two sisters ruled this town with an iron fist and matchmaking with a side of oatmeal cookies. They'd set up countless couples through the years, his best friend Jason being their latest casualty. Parker's sister, Paige, was Marie's personal assistant. It was exceedingly rare for her to dispute him on any police matter.

Because he was good at his job.

"That's well within your rights to do so." He waved again. "I'm sorry I couldn't be of more help. You ladies have a wonderful day. Lovely weather we're having."

He strode to his PD-issued dark blue Charger at the curb and climbed behind the wheel. Glaring at the radio, he hesitated picking up the mic. He could all but hear his officers at the station laughing like hyenas.

Another sigh, and he snatched the mic. Why not? If you can't beat 'em… "Curtain is closed on the shit show. En route to the station before they decide on an encore."

The radio crackled and multiple rounds of laughter emitted a good ten seconds before Sherry, their dispatcher, answered. "Ten-four. Were there any victims, sir? Perhaps a fan as it was hit?"

He rolled his eyes at the pun. "Negative."

His cell rang and he tilted his phone on the passenger seat to read the screen. Paige. His sister didn't typically call during the day. Swiping, he answered while turning the volume down on the CB to drown out the chuckles.

"Hey, sorry to bug you, but I have a problem. Two problems, actually."

That was him. Solver of problems. "What's wrong?"

"I think Marie is up to something."

He grunted. "This is the mayor and head Battleaxe we're talking about. She's always up to something."

"Well, I think this time it involves me. I suspect I'm their next matchmaking victim."

It took everything in him, but he didn't laugh. People of Redwood Ridge always referred to themselves as victims when they were found in the path of Cupid's arrow, wielded by the sisters. They ran. They hid. They resisted. In the end, they succumbed.

He was the sheriff. He got around. He saw and heard things most didn't. And the truth was, not a solitary "victim" was unhappy after The Battleaxes were through with them. He had to bow to the women. Absurd as the matches appeared and odds seemingly not in the couples' favor, they wound up with their soul mates. He should be so lucky. The trio were single-handedly lowering the depression rate. It was uncanny.

And Paige? She could use a little happiness in her life. Her douche canoe ex-boyfriend had bolted when she'd told him she was pregnant. She'd given him two choices. Stay and raise their daughter or leave and don't come back. He'd picked the second option. That had been almost eight years ago. Since then, she'd dated here and there, but nothing serious until…

Wait a second. "I thought you and Erik were seeing each other." Erik ran the kitchen at Shooters. He and his sister, Emma Jane, had taken over the bar when their uncle retired. First time Parker recalled Paige mentioning Erik's name had been early this summer.

"We are! Thus, the problem. We've moved from casual to committed. I can't be set up with someone else."

Parker pinched the bridge of his nose. "If Marie knows you're dating someone, she wouldn't interfere."

"Oh yeah? Then why did she ask me to stay late tonight?"

"It's not that unusual for her to—"

"Rearrange her office. She wants me to stay late to *rearrange her office*, Parker. She said she needed to *feng shui*. She hasn't changed so much as a paperweight in the seven years I've been her assistant."

That did sound sort of suspicious. Marie was meticulous about not overworking her staff, even during re-election years. Plus, Paige was not a creative person. Hell, when she'd bought her cozy two-bedroom down the road from Mom and Dad, Parker had been the one to pick out furniture and wall color. On *her* insistence.

"I got nothing, sis. Sorry." He briefly cranked the CB volume to make certain the station wasn't trying to radio him. They were still cracking up and joking at his expense. He sighed and turned it back down again.

"What was that?"

"A hazardous contagion known as laughing stock."

"What?"

"Nothing." He leaned his head against the seat. "I'd just mention to Marie you're still dating Erik. It'll blow over. What's your other dilemma? You said you had two."

"Problem one bleeds into problem two. Can you pick up Katie from school? I wasn't expecting to work late so I didn't book her a spot at the Rec Center. Marie suggested I call you when I tried to wheedle out of tonight. Which is also weird."

That *was* strange for Marie to offer his services in such a manner. Katie was Paige's daughter and Parker's favorite person on Earth. He spent a lot of time with his niece, but he couldn't ever recall Marie trying to unload her on him.

Regardless…"Now that is an easy fix. Yes, I can…" He glanced at his watch. "School's out in five minutes." He'd never get across town in time.

"Her teacher said she'd stay with her until you got there. She's grading quizzes anyway." Paige paused, and he could tell by the length of it she was still frustrated. "Sorry for the late notice. Mom and Dad are on that cruise and Erik's already at work for the night shift. I don't know how long I'll be. Last time I had to rearrange furniture was never."

Grinning, he put on his seatbelt and connected Bluetooth. "Relax. I got this. She can spend the night at my place." His guest room was catered to his niece for just such occasions. He checked his blind spot and pulled away. "Don't go moving anything too heavy on your own."

"I won't. Thanks, Parker."

"Thank me after I overdose her on sugar and send her home."

"Payback's a bitch." Papers shuffled in the background. "Luckily, I love you."

"Love you harder. Have fun."

After a few muttered curses, she disconnected and he radioed the station to let them know he was signing off. The hysterics had apparently ended because Sherry's voice was back to its chipper, pleasant tone and the hyenas were absent in the background.

He drove out of the subdivision and down Main Street's cobblestone road at a snail's pace. Lampposts were decorated with cornstalks and pumpkins while the flower boxes held mums of varying colors. Residents waved to him from awning-covered storefronts and he nodded hello from behind the wheel.

They were the same people he'd grown up with, same sights and sounds and scents. Little had changed since he was a boy. Some faces had aged, others were seemingly untouched by time, and a few were new, but the idealistic town mentality remained. The Ridge took care of its own. All one had to do was ask, and a hundred hands would show up to offer assistance.

Parents could let their children play freely, roam and explore as kids were meant to do. Everyone knew everybody's name, backstory, and each other's business. One person's grief, accomplishments, or happiness were not just theirs. They were everyone's. Privacy was more of a smokescreen, confidentiality an illusion. Gossip was a way of life, the fuel that kept the torches burning. If he were to so much as sneeze, ten Tupperware bowls of soup would pop onto his front porch. All homemade and still warm from the pot.

Yes, at times, there were closed minds. Yet, here, humanity wasn't merely a word in the dictionary.

There was nowhere else he'd rather be, not a thing he'd change. Once, he'd briefly tended the notion of moving to a larger city, seeking more action. That had lasted point-seven seconds. There might be adventure beyond the town limits, but he'd take the safety of ordinary and the sense of family over adrenaline any day of the week, and twice on Sundays.

He turned into the elementary school's nearly empty lot and climbed out. A wave of nostalgia smacked him in the face despite the number of times he'd been here since his school days or he'd picked up Katie. The one-story brick building faced East to start every morning, and the interior forever smelled like glue and chalk.

Around back was the playground, not visible from the lot, where he and Jason had wreaked havoc on the teachers by doing pranks. He'd had his first kiss at age fourteen under those monkey bars. A dare by other kids, of course.

Madeline Freemont. He smiled. Now there was a name he hadn't thought about in a long time. He wondered what made him conjure her now. She had been an adorable blonde-haired, blue-eyed terror as a girl. And by terror, he meant the very word and meaning had been cited after her. She'd stolen his hat at recess and run off with it. Every day. She'd teased him relentlessly with taunts and petty insults. She'd kicked his seat in class. For hours. All that aside, the kiss had been swift, sweet, and merciful. Everything she wasn't.

Shaking his head and wiping away the stray memory, he yanked open the front door and stepped inside the building. His shoes squeaked as he strode through the front entry, past the office, and down the hallway toward his niece's first grade class.

Peeking in the room, he spotted the teacher at her desk, papers and a red pen in hand, and Katie on a play mat in a corner with a plastic tea set. "Knock, knock."

"Uncle Parker!" Katie launched to her feet, ran across the short distance, and leapt into his arms.

Grinning, he stared at her vivid green eyes and wavy black hair, cut just past her shoulders. Both were Maloney family characteristics on his dad's side, but those round cheeks and smile were all his mom's. Infectious little devil. A pang reverberated behind his ribs as he held her to him. He wanted a litter of tiny humans just like her one day. Alas, he hadn't met the right woman yet. He'd come close, but not quite. Though he desired a family of his own, settling wouldn't do anyone any good.

"What's up, bratty-cake?" A nickname he'd given her as a baby, a twist on the game because she'd loved patty cake. She wasn't fond of the moniker so much nowadays.

She rolled her eyes, looking more and more like Paige by the second. "Just waiting to go home."

He laughed. "How about you go home with me tonight? I require your assistance with Domino. The poor dog keeps going on and on about how he misses you. I can't stand it anymore."

"Mom has to work late, huh?"

He rested his forehead to hers and chuckled. "That, too. But I'm serious about the dog. All day and night, it's Katie this and Katie that."

Up went her brows. "Dogs can't talk."

"How do you know? Maybe he's really smart and keeping it under wraps."

"He drinks out of the toilet and chases his tail. I don't think so."

That earned a laugh from her teacher.

He waved over Katie's shoulder to the young, fresh-out-of-college brunette. It was her first year on the job. The students seemed to really like her. She'd left Redwood Ridge for college in Washington, but like a lot of others, she'd returned to her roots. "How are you, Ms. Reilly? Thanks for staying until I could get here."

"Oh, no trouble. She's a sweetheart."

"Pfft." He looked at his niece. "You've got her fooled."

"I'm charming." She shrugged. "Everyone says so."

He tilted his head back and laughed. Straight from the gut and erasing all tension from his day. Damn, but did he love her to no end. Seven-years-old, going on seventeen. He feared the day she started dating. "That you are. Ready to go? Get your backpack so we can let Ms. Reilly head home."

As he set Katie on her feet, a woman stepped into the room wearing gray coveralls and pulled up short, a broom in her hand. Wide, familiar blue eyes rounded to saucers as she glanced from Ms. Reilly to him and back again.

Speak of the devil.

"Maddie?" Damn. How crazy he'd just been thinking about her on the way in, and here she was in the flesh. And...in a janitor's uniform? "You work here?" Since when? And why? She was a trust fund brat. Hell, at one point, before the scandal, her family had owned half this town. She'd rarely let anyone forget it, either.

She ducked her head, causing the knot of blonde hair on her head to shift, and avoided eye contact. "Hey, Parker. Long time, no see."

Understatement. Last he'd heard, she'd been living upstate after college. Then again, that had been three years ago when her father and fiancé had been sentenced. When the hell had she returned? And how had it slipped past his notice?

Before he could drill her with questions, she whipped her attention to the desk. "I'm so sorry to intrude, Ms. Reilly. I thought everyone was done for the day. I'll come back."

The teacher opened her mouth, but quickly snapped it shut when Maddie disappeared from the room as fast as she'd arrived.

"I've tried being friendly to her, but she just ignores me." Ms. Reilly sighed and dropped her chin in her hand. "I know she's not supposed to socialize with the staff, but running away is kind of extreme."

All right. Somehow, he'd landed in an alternate dimension. The Maddie Freemont he knew and—frankly, feared—didn't run from anyone or anything. She didn't lower her head to avoid engagement, didn't take jobs she'd consider beneath her, and she'd never, ever be seen in public without her hair and makeup done with flawless precision.

"I didn't realize she was back in town. I barely recognized her."

"How the mighty have fallen." Ms. Reilly straightened papers. "I never believed she had anything to do with her father's scam, but I'm in the minority. The only way the school board would hire her was under a permanent trial basis. One misstep, and she's gone. That's about all I know, other than she's been a custodian for nearly three years."

"Three…" He choked. "Three years?" And he'd had no clue? Now, granted, he didn't know every single tidbit of info in town, but certainly he'd recall gossip about a Freemont within the borders. "As a janitor?"

Not that there was anything wrong with the profession. Of course not. Hard work was hard work. It was a respectable job. But when a woman like Maddie, who'd mocked the custodians when she'd been a student, took such a position, he had a serious case of WTF brewing.

"From what I hear, it's the only job she could get. She needed the money and all but begged in her interview to be hired."

No way, no how. Sure, gossip often held a smidgen of the truth, but God Himself coming down from On High and telling Parker this version of the story would come off as bogus.

Frowning, he glanced at the teacher, then his niece. Maybe he'd make a little pitstop before heading to his car.

Chapter 2

"Kids are disgusting creatures."

Rubber-gloved hands on her hips, Maddie Freemont glanced at the rows of urinals in one of two boys' bathrooms inside the elementary school and shook her head. It didn't matter how often she cleaned and disinfected, it chronically smelled like urine. Could be because the hit or miss phrase tended to miss more than hit.

She'd attempted once before to get the principal to order air freshener that scented every time someone flushed, but the woman wouldn't allow it. According to her, if Maddie was doing her job correctly, then air freshener wouldn't be needed.

Whatever. She sprayed cleaner over the tile and urinals. While that sat for a minute and soaked in, she moved into the stalls and dumped toilet bowl solution into the tanks. And, lovely. The last stall had a present just for her.

Grabbing the plunger from her rollaway cart, she went to work pumping. She swore, *gurgle, whoosh-whoosh* was the most vile sound in the history of ever. Luckily, the tank drained rather quickly and she finished cleaning the toilets.

On her hands and knees, she scrubbed urinals, and the brief exchange with Parker in the classroom from a mere ten minutes ago slammed to mind. Heat scoured her cheeks and her hand holding the sponge shook.

The last time she'd seen him had been at the courthouse in Portland during the sentencing phase. His father had been sheriff then. After logging numerous complaints by townsfolk, Mr. Maloney had brought in the Feds. Parker hadn't been a part of the investigation at all, yet he'd been in court in support of his father and Redwood Ridge residents who'd been scammed out of hundreds of thousands of dollars.

She'd been in her fourth year of college and had wound up dropping out during the whirlwind. She'd intended to go back and finish one day, but that day had never come. Though it had taken the FBI a few years to build a case, and her fiancé David and her Daddy had the best attorneys, they'd pleaded guilty to avoid a trial. They'd said because the evidence had been too damning.

A day. Thirty-eight months of them reiterating to her and insisting they were innocent, and in *a day* her world had crashed into oblivion. She'd stupidly, blindly believed them, that they couldn't possibly have done what everyone had said. The kicker? She'd found out about their plea deal in court with the general public.

Her last memory of walking out of the courthouse was Parker Maloney, hands in his suit pockets, sun at his back, solemnly watching her.

Today, he'd stared at her with shock and awe, pity heavy on the undercurrent.

Every second of every hour she was reminded of her place. Where she'd come from and where she'd landed. The two worlds were night and day. She had nothing to call her own and not so much as a soul to bitch to about the circumstances. She'd learned to live with it, had even accepted her fate.

But one encounter, one glance at Saint Parker Maloney, and her mind backtracked to a place so dark, it was hard to recall what light had once looked like. Shame that shouldn't be and wasn't hers to own had filled her until it seeped from her pores.

She'd done her level best to avoid him and stay off his radar since moving back to town. It appeared as if her luck on that account had run out. Which meant she had none. She could handle townsfolk talking behind her back, to her face, or the way they treated her with hatred and contempt. But there was something especially devastating about the first boy she'd crushed on viewing her the way the world did.

As if she were nothing. A liar. A thief. Worth less than the gum they scraped off their shoes.

Footsteps squeaked in the hallway, and she focused on scrubbing. She wasn't allowed to be on the premises until at least an hour after school adjourned. Typically, the building was empty when she arrived, though it wasn't unheard of for a teacher to stay late once in awhile. She kept her head down, evading whoever might be left and passing by. Biting her tongue and being invisible had allowed her to skate through the job without complaints so far.

Except the footsteps halted outside the bathroom. A shadow of a person filled the doorway in her peripheral, but she stared at the urinals she was cleaning, bracing for the inevitable jab from the few staff who sometimes brought it upon themselves to mock her. That didn't happen as often anymore. Not like it had her first few months. Nevertheless, she was prepared.

"I wasn't aware you'd moved back to town."

Ah hell, no. Not him. She'd recognize that soft, yet authoritative voice anywhere. A deep rumble with a universe of affliction in the tone.

Eyes burning, throat tight, she scrubbed harder. Maybe he'd get the hint and just leave. Pretend he'd never saw her.

Silence clanged heavy for a beat.

"You can't spare a glance for an old friend?"

Who was she kidding? When had anything gone her way? Of course, he'd stop to chat. Poke at the bear. Gawk at the former prom queen and princess in her reverse rags-to-riches story.

She cleared her throat, gaze still on her task. "We were never friends."

Honestly, she'd not had any true friends. Ever. A couple of girls in high school who might've pretended for stature purposes, but they'd turned on her right along with the town. Parker certainly wasn't the slumber-party, up-all-night-telling-secrets, defend-her-honor, had-her-back kind of pal. If memory served, and it did, he'd dodged her at all cost.

There was a time she would've given anything for a look from him. A glance, a gaze. Anything to acknowledge he'd known she was alive. It hadn't happened.

"No, I don't suppose we were." He leaned against the doorjamb, his niece next to him. "I don't recall animosity, either, Maddie."

She closed her eyes at the nickname. It had been so long since she'd heard it uttered. Everyone called her Madeline. The only souls who had used the shortened version with consistency were her mom and Parker. And her mom had been dead for fifteen years.

Urinals cleaned, she rose and switched to the sinks, spraying them with cleaner.

Unrelenting, he kept at the small talk. "How have you been?"

How had she been? *How had she been?* She nearly brought out her claws and snapped at him, an old habit born from self-preservation, but then it dawned on her this was Parker. He probably had zero clue what her life had been like the past few years. His genuine surprise at seeing her earlier proved he hadn't been lying and had been unaware she lived in town again. He was and always had been a wonderful guy. Nice when he didn't have to be, when it wasn't necessarily expected.

"Fine," she muttered, rather than spouting the truth. She was pretty certain he wasn't seeking answers like *lonely, scared, sad,* or *ashamed* when he'd asked his question.

He didn't respond immediately, and she made the epic mistake of glancing at him in the mirror over the sink. He'd been a handsome devil in his youth, but he'd aged like the fine wine her father used to drink with meals.

Parker had the lean, athletic grace of a ball player with wide shoulders, a narrow waist, and hands large enough to make a woman wonder if the sayings were accurate. He wore jeans like the second coming and a plain white tee that emphasized his sculpted biceps. An empty holster was attached on his belt, the weapon no doubt locked in his car, and his badge fixed next to it. Hair, black as midnight, was cropped close to his ears and nape, longish and wavy on top. Dark overgrowth dusted his jaw around a full, unsmiling mouth. But, his eyes? Oh damn, those eyes. Emeralds in sunlight.

Intuitive. Charismatic. Solemn.

"Who is that, Uncle Parker?"

Maddie quickly averted her attention to the sink and wiped the porcelain.

"That's Maddie, silly. You know, your school's janitor."

"Nuh-uh. Mr. Ben is our janitor. He cleans up puke and cuts the grass and stuff."

Parker sent a questioning glance Maddie's way.

In the mirror, she briefly looked at him and away, focusing too hard on wiping the faucets. "Ben is the daytime custodian and maintenance supervisor. I come in at night. I'm not allowed to see or speak to the students, so she's not met me before."

His eyes narrowed to slits. "Why aren't you allowed to be around the children?"

She turned around and whipped him a you've-got-to-be-kidding-me glare, then snatched a stack of paper towels from her cart to put in the dispenser.

"Not because of David and your father? Is that what you're telling me?"

Keeping mute, she locked the dispenser and gathered supplies to clean the mirror since the soaps didn't need refilling yet.

"That's asinine."

"Uncle Parker! Swearing is naughty!"

He sighed and set his hand on the girl's shoulder. "Right you are, bratty-cake. Asinine is a regular word, though, even if it sounds like a curse. It means goofy or ridiculous."

"Oh. Asinine is an asinine word."

A grin split his face from ear to ear and exposed a row of straight white teeth.

Maddie's heart somersaulted, barely sticking the landing.

Damn this day, anyway.

Finished with this bathroom, she gave it a onceover, satisfied it was cleaner than she'd found it. "Excuse me. I have to get back to work." Her shift was only four hours long, three days a week, and this was a big building. Funny how it seemed so small when she'd been young.

She brushed past him, dragging the cart behind her, but before she could get far, he gently touched her arm.

"Why don't we get coffee sometime? Catch up and whatnot."

There was the saint everyone knew and adored. Kind and friendly, he'd go out of his way to help anyone or make them more comfortable.

Though the offer was probably an empty one and it implied nothing romantic, it was best she nip it in the bud. Swiftest way for him to lose the respect of the townsfolk was to be seen associating with her. And, let's face it, she'd been hiding in the shadows for a long time. Reminding people she existed by going out in daylight would only end badly.

Besides, no one actually wanted to drink coffee and chat with her, amazing as that sounded.

She cast her gaze over him, pausing on the pink, sparkly backpack slung over his shoulder. The sexy, adorable man. "I don't think you bat for my team, sheriff."

While he glanced at the bag in question, she used that opportunity to start high-tailing it down the hall.

"It's Katie's backpack," he called to her from a few feet away.

"Uh-huh." She smiled, not turning from her retreat. "If you say so."

She half expected him to follow. He didn't.

Figured. Not like anyone had bothered to chase her before. They certainly wouldn't now. Not with her hands dry and cracked, nails to the nub, zero cosmetics, and her hair up in a loose bun on top of her head. Her perfume was eau de Lysol. Then there were the gray polyester coveralls. That wasn't even accounting for her reputation.

Yeah, the guys were lining up.

By the time she finally got done with her duties, it was pushing the envelope on when she needed to clock out. The other boys' bathroom had contained a multitude of surprises for her, not including but limited to wads of wet toilet paper thrown against the wall. Cleaning it had taken time off her orchestrated routine. If she went so much as a minute over her shift punching out, it would give them reason to fire her.

She felt disgusting. Unfortunately, she wouldn't get to shower until her night shift at the youth recreational center tomorrow night. Such was life.

In the janitorial office, she clocked out, stripped out of her coveralls, tossed them in the laundry bin, washed her hands, and checked her staff mailbox on the wall. Paydays were both awesome and sucky. Awesome because, well, money. Money got her closer to her goals. Sucky because she'd have to go a few blocks out of her way on legs that were already exhausted to the bank where she could deposit the check by ATM. At night, no one could complain that she walked up to the drive-through machine. Going in during business hours was out of the question.

Checking the weather app on her phone—her cell was the only amenity she had since it was instrumental for employers to contact her—she noted it had cooled off. Still, the temp at fifty-three was tepid for autumn. Good thing she'd brought her sweatshirt.

She pulled her hoodie from her backpack and dropped her check into the side pouch before flipping through the other papers in her mailbox. Nothing from her immediate supervisor. The rest looked like mass communication flyers they gave to all staff. The last in the stack was the trick-or-treat schedule and Halloween costume party announcement.

Written on the back, in black marker, were the words: *You're not invited.*

Staring at the note, her belly cramped and her heart sank. It wasn't as if she planned on attending. Heck, she hadn't shown her face at any of the town functions from the Firefighters Ball to the Easter Bunny Hop to the Valentine's Dance to the 4th Fireworks. She hadn't even dared to visit the Christmas display in the park last year. How catty and unnecessary to remind her she wasn't wanted. It was a blatant fact she already knew.

Still, it hurt. A lot.

Tossing the bulletins in the trash, she locked the office behind her, did a sweep of the building to turn off lights, then made her way out the front door.

This time of the evening mid-week, the sidewalks were rolled up and most of the town was quiet. Lampposts lit her way as she walked the side streets until coming to Main. She turned left instead of right and trudged the two blocks to the bank. Once finished, she headed toward the edge of the park.

Though it was warmish, she pulled her hood over her head to ward off the breeze from the Pacific just on the other side of the rocky bluffs. Saltwater tinged the air and mingled with pine the closer she got to the hiking trails in the forest. Leaves shushed under her shoes as she stepped from the pavement onto a path. Darkness engulfed her, save for the light of the moon, and she was surrounded by hundred year-old cypress and redwood trees. Animals scurried. An owl hooted.

Long ago, when she'd been desperately searching for a safe place to land since none of the apartments had accepted her application and everyone else had turned her away, the trek through the forest had been daunting. She'd since grown used to it and could navigate the way while asleep.

One day, she'd have an actual roof over her head again. Alas, it was a luxury she couldn't afford. Yet. For now, she enjoyed the peace of nature.

Quarter of a mile up the incline, she veered left. Tourists and townies never strayed from the trails for fear of animal activity or getting lost. Both were legit concerns and threats. She'd taken precautions, though.

Coming to a stop, she eyed the tiny clearing. A two-man dark green tent stood amongst boulders and between giant redwoods. Fastened at the corners to four tree trunks over the tent was a tarp serving as extra cover from precipitation. Grounded railroad spikes with a crude four-foot barbed wire fence spanned the perimeter, deterring creatures from entering. In front of the tent's opening was a small fire pit dug into the soil like a fishbowl and lined with rocks.

Home sweet home.

She'd carefully picked the location. It was close enough to town for her to get to or from, yet off the beaten path. Predators didn't typically roam this far down the mountain, though the risk was always present. Worse she'd encountered the past few years had been a raccoon. Regardless, after her first night, she'd bought a BB gun and a taser. Neither would kill a mountain lion or a bear, but it would give her the opportunity to get away.

Not a bad getup for a chick who'd never gone camping a day in her life. Considering she'd been raised in a ten thousand square foot mansion overlooking town with servants who'd done everything for her, she was pretty damn proud of herself. Hey, she might be the only one, but whatever. Yeah, over the months, things had been by trial and error, but she'd made it work.

She'd kill for a hot bath, though.

Lifting a makeshift post, she swung the gate open and shut it. Of course, she used the term "gate" loosely. She'd connected railroad spikes in a square with zipties and fastened them to a grounded spike with barbed wire. It worked and beat her having to step over the improvised fence, accidentally cutting herself.

Using her phone's flashlight, she checked the tent for creepy crawlies, finding none, and ducked inside. She sat on top of her sleeping bag and switched on the battery-powered lantern, filling the tent with a warm yellow glow.

Prying the lid off of a large tote in the corner, she surveyed her options. She'd eaten prior to going to work, but she needed something before lying down or her stomach would grumble all night. Her canned tuna, chicken, veggies, and fruit stash were getting low. Which sucked because that meant dealing with the market employees and lugging the stuff back. She had one granola bar left, however.

Score.

Taking a bite, she opened one of two notebooks from another small tote and logged her paycheck amount in the column. She had a little more funds this month because she hadn't needed supplies like batteries, shampoo, soap, or toilet paper, plus her cell bill had gone down because she'd finally paid off the phone, but she would need to go food shopping soon. Tapping the pen to her cheek, she estimated the total she figured she'd spend and flipped open the second notebook.

There were ten pages of the wide-ruled lines filled front to back with names. It had taken some sneaking around and terrible detective skills to gather the intel, never mind the dollar amounts, but she'd managed. Hours of reading police interview notes, lawsuits subsequently filed afterward, and court transcripts of the charges. She'd obtained them all. Every last person David and Daddy had hurt with their scheme.

Some names had checkmarks. Too many didn't. She'd made a dent in the list, though. Baby steps.

She scrolled through the numbers and compared them with what was in her account. Some amounts weren't a lot because families only had so much to invest at the time, others were four figures. Those were harder to amend. If she waited until her next paycheck, she could pay off one of the larger sums. Or she could knock off two smaller ones now. Possibly three if she was careful.

Debating, she finished her granola bar and snatched a bottle of water from her drink tote. She usually reserved bottled water for the weekends when she didn't go into town, but she'd forgotten to fill her reusable one at work today.

Glancing around, she took stock. Her laundry bag wasn't full. She always wore her work jeans and t-shirt for a week at a time to conserve, and she had two of each. The sweatshirt and pants she slept in for about a month. She had a pair of khakis, two nice sweaters, and a few polos in a clothes tote for interviews or if she had to look nice. Those were still clean. She'd only soiled three of her eight pairs of socks so far.

All right. No extra expense at the laundromat for a few weeks.

She looked at the notebook again. Three. She'd clear three names. It would mean being very careful until her next check, but she could do it.

Nodding, she reached over and grabbed envelopes from her documents tote, then began writing the letters to put inside.

Chapter 3

"You're never going to believe who I ran into the other day." At a scarred pine table in the corner of Shooters, Parker glanced at his best friend since the age of diapers over the rim of his beer as he took a sip.

Jason's brows furrowed. "Must be good if you're mentioning it."

"Madeline Freemont."

A puff of his cheeks, and Jason ran his hand through his dark blond hair. "Damn. There's a name I wouldn't mind never hearing again. Did you go to the clinic to get vaccinated afterward?"

"Funny." Parker set his mug down, skimming his fingertips over the condensation on the glass. "I thought she was living upstate somewhere."

Jason tilted his blue eyes toward the ceiling as if in thought. "I seem to recall rumors about her presence a couple years back, but haven't heard any since. Where did you see her?"

"At the elementary school." He paused. "Where she's a janitor."

Up went Jason's brows. A full second later, he slammed his palm on the table and laughed. Deep, uproarious laughter that might require a respirator afterward. "No effing way. How's that for karma? The princess turned into the pauper."

At the time, Parker had been so shocked, he hadn't known what to think. Growing up, she did have the reputation of being a princess. Snooty, looking down her nose at everyone. He had always gotten the impression it was an act, but he hadn't been close enough to her circle to verify his theory. Nor had he really wanted to. The girl who'd made his childhood miserable had grown into a woman he'd barely recognized.

And still, she was intimidating. After all these years.

Give him Bigfoot with an AK-47, a room full of sugar-induced five-year-olds, or any supermodel on the circuit in a little black dress playing a private game of cops and robbers with his fly, and he'd be fine. Wouldn't break a sweat. But, put him within fifty feet of Maddie Freemont? He turned into a tongue-tied, forgot-his-own-name, card-carrying member of the idiot brigade.

Hell, and he'd invited her out to coffee, for the love of God. Coffee. Him and her. At a civilized table for two. Where she probably would've asked, *do you want arsenic with that?*

Thankfully, she'd declined his offer. After she'd questioned his manhood.

"Christ, she used to scare the bejezus out of you."

"Still does." Why, he hadn't a clue. There was just something nerve-wrackingly daunting about her. Perhaps it was her inapproachability.

"Okay, seriously. Why on Earth is she a janitor? She does know that'll make her break a nail."

"I don't know. Katie's teacher said Maddie's been there almost three years and she had to beg to get the position. That she needed the money."

Jason grunted, a sneer on his lips. "Her family hasn't conned enough dough from the residents? She needs more? You know most of those people never got that money back."

Yeah, Parker knew all too well. It was his father who'd brought evidence to the FBI in the first place. To date, it was the only true scandal Redwood Ridge had ever faced. Townsfolk might argue otherwise. A lot of things passed as scandalous in a place this size. But Rachel Johnston getting drunk at the New Year's Eve Ball and hitting on Diana Colebrook's husband just didn't seem on the same caliber as one of the founding and wealthiest families in the Ridge scheming ninety-eight people out of more than three-hundred thousand dollars in a real estate con.

His sister had been one of those people. Ninety days after David Weaver and Nicholas Freemont's sentencing, Paige had received a check in the mail for a whopping four out of the three-hundred dollars she'd doled. Like many others, she'd thought she was investing in land farther up the mountain where a resort had been proposed. The land purchase itself was coming from Redwood Ridge residents, the resort from other investors Nicholas and David had procured from Havencrest, a town north of here. The resort was supposed to bring in tourism to both areas. Except the property was owned by the state Wildlife Commission and not for sale, nor was it buildable due to unstable terrain.

"All their assets got liquidated after they pleaded guilty. The house, the businesses, everything. Once the attorneys and back taxes got paid, the rest was divided between the victims." Parker scratched his jaw. Unfortunately, there hadn't been much left and people received a small percentage of what they'd handed over to a man they thought they could trust. "They never pinned anything on her, though. She was probably left broke."

Jason offered him a withering glare. "You don't honestly believe she had no clue what they were up to, or that she didn't stash money away. Her own father and her fiancé? She was six months from walking down the aisle, man."

"Actually, yes, I do believe she was innocent." Which meant they'd left her barren since she wouldn't have known to put funds aside. He assumed. Parker sighed and glanced around the semi-crowded bar that smelled like French fries, cheap perfume, and boredom. Pool balls clacked from the adjoining room and darts smacked boards. People danced in a cleared area near the back wall to some 90s hair band song that was giving him a headache. No one seemed to be paying them any mind. "I've read statements and reports that never went public. I watched her interviews from behind the two-way glass. She had no idea what was going on. Not to mention, she'd been away at college during most of the investment hunting."

Worse, so much worse, was the look on her pretty face when she'd walked out of the courthouse. It was apparent by her shell-shocked, despondent expression that she'd believed she would be leaving with her father and the man she'd loved. Instead, she had stood on the stairs, alone, bathed in golden sunlight, hunkered within herself like someone had stolen her warmth. Utterly, utterly lost.

The bastards hadn't even bothered to tell her they'd struck a deal, that they were, in fact, guilty.

It was a memory that had stuck with him the past few years. Every once in awhile, it would resurface just to screw with him.

And since he'd seen her at the school, it had been on a constant loop.

"If you say she's innocent, then I believe you." Jason shrugged. "She's still a Class-A bitch."

She certainly used to be. No argument there. Again, though, the Maddie he'd met two days ago was not the same Madeline he'd known. It was as if circumstances had zapped all her spitfire and left her with nothing but ashes to sift around. Damn, but he'd almost felt sorry for her.

"That may not be the case anymore." Parker rubbed his eyes, not caring for the ache in his gut. He was done with this conversation. "Why are you solo tonight?" Typically, as of late, Jason's fiancé joined them in whatever they did.

"Ella's finishing up with the event committee meeting." Jason glanced at his phone. "She should be here any minute. They're finalizing the Halloween Party or something."

Parker grinned. "And what are you going as? I know she has some adorable couple costume in store for you two."

"Does not."

"Liar."

In Parker's expert opinion, Ella was the best thing to ever happen to Jason. He'd do anything and everything for her. Just as it should be when a man had been smacked upside the head by love. His father had died fighting a fire when they were boys, and Jason had developed an aversion to commitment, of any kind, as a result. It had taken twenty years and three meddling matchmakers to get him out of that mindset. Enter Ella Sinclair, soft-spoken and kind kindergarten teacher whose parents happened to have died in the same fire that had killed Jason's dad.

The world was a rather small place sometimes.

"Shut up." Jason popped a pretzel in his mouth. "I'm not dressing up for Halloween, town event be damned. Not happening."

Ella strode in and leaned over Jason's chair, her long brown hair cascading. She smacked a kiss on his cheek and grinned. "Guess who picked up our costumes for next week's party."

Parker threw his head back and laughed. He looked at his best friend, and about lost his ability to breathe as he laughed harder. His side splitting open, he placed his hand there. "What were just saying?"

"That you need a high-five to the face."

"With a chair?" Parker kicked one away from the table for Ella. "Have a seat. We were just discussing costumes."

She sat and eyed the two of them. "Now what did I miss?"

"Nothing at all." Jason winked. "Parker was just telling me he's striving for best costume award by going as a naughty school girl. Know where he can pick up a short plaid skirt?"

"He's just pissy because I was right. Again."

"And by again, he means never."

"I was right about the Battleaxes matching you, wasn't I?"

"Coincidence." Jason leaned over and pressed his forehead to Ella's. "A wonderful coincidence."

The sap. Jealousy crawled up Parker's spine, but he couldn't be happier for his friend. They both deserved it. "What are you two dressing up as? Pray tell."

She tilted her head, obviously pleased with herself. "A firefighter and a Dalmatian."

Clever, especially considering Jason was a lieutenant at Redwood Ridge's fire station. "He's going as the dog, I hope."

"No." She smiled through a sigh. "Are you attending the party? What are you wearing?"

"I might sit this one out." He went to all functions, if only to make an appearance, but he just wasn't in the mood for it this year. Events like that one were more fun with a better half, and since he hadn't found his, he'd rather take Katie trick-or-treating and watch silly kid movies while getting cavities, if it was all the same to him. "We'll see."

Jason braced his forearms on the table and leaned forward. "Worried the Battleaxes are gonna set you up?"

At this point, Parker would welcome the sisters' interference. It had been a handful of years since he'd been in a relationship that lasted longer than the third date. Especially now that Jason had found Ella. He was kinda feeling like the third wheel.

"Speaking of Battleaxes, Paige thinks they're trying to match her."

Jason frowned. "I thought her and Erik were a thing."

"They are, but a few nights ago, Marie asked her to work late for a very weird reason, and suggested I pick up Katie from school."

"Did anyone randomly go visit Paige at the office? Security guard or something?"

"Not that I'm aware." Parker shrugged. "Told her it was probably a fluke."

"Maybe." Jason rubbed his jaw, then suddenly froze. "Marie suggested *you* pick up Katie so Paige could work late?"

Suspicion in his friend's eyes had Parker on edge. "Yeah, why?"

"This wouldn't happen to be the day you ran into Madeline, would it?"

Shit. Double shit. No way, no how. The Battleaxes had cooked up some crazy couple concoctions before, but he and Madeline would cause a chemical explosion. It had to be another coincidence. Nothing more.

"I saw Katie's teacher, too. Doesn't mean anything."

"It means it's more likely *you're* their next target, not Paige. And she's dating someone already." Jason looked at Ella. "Thoughts?"

"I don't know. They don't exactly consult me." A baffled expression, and she pulled her phone from her purse. "Let's check Twitter or Pinterest."

Because the town had an account on both social media sites. Tweets were about anything and everything, but the "word on the street" teasers were the key phrases to spot who was being matched. Pinterest had a board for every couple that had been paired, beginning with the first encounter of set up.

After multiple pulse-pounding beats, Ella slowly shook her head. "Nada on both accounts. You're not mentioned at all."

Parker exhaled hard. He hadn't even realized he'd been holding his breath. "See? Coincidence."

Up went Jason's brows. "Why do you look so relieved then?"

Ella put her phone aside and set her golden-brown eyes on Parker. "When you said Madeline, did you mean Freemont?"

"Yeah. We went to school together. It was a surprise running into her. Why? You know her?"

"A little. Not well." She chewed her lip. "I tried talking to her once or twice, but she just tucked her head and pretended not to hear me. Some of the staff aren't very nice to her."

He narrowed his eyes. "How so?"

"She was hired a couple weeks before me. During my orientation, the vice principal said to take home all personal property at night and lock up everything because Miss Freemont was a thief. Something about giving her the job to stick it to her. Of course, he said this very hush-hush, under his breath." She swallowed, glancing at the table. "A few of the teachers purposely left their classrooms a mess so she'd have more work to do. Best of my knowledge, that kind of thing has tapered off, though. Honestly, I think she's doing a good job. I hardly ever see her."

As silence hung, Parker stared at her with pounding temples, disheartened and, frankly, pissed off. No matter what Maddie's family had done, that didn't mean she should be punished for the sins of her father. No one deserved that kind of treatment, especially if she'd been doing her job well, kept her nose clean, and didn't bother anyone. Which was precisely what it sounded like she'd been doing.

"Okay, I can't stand the woman, and even I think that's crappy." Jason pivoted his head between Ella and Parker as if seeking verification. "Can you do anything?" he asked her.

She shook her head and helplessly waved her hand. "I said something once to the principal, but I don't think it was taken seriously. I was new also and trying to fit in. Most people didn't know I was there, never mind committed my name to memory. Who was I to say something?" Her shoulders sagged. "I guess that makes me no better than them."

Jason set his hand on her back, rubbing circles, and eyed Parker. "What about you?"

"Not without a formal complaint." He could, however, pop into the office and whisper in certain ears.

Which was what he intended to do first thing Monday morning.

Chapter 4

As opposed to her custodian position on Mondays, Wednesdays, and Fridays at the school, Maddie liked her three to eight o'clock job at the Rec Center on Tuesdays and Thursdays. For the most part. They required her to go to and from the back door and stay in the kitchen out of sight, but at least the staff were relatively pleasant. And by that, she meant they sometimes said hello or goodbye, or looked her in the eye. Once in awhile, she felt a part of the human race and worthy of a semblance of respect.

The only reason they had accepted her application two years ago was because their full-time cook's doctor had made her cut back on hours after a mild heart attack. Maddie had lied and told them she could cook. She hadn't boiled a pot of water in her life. The cook had left specific recipes and a menu for her days off, and in no time, Maddie had gotten the hang of it. Once she'd learned the groove, it was kind of relaxing.

The employees and kids were gone by seven, and that meant she had the building to herself for a blessed hour. If there was food leftover, she could even have a hot meal. Miles, the center's director, had given her permission to use the shower facilities, too, as long as she didn't tell anyone. He didn't know her situation, but when she'd asked and he'd looked confused, she'd said it was so her car wouldn't smell like a kitchen. Little did he know, she didn't own a vehicle.

Today had been mac and cheese with hotdogs and carrots. The carrots were the only part of dinner that remained. At least it was a fresh vegetable.

She cleaned up the kitchen while she munched on carrot sticks, waiting for the clock to hit seven. Last night, it had cooled off significantly. She'd been forced to pull her heavy blankets from the tote in her tent. A hot shower sounded like heaven. If she rushed, she'd have time to blow dry her hair before the long hike home.

The door to the main dining room swung open and she turned to find Miles standing inside the kitchen. He was a good-looking guy with mulatto skin and sharp blue eyes. His dark brown hair was curly and cropped close to his head. If he weren't gay as the day was long and dating Brent from the vet clinic, she might swoon over him. Not that he'd go for her if he were straight.

Semantics.

"Hey. Is everything okay?" She did a double-take when he just rubbed the back of his neck and awkwardly smiled. "Did I do something wrong?"

"No, no. I'm just…really sorry there wasn't any dinner left for you to eat also. We had a full house today."

The center was open after dismissal on weekdays from two to seven, a full day if there was no school. Those were nice because she got to work an extra amount of hours and her paycheck was bigger. The number of kids they had at any given time was hit or miss, and often dependent on if there were any practices in the gym.

"It's okay. I'll eat when I get home." Probably a can of tuna since she hadn't had protein today. Or yesterday.

He studied her as if he didn't believe her. "Still, I feel bad. I hate that you can't leave the kitchen, either. The parents have to be comfortable bringing their kids here, though. If they—"

"I get it, Miles. If they knew I was here, they'd pull their children or you'd have to let me go. I understand." Such was life.

Sad that the longest conversation she'd had in months had been this one, save for the brief interaction with Parker the other day. She was starting to lose her social skills altogether because of isolation. It felt weird opening her mouth and speaking.

"I wish things could be different. You're doing a wonderful job."

Throat tight, she smiled. She absorbed the compliment since they were hard to come by. "Thank you."

He was a nice guy and one of the rare breed of townsfolk who hadn't believed she'd been a part of her father's scam. He'd done a lot by giving her a job and allowing her to use the facilities. If not for him, she didn't know how she'd bathe. For a year before being hired here, she'd washed up in the bathroom sink at the school. She swore, she'd stood under that nozzle in the locker room for thirty minutes straight that first shift, weeping in relief and for her good luck.

"Have a wonderful night."

"You, too." She watched him leave, then did a scan of the kitchen to be sure she'd cleaned everything.

Finishing the last carrot stick, she walked out of the kitchen, through the main lobby, and to the locker rooms. She turned the combination to her locker in the corner, fished out her shampoo and bar soap, then snatched a towel from the cart. The adjoining room had ten shower stalls, five on each side, and was still humid from the high school basketball team who'd used it last.

Starting the shower, she undressed and neatly folded her clothes to put back on when finished, setting them on a bench. The white tile was cold, despite the warm air, but she got under the spray quickly.

Yessss. Heaven.

Summer days had dwindled, leading to late fall, so she couldn't linger like she wanted. If she didn't dry her hair before walking home, she'd get sick or spend the night shivering. None of her jobs had health insurance. She couldn't afford a clinic visit.

Alas, she gave herself a brief moment of comfort, letting hot water run down her back before reaching for her shampoo. To save money, she bought the bargain brand with a conditioner mix. It smelled like strawberries and reminded her of the patch that grew wild behind the Freemont Manor. As a girl, she'd often snuck back there to read or cry over a boy or just get away from her father's harsh, rigid rules.

Hair washed, she lathered soap over her body, rinsed, and reluctantly shut off the nozzle. By the time she'd dressed and dried her hair, it was pushing eight o'clock.

Donning her coat, she geared up for the chilly air and the long trek home. It was the only thing she didn't care for about coming to this job. The center was clear on the other side of town from the park.

Head down, she stepped out the front door and bumped solidly into someone.

A low, manly *oomph* sounded just as the mysterious someone grabbed her upper arms to steady her.

Face buried in a gray tee against a solid wall of a chest, she reached up to push away, and wound up fisting the lapels of an open leather jacket instead. The scent of pine and fabric softener filled her nose, making her pause just long enough for the moment to become more awkward. Who the heck...?

"You okay, Maddie?"

Ah, crap. Seriously?

"Sorry about that. I don't normally have a habit of plowing down women."

Could have fooled her. She was feeling particularly flattened at the moment.

Gently, he set her away from him, hands cupping her shoulders, and ducked to look in her eyes.

She got the briefest glimpse of green framed by thick black lashes before she lowered her head and stared at his sneakers. There was a scuff mark on the toe of the left one. She focused on that while mentally trying to cool the heat in her cheeks. Why she'd blushed, who the heck knew, but this was twice in a week's span she'd run into him. Literally this time.

The universe had a terrible sense of humor. Nothing she hated more than being the punch line.

This wasn't happening. It wasn't.

"Earth to Maddie. Cat got your tongue? You always had a lot to say growing up."

Okay, it *was* happening. Who did she have to bribe to get off Karma's hit list?

Clearing her throat, she glanced over his shoulder. "Hey, Parker. I'm fine, thank you. I don't have a cat. And you'll find I don't talk as much as I used to. Behind backs or to faces." There. That should answer all his questions.

"What are you doing here?"

Or not. So much for going on her merry way.

She brushed a strand of hair from her cheek, frustrated. "Not breaking in, if that's what you're suggesting."

"I don't believe I said anything of the kind."

He didn't have to, did he? Implication was unanimously tied to her. Forever would be. It was a sentence handed down by the people, without any evidence of wrongdoing on her part, and all because she shared a name or had naively fallen for the illusion of love.

Her mistake. Punishable by banishment, it seemed.

Jaw clenched, she continued to stare over his shoulder. "I work here."

He reared. The slightest of movements, but the obvious tell of disbelief wasn't lost on her. "I thought you worked at the school. In fact, correct me if I'm wrong, but we just bumped into each other there last Wednesday."

Smart ass. "I work there three days a week, two here." And speaking of... "What are *you* doing here?" All up in her orbit and flustering her. Again. Was catching a break too much to ask?

"Marie was on her way home and noticed the lights were still on. She called me to check on things."

Marie the mayor. Oh. Well, then. "I stay an hour past closing to clean up. As you can see, everything's fine." So, go away.

"What do you do here?"

Screaming at the top of her lungs would probably be counterproductive. Nevertheless, it was tempting. "I cook."

"You? *Cook?*"

She whipped him a steely glare, seething at his raised brows and grinning mouth. It was a damn crime he was so attractive. The fact he was the sheriff was probably the only reason he got away with it. He looked like a wicked Celtic hellion with his black hair and bright green eyes and dark dusting of overgrowth on his jaw. The jeans and leather jacket added to the conjecture. Except, he had the patience of a saint and a good ole boy personality to contradict appearances.

"Sorry." He threw his hands up in surrender, expression dialed to aw-shucks. "You surprised me. I just can't picture you cooking."

As if he pictured her at all. If he did, it would be behind bars. "I don't poison the children. They're simple meals. It's not that hard."

He nodded slowly, studying her and shoving his hands in his pockets.

Not caring for the perusal, she focused elsewhere, hoping he'd leave so she could start the long walk home. Without an audience.

Stars poked through a deep navy sky, accenting a crescent moon. The stiff breeze held traces of snow, indicating the direction was coming from the east off the mountain instead of west from the Pacific. Soon, fog would roll in, thick and heavy, to blanket the Ridge. For now, it was clear.

The basketball courts to their left were empty, as was the playground to the right and the parking lot that stretched three rows deep between the building and the road. Red and orange leaves crackled overhead, some falling like snowflakes to the damp asphalt and wet grass.

He was still staring at her. She could all but feel his gaze like an imprint branding her through the outer layers of clothing to her skin. One thing she recalled with ease about him was his ability to make excellent use of silence. She just wished he'd do it to someone else, some*where* else. She had to be up early tomorrow for her weekend job and it was going to take her at least ninety minutes to walk across town and a quarter of the way up the mountain to her tent.

"Maybe we should just hash it out now."

For the second time, she jerked her gaze to his. She was beginning to suspect this was an interrogation. "Hash what out?"

His jaw ticked as his gaze roamed her face. "Whatever it is that's bothering you so much you won't look me in the eye for more than five seconds or speak but a couple fragmented sentences."

"Oh, I'm so sorry, Saint Parker. Is my disinterest wounding your delicate ego? Standby while I swoon to make up for my obvious inadequacies."

"All right. That's a bit better. Now you're sounding more like the terror I know and remember." He inhaled hard, his gaze harder. "And I'm not a saint."

"Please. You all but walk on water. I'm not a terror."

"Please," he mocked. "You all but ate my soul for breakfast every day of our childhood."

So that's what this was about? Her stupid girly ploys to get him to notice her? Peachy. She took it all back. Every proverbial hair yank she'd attempted for attention. She'd needed it so very badly back then and didn't want it now. Not that she ever got what she needed, wanted, craved, desired, or required. She had no clue why it suddenly upset her or why she was letting him scratch at a scab that she was trying desperately to heal.

But hell if she'd let it continue.

Huffing a laugh, she strode around him. "One shouldn't live in the past, Parker. You'll smack into something in the present looking backward and not get a clear view of your future. Trust me."

She got two steps before his hand wrapped around her arm to stop her. Closing her eyes, she tilted her face heavenward, praying to a God who'd never been merciful on her to, just once, grant her a break.

"Where are you going?"

For the love of all the Gobstoppers in Willy Wonka's Chocolate Factory, would he please just leave her alone? "Home, sheriff. I'm going home."

He released his hold on her arm. "Where's your car?"

"I don't have one."

Once more, with feeling, she started walking.

He stepped in front of her. "What do you mean, you don't have one?"

"I don't recall you being this dense as a kid. Have you suffered brain damage since high school? Hit your head one too many times on your halo or something?"

He crossed his arms, the leather of his coat crinkling in the otherwise quiet night. "I thought I was a saint. Angels have halos. Saints have status. Sometimes with beams of light behind them while depicted."

Crap. She almost forgot he had a great funny bone. The jerk.

"See that streetlight over there?" She pointed to the curb where he'd parked his car. "That's your beam of light. Go there. Go on. Shoo. Stand over there and look pretty."

A grin split his face, and damn if her knees didn't nearly buckle. He had such expressive features, but that grin, that stop-the-presses, her-panties-were-damp, rapid-flash-of-unbidden-amusement grin was the very reason she'd developed a crush on him at age twelve. First of many reasons, anyway. She was beginning to wonder if she'd ever gotten over it.

"You think I'm pretty? I'm humbled."

She rolled her eyes. "Yes, sheriff. It's such a shame you bat for the other team. Now, if you'll excuse me, I really have to get home."

And the grin disappeared. Just like that. "I do not bat for the other team."

Duh. He'd dated the popular, and some not-so-popular, girls in high school. All except her. "Okay," she said, riddling her tone with disbelief.

"The backpack was my niece's."

"So you've said." She crossed her arms against a stiff breeze and turned, putting one foot in front of the other until something dawned on her. He had his hand on the pulse of this town. If he were to even casually mention to anyone he'd seen her here, it could mean trouble. "Oh, Parker?" She faced him. "Please don't tell anyone I work here. I like Miles. I wouldn't want him to lose his position or cause problems for him."

A dumbfounded, perplexed crease of his brow, and he opened his mouth.

She retreated before he could stop her. "Goodnight."

Ten seconds passed. Twenty. She started breathing at thirty, then...

"Hold it, hold it." Shoes tapped asphalt as he jogged over. "I'll drive you home."

Yeah, not happening. She kept going. "I'm good, thanks."

"It's chilly and I'm here." He matched her brisk pace. "No sense in you walking."

"Totally fine, Parker. Goodnight."

His harsh sigh could've brought down the Klamath Mountains. "Where do you live?"

"By the park." Or close enough.

"By the...?" He growled at her retreat. "That's an hour walk from here. Get in the car, Maddie."

Almost ninety minutes, actually, but why point that out? It wouldn't help her cause. She didn't respond, save for the sound of her too-worn shoes with a hole wearing on the right sole.

"Get. In. The. Car, Maddie Freemont."

Damn it. She turned around, eyes narrowed. "Is that a direct order?"

"Yes. Don't make me tase you. I'll have to write up a report. It'll just piss me off and ruin my evening."

Hardy, har-har.

Sighing, she glanced at his blue Charger. It would be nice to get a ride for a change. Her legs were tired. Her everything was tired, but wouldn't that just make the town's day by watching her drive past in a squad car. It was dark, though, and his windows were tinted. She could pull her hood up to cover most of her features and tell him to drop her off at the apartments next to the park. When he drove off, she'd just hike the rest of the way without him being the wiser.

"Please?" He looked at her, eyes pleading and shoulders braced for her answer. "I'm not comfortable with you walking in the dark alone that far."

Yep. Saint Parker.

"I walk to and from work every day. What exactly do you think is going to happen to me in Redwood Ridge? A Halloween display falling on me? Blown over by the force of someone waving hello? No, no, I got it. I'll get diabetes after I'm forced to eat a cookie from the free sample display by the bakery. I hear sugar calling to me now. Dangerous stuff."

Expression deadpan, he ran his tongue over his teeth. "Taser's sounding better by the second. Get in the car."

"Fine."

Chapter 5

The blasted woman smelled like strawberries. Of all things, strawberries. The fragrance filled the small cab of Parker's car and made it extremely difficult to focus on driving her across town. Or concentrate on anything, really.

She'd put her hood up, too. Like it was cold inside his car or something. He'd cranked the heat, but she hadn't put it down, making him suspect she was hiding, not chilly.

He wove out of the short cul-de-sac where the Rec Center was located and turned down a series of streets until getting to Main. Regardless of all the shops being closed and people at home with their families, he drove slowly on the cobblestone road. He snuck a glance at her out of the corner of his eye, but the yellow glow from the lampposts only illuminated her thin frame. Her face was still obscured by the damn hood.

For the hundredth time in five minutes, he resisted the urge to squirm. That subdued version of her from their encounter at the school and again at the center tonight was fifty times more frightening than the girl who used to call him names while chasing him at recess. There'd been a brief blip of her former sass when he'd challenged her, but she'd put it back in a box once they'd gotten in his car.

She'd been a very pretty, well-polished girl in high school with legs for miles and insults for days. He couldn't remember ever seeing her without cosmetics or wearing an outfit that cost as much as a month of his dad's salary. Her hair had been shorter then, resting on her shoulders, and loosely curled. She'd been slender, too.

Not like she was today, though. Then again, she was currently bundled in a heavy coat, and last week she'd been in coveralls. He supposed it was hard to tell, but she seemed thinner. All angles and edges like her personality. Her once brassy blonde hair was nearly down to her backside and caramel in tones now.

Stick straight to boot. Besides some slight color in her cheeks from the wind, she hadn't a trace of makeup on.

He much preferred her this way. No masks or fluff. Just the real woman. Not that he preferred her at all. That was insane. He was just saying, the genuine article was more catered to his taste. A woman he could kick back with to watch a game on TV, or pop into Shooters to meet up with Jason, or take home to his folks' place for dinner. He wasn't high-maintenance, thus he didn't know what the hell to do with females who were.

Maddie, most definitely, had been as high-maintenance as they came. Straight from the factory, all shiny and new, with bells and whistles and gadgets he wouldn't have a clue how to operate. Weird how his two encounters with her in the past three years had been this week, and it was as if someone was attempting to demonstrate that she was more his speed than he'd realized.

He inhaled, attempting to shake off the jitters she instilled, but...

Yeah. Strawberries.

If someone had asked him an hour ago what scent he'd tie to Maddie, a sweet, juicy fruit that brought about memories of summer and shortcake wouldn't make the cut. Expensive perfume direct from Paris? No doubt. Brimstone? Probably. Rotting innards from her prey? Likely.

But, strawberries? Just what was he supposed to make of that?

And how narcissistic was it of him that he wanted to take a bite? Of that pouty lower lip. To shut her up, of course. Of her earlobe. Only so she would have to listen solely to him for a change. Of...

All right. What the actual fuck? He was not thinking of Maddie I-Live-To-Make-Your-Life-Miserable Freemont in terms of sexuality. He was not attracted to her in the least. Period and exclamation point.

Breathe. He just had to breathe and...

Strawberries.

"What's wrong?" She shifted slightly in her seat in a half-assed attempt to face him.

"Nothing." Everything. Nope, nothing.

"You always growl when nothing's wrong?"

He tapped his fingers on the wheel, grinding his molars. Had he growled? Sure, he was frustrated for no apparent reason, but he would've been aware if he'd made an animalistic utterance. Right?

Right. "I didn't growl."

"Yes, you did."

"No, I didn't."

"You have a very loud stomach, then. Maybe consider eating something."

"I ate earlier. I'm not hungry and I didn't growl."

"Hmm." She pressed her lips together as if pondering a conundrum.

He glanced at her, to the road, and back again. "What's that mean?"

"That? It's a pronoun, depending on context. Sometimes the word *that* can be a conjunction or adverb. Did you not pay attention in English class? You sat right behind me."

He glanced at his steering wheel just to make sure there wasn't a sign that said, *bang head here*. "Not the word *that*. You *hmm*-ed as if in thought. What were you thinking?"

"Oh." She shrugged. "I was just assuring myself I was safe in your car. They wouldn't give someone the job as sheriff if he had mental illness or a habit of randomly uttering noises with no recollection of doing so. I convinced myself there was a cougar in your trunk, thus the culprit for the growling I heard. Because there was a growl."

Give her a ride home, he'd said. *It was the nice thing to do*, he'd said.

There wasn't enough tequila in Margarita-ville to deal with her.

"There's not a cougar in my trunk."

"I meant the animal, not the euphemism for an older woman attracted to younger men. Unless that's what you're into. Do you have that kind of cougar in your trunk? Does she growl?"

His left eye twitched. It hadn't done that since high school graduation when he'd had to sit next to her in a full auditorium, but there it went. Twitching like a strung out addict without a fix.

"Fine. I growled, all right? Satisfied?"

"I regress to my original question. What's wrong?"

He thought about responding with, *I forgot*, but she wouldn't let that fly. Answering with, *for a fleeting second, I caught myself thinking about you as more than a perpetual thorn in my side that I thought I'd extracted years ago*, wouldn't be wise. Muttering *strawberries* wouldn't help, either. How was he supposed to reply and still maintain self-respect?

"Do you care?" Not bad. Kind of a jackass comeback, but he could have done worse.

"I wouldn't have asked if I wasn't interested in an answer. I could've just let it go at a cougar in your trunk. Wildcat or the mature woman version. Either. Though, the latter could be considered a wildcat if—"

"I'm irritated with myself because you still have the ability to unnerve me." He exhaled through his nostrils and gripped the wheel until his knuckles popped. "Twelve years since we graduated high school. I've been a police officer for the better part of ten years, sheriff for three, I answer dispatch calls ranging from dogs poo-pooing in neighbors yards to coffee trapped in locked cars to lost keys in a purse, and somehow, *you* of all things is what flusters the ever-living, holy-crap outta me."

And, shit on a shingle. He just went off on a raging tangent and admitted weakness to the one person on earth who had ever been able to get under his skin or make him flee screaming. Splendid.

It had been a good span, he supposed. What? Ten minutes alone in an enclosed space? He glanced at the dashboard. Make that fourteen minutes. He'd lasted thirteen and a half minutes longer than he would've twelve years ago. At this rate, he'd be able to spend quality time with her for a whole day without flipping his gourd when he was ninety. Something to look forward to.

"Feel better?"

He sighed. "No." Honesty for the win. "No, I sure don't."

She went silent for a moment. Then, *of course then*, she said, "Poo-poo?"

Next time the mayor called and said something looked suspicious, he was telling her to go check it out herself. He could be at home right now, drinking a beer, bingeing *The Walking Dead*. Was he doing that? Nope.

"Don't ask," he grumbled.

"Okay." Tick-tock. "Why do I fluster you? We haven't spoken in ages. It's not like I'm intimidating or anything."

He barked a laugh and glanced at her, only to triple-take because she actually appeared like she was being serious. "Are you kidding me? I'd rather be in a high noon shootout with Clint Eastwood than the same room as you."

"Ouch." Saying nothing more, she glanced out the passenger window, her face completely obscured once again by her hood.

Damn it. "That didn't come out right. What I should've said was, my odds of survival are better in a high noon shootout with Clint Eastwood than the same room as you."

Slowly, she turned her head and pushed the hood back to reveal pursed lips and narrowed eyes. "Look at me. I'm not a threat to anyone. Never was."

Threat? No. Scary as hell? Yep.

"Your memory needs a reboot. I couldn't pass you in the halls without ducking. You used to call me Parker Penis."

She did the damnedest thing. Right there in the passenger seat of his squad car. The damnedest thing. She...*laughed*. Head thrown back, blonde hair flowing around her shoulders, hand pressed to her chest kind of laugh.

How unexpected. If under oath in a court of law while testifying, he would've guessed her laugh was a cackle with, *my little pretty*, spewing from her mouth afterward. Perhaps he even would've stated she didn't have the capability. As it turned out, he would've perjured himself.

Throaty, raw, and infectious. That's what her laugh sounded like.

"Oh, gosh." She fanned her face. "I totally did, didn't I? Those were good times."

"Yeah, the best," he drolled.

"Ah, Parker." She let out a contented sigh. "I wasn't that bad."

"Uh, the hell you weren't. You snuck into the locker room and changed my baseball jersey number to 666. Mrs. Garrett still makes the sign of the cross when I walk past."

She rolled her lips over her teeth, but it failed to hide her grin. "You have to admit, that was funny."

"I'm pissing my pants in laughter. Or how about the time you rigged my locker to explode with glitter when I opened it. Weeks, Maddie. It took weeks to get that shit cleaned up."

"But you looked so pretty afterward."

He offered her an unamused side glance. "You put crime scene tape around my car. Covered in Vaseline."

She buffed her nails on her coat. "One of my best moments."

"Are you getting the picture? So, yes. You unnerve me. I'm half expecting to get out of my car with post-it notes glued to my ass."

"Why didn't I think of that? Damn. That would've been hilarious." She looked at him and rolled her eyes at his baleful glare. "Oh, come on. You can't possibly be telling me those foolish little girl antics to get your attention still bother you now. That was over a decade ago."

Tongue in cheek, he spun that response around in his head until his brain was drunk and giddy. Yeah…and no. Regardless of how he tried to dissect her words, she'd actually said… "Get my attention?"

Why in the name of all that was holy would she…?

"Duh. I had a crush on you."

The car swerved. One second they were merrily cruising along, squabbling about the difference between good ole days versus good ole nightmares, depending on the viewpoint, and the next thing he knew, he was practicing driving in Europe. Just jerked the wheel so hard out of sheer shock that he wound up on the other side of the two-lane street.

"Your lane is over here."

Heart pounding, hands shaking, spots in his peripheral, he gradually began the process of easing back to the correct lane. It was a hell of a blessing there was no one else on the road.

He sucked oxygen. "Are you joking?" Crush? *A crush?* Certainly, she'd meant crush *him*, not crush *on* him. She had to have been playing another prank with that BS answer.

"Totally not. Driving 101. You maintain the vehicle to the right of the yellow dotted line and to the left of the white solid one. Or the shoulder. I would think as sheriff you'd have a valid driver's license, not one procured as a prize in a cereal box. I'll have to bring that up at the next town meeting."

His left eye twitched harder, transitioning from junkie to full-blown seizure. "Define what you meant by *crush*."

Her sigh shook the heavens. "Crush, Parker. You know, to have idealistic romantic interest in a person, typically someone unattainable or inappropriate, and fleeting in length of time."

Sweet Lord. He had heard her correctly. He hadn't, contrary to how it seemed, been hog-tied and forced into a Stephen King novel on a whim for her amusement. Or perhaps, for grins and giggles, she was still a terror and trying to get a rise out of him.

He was a fully-functioning grown adult male with a badge and a gun. Surely, he could handle one waifish and smartass Maddie Freemont.

"You did not have a crush on me." Denial, his new defense system.

"Whatever makes you sleep at night. Think what you want."

He pulled up to the curb outside the apartment complexes by the park. "Which unit?"

She pointed to the building he'd stopped in front of, directly across the street from his friend Jason's. Ella used to live in this complex until she'd moved in with Jason last month.

Maddie reached for the handle.

Parker set his hand on her arm. "Why didn't you ever say anything?" If she had, maybe she wouldn't have harassed him to the point of his outright avoidance. Who knows how he might've responded back then, but at least they could've been friendly instead of mortal frienemies.

She climbed halfway out of the car and glanced at him over her shoulder, her expression incredulous. "I did. You ignored me."

He opened his mouth to contest that claim because he sure as hell would have remembered the rich princess of the Ridge saying she had a thing for him. Five concussions and ten hangovers wouldn't erase that from memory. But she was already out the door. It slammed behind her, shutting out any rejoinder.

He watched her cross the front of his squad, walk up the short sidewalk, and stop under the awning by the front entrance.

An impatient press of her lips, and she waved him off like she were flicking a flea.

Proving she wasn't the boss of him—anymore, anyway—he pointed to the apartments, indicating he'd wait until she was inside.

She defiantly crossed her arms.

He shrugged.

She tapped her foot.

He grinned.

A stalemate ensued for what he guessed was a good two minutes until she finally threw her hands in the air and opened the door, disappearing inside.

He was halfway home before he breathed, and three quarters of the way before it dawned on him the other thing she'd said. *Unattainable.* That was the exact word she'd used to describe him in regards to her "crush."

And damn her, that one flipping word haunted him the rest of the night.

Chapter 6

Maddie looked up from her task at the worktable in the back of the flower shop when Harriet Nunez strolled in from the front section of the store. She raised her brows in interest at the middle-aged woman's grin of delight.

"Great news."

"Oh, yeah?" Maddie smiled, gaze retrained on the funeral display she was preparing for Fran, the former librarian's, funeral. Like with Betty White, Maddie had never expected Fran to ever pass away. She'd been a timeless fixture in town for as long as Maddie could remember. Alas, the elder lady went last night, peacefully in her sleep.

"Remember that arrangement you did for Gary last week?"

"Sure. The one that was supposed to say, *sorry I forgot our anniversary, but I hope this makes up for it?*"

"That's the one." Harriet eased onto a stool on the other side of the table and crossed her arms.

Like usual, her makeup was flawless, if not a tad heavy on the blue shadow, and her short salt and pepper hair was sprayed with enough schlack a category five couldn't ruffle the strands. Fine lines and wrinkles, some deeper than others, creased her forehead, around her eyes, and her bright pink lips. A testament to a life lived smiling for customers and getting joy from her career.

She'd owned Ka-Bloom for over thirty years and, up until last year when she'd fallen and broken her arm, she'd been the sole employee. Maddie had walked past one night on her way home from the school and had spotted the Help Wanted sign. Harriet had asked her to create a Welcome Baby basket by way of an interview, then had given Maddie the job on the spot after liking her work. Maddie had a condition, though. She stayed in the rear of the store, letting Harriet answer the phone and greet customers.

Since then, after Harriet's arm had healed, Maddie came in on weekends to complete advance orders or ready-made bouquets for the glass refrigerated display cases. Once in awhile, she did special projects like wedding arrangements or the funeral one currently before her.

She adored the woman to no end. Her husband had passed away not a year after she'd bought the store, and she'd never remarried, nor had kids. Her whole life was dedicated to making others happy with her blooms. She treated Maddie like a human being, often bringing in muffins for breakfast, and tried to give bonuses when she could. There wasn't a week that went by since she'd hired Maddie that Harriet hadn't told her how wonderful a job she'd been doing.

Honestly, until this position, Maddie hadn't played with floral arrangements since her second year at college when she'd had a class on it for her interior design degree. She'd forgotten how much fun it was, and her creative side was finally being put to use. She just wished Harriet needed her for more hours.

"Was there something wrong with the order?" Maddie brushed her hair from her face. She should've put it up like she normally did, but the fresh cup of hot coffee and banana nut muffin waiting for her when she'd arrived had distracted her.

"Not at all. Gary's wife has been gushing all over town how amazing it was and how she had no idea I could design something so detailed. I have half a mind to ignore your wishes and tell the truth that it was you who made it."

"Please don't," Maddie pleaded. If townsfolk knew she was working behind the scenes here, Harriet's sales would decrease or they'd treat her poorly. "I'm just glad they liked it. That's all the credit I need."

Actually, that project had been quite fun. She'd sculpted a couple out of floral foam and had used dyed carnations to cover the model. It wound up resembling a tiny parade float. So cute. It would've made a great cake topper.

Harriet frowned. "If you say so. That's coming along nicely." She gestured to the table, where Maddie had a mess going on.

"Not bad. It's not exactly as I designed it in my head, but I think it'll be a nice tribute to Fran." She'd taken a tall basket and created a paper-mache form that looked like an open book to adhere to the front. The flowers in a vase inside the basket were white calla lilies, daisies, and tulips with fern accents.

The jingle of the front door chimed, and Harriet straightened. "Be right back."

Maddie fidgeted with the tulips again. They seemed to be attention-hogging the callas. Removing them, she snipped a half inch off of two, an inch off five more, and placed them back in the vase. There. Better.

Setting the arrangement in the cooler, she started cleaning up, half-listening to the mumbles from the front shop. The other voice sounded male and she wondered if she'd need to do a quick special order before preparing some bouquets for the display case. They were down to just a few out there.

Harriet returned, followed by...

You have got to be kidding. "Parker?"

He stopped inside the doorway, hands buried in his jeans pockets, and a dumbstruck expression sliding toward WTF. He had his badge fixed to his belt and a gun in a holster next to it, indicating he was here for police business. His open leather coat revealed a yellow tee molded to his hard chest, which only made the green in his eyes a starker emerald.

Damn, he was an attractive man. As a boy, he'd been tall and wiry. He'd since grown into his height and filled out, especially in the shoulders and chest. He packed the room with his presence and still didn't seem imposing.

Her heart thumped just to be argumentative.

While he cast his gaze around the small workshop, she noted the shadows under his eyes and how his black hair looked more finger-combed than styled. She wondered if that meant he'd slept as poorly as she had last night.

Heat infused her cheeks. Their back-and-forth banter outside the Rec Center and in his car had kept her tossing and turning in her tent. Every stupid thing she'd said repeated like a terrible rom-com in her head. Ugh, including, but not limited to, her admission of a past crush.

What the heck had possessed her to spout that tidbit, she hadn't a clue, but she'd gladly cut out her tongue if it meant taking it back. *She* flustered *him*? Please.

"Let me guess. You work here, too?" His gaze slid back to hers, methodically, like he was connecting the dots on a puzzle she couldn't see.

Quickly, she glanced down to the table, grabbing the remnants of cut stems. "On the weekends." She tossed the stems away in the bin next to her and reached for the ribbon fragments next.

"Just how many jobs do you have, Maddie?"

"Three." Not including the occasional ones when people called her as needed.

Tonight, she'd have to go to the beauty parlor, Hair Lair, to do their quarterly deep cleaning. None of the employees knew it was her who came in, just that it was a maid service, because the owner wanted it that way. She was tasked with taking products off the shelves, wiping them down, dusting, and replacing items. She also took apart the stations to get hair out from the nooks and crannies, plus she cleaned mirrors.

"And how long have you been here?" Suspicion riddled his tone, even if he didn't move a muscle.

"A year or so." She glanced at Harriet, but the woman just shrugged. "Why?"

He inhaled, stared at the ceiling, and gradually released his breath. "Mrs. Nunez," he said, gaze still heavenward, "the disturbance you reported this morning out back in the alley, the one you just told me a few minutes ago was probably nothing. You didn't happen to mention it to our beloved mayor, did you?"

"Um, yes." Harriet, obviously confused, ping-ponged her attention between Parker and Maddie. "We ran into each other at the market and got to talking. I told her the dumpsters have been messed with every night for a couple weeks and garbage was strewn around the alley. I also said it was, no doubt, those pesky raccoons again. They come around every fall. Marie insisted I call it in to you personally first thing this morning."

His lips flat-lined and he nodded slowly, still glaring at the ceiling tiles. "That's what I thought."

"Was that wrong?" Harriet clasped her hands, concern evident. "I thought it was silly calling you, but—"

"No, no." He lowered his head and closed his eyes as if seeking patience and failing miserably. "I am always readily available for townsfolk in need." He huffed a laugh that was drier than the Sahara. "Why don't you show me this disturbance, Mrs. Nunez?" He looked at Maddie. "Are you going to be here for awhile?"

Crap. Why? "Yes. I didn't make the mess in the alley."

His eyes narrowed. "No one's accusing you."

That would be a first. "Okay. I'm here until two."

"Awesome," he said, his tone suggesting it was the farthest thing from it. "Mrs. Nunez, after you."

She watched them exit the back door and into the alley, a knot in her gut. Three times in a week he'd shown up to her place of employment. For nearly three years, she'd managed to avoid him and stay off his radar. Everyone's radar, for that matter. With the exception of a handful of people who saw her only when necessary, she'd been an invisible non-entity.

Much as she liked Parker, being around him brought up the constant reminder of who she used to be and that empty sensation of not having her feelings reciprocated. It was also a slap in the face of what she could never have. On top of that that, he was the presence townsfolk recognized and loved. He was noticeable, and that meant she'd be more likely to be noticed.

She moved to the sink, washed and dried her hands, then put her hair up in a loose knot so at least one thing wouldn't annoy her for the rest of her shift. From there, she cleaned up the worktable and pulled fresh flowers from the cooler.

When she arrived for her shift, she made a habit of sizing up what bouquets were left in the display cases out front. That way, she didn't accidentally run into a customer by having to check. There was a bunch of colored daisies and one of yellow roses left, both made by Harriet.

Autumn tended to draw a target group of clientele, as did Christmas and Valentine's Day. Maddie was pleased to see the items she'd requested had been delivered. Harriet was great about letting Maddie have a say in what product got used.

She glazed over the advance order list and nothing jumped out as unique, other than the funeral one she'd completed, except the ten pre-orders for the town's Halloween Party, which had been on the docket for a month. Those needed to be made today.

She began gathering supplies when Parker and Harriet came back inside.

Crossing his arms, he glanced at Maddie out of the corner of his eye, then back to Harriet. "I'll make a quick run up to the hardware store and come back with a latching mechanism for you. That should keep critters out." He cleared his throat. "Would you mind if I had a quick word alone with Maddie first?"

"Not at all. I'll be in the shop if you need me."

Maddie tried to swallow and couldn't manage. Instead, she focused on putting a cotton ball inside a two-inch by two-inch white satin square piece of fabric and tying a rubber band around it for makeshift ghosts. The attempt to ignore the rapid plummet of her stomach failed.

Feet shuffled, and he moved to stand on the other side of the worktable. He set his hands on the surface and leaned into them.

She glued black sequins for eyes on the ten sets of ghosts.

He watched her.

She inserted plastic stake sticks into the ghosts.

He watched her some more.

She snatched black pipe cleaners and switched to making spiders after the ghosts were done.

Five minutes passed. Then ten. He never stopped staring.

Though she didn't look at him or encourage his company, she could feel the weight of his gaze, heavy and cumbersome. She had no idea what he wanted, but she refused to shove her foot in her mouth like she had last night. If she ignored him, perhaps he'd leave.

"What are you making?"

Or not. Dang it. "Halloween arrangements."

"Seems like you're making a lot of them."

"It's for the party next week."

"Gotcha." He paused. "I figured Mrs. Nunez would do them. It's her shop."

Irritation pounded her temples. "It is her shop, yes. She likes my work, so I typically design the special orders." She inserted sticks into the spiders. "Keep that to yourself. There's a reason I'm in the back and she's up front."

She could all but hear his frown. "And what reason is that?"

A roll of her eyes, and she bent to pick up the box by her feet. She wanted to slam it on the table for effect, but the contents were fragile. One by one, she set out the small square black vases.

"You're not going to answer me?"

"Stupid questions don't require a response."

"It's not a stupid question and I want an answer."

The frustrating man. She unwrapped orange lilies and dark purple carnations. "Think, Parker. You'll figure it out."

He swiped a hand down his face like she'd asked him to dance a jig while solving the energy crisis. "First, you high-tailed it out of Katie's classroom as if you had done something wrong by being there and barely acknowledged me when I stopped to say hi on my way out. Then, you tell me not to mention your job at the Rec Center to others for Miles's benefit. Now, I'm supposed to *keep it to myself* that you work here."

"MmmHmm." She turned to the sink behind her and reached in the overhead cabinet, extracting the powdered plant food. Measuring a teaspoon, she dumped it into the ten vases, closed the container, and put it away. "Nice to know you're paying attention. That puts you several bars above most males."

While he stewed on that, she filled the vases halfway with water and placed them on the table once more. She stirred to dissolve the plant food, keeping her gaze on her task. She hadn't dared look at him since he'd returned from the alley. Doing so would encourage him to stay.

And she needed him to go.

"Oh, I'm paying attention, all right, and it seems to me you're attempting anonymity like you don't exist. What I don't know is why."

She trimmed flower stems.

He drummed his fingers on the table.

She put the flowers in vases.

He leaned over and ducked his head, forcing her to look at him. "Why, Maddie? I would think you'd want people to know that you're making an honest living and working hard."

"Damn it, Parker." She pounded her fist on the table. "I'm a reminder. That's why. Every time they see my face or hear my name, it's a reminder to them what David and Daddy did. Or they think I took part in the scheme also. They hate me. They don't want me here. And I can't blame them. What I can do is go about my day, *quietly* in the background, and leave them to live their lives in peace. Which," she ground through her teeth, "I wish you'd let me do."

Closing her eyes, she took a calming breath before opening them and going back to her arrangements. She had the ghosts inserted and was halfway through the spiders, all while he solemnly watched her, when he finally straightened as if to leave.

"You didn't do anything wrong."

She froze, her arm extended mid-task. Her breath caught and her eyes watered.

Not once had anyone ever deigned to say that to her. Even those who believed she was innocent still kept mum on that particular subject. Like the mere mention of the crime would alter the circumstances. Some people treated her decently, gave her a break or a job if she'd asked, but not a soul had actually said the words or acknowledged her in public.

Was this a trick? Payback for all the pranks she'd pulled on him in their youth? His very father had started the dominoes tipping. Truth be told, she'd always assumed Parker thought she was guilty, just as most of Redwood Ridge did, and that the authorities just hadn't found enough evidence to convict.

Throat tight, she slowly lifted her gaze to his. It took everything she had, but she didn't set the tears free. Parker didn't lie or mislead. He didn't speak for the sake of talking. And he wouldn't fluff his commentary to make her feel better. Which meant he believed what he'd said.

Contemplative and somber, he studied her. "You didn't do anything wrong," he repeated. "I have to run down the block to the hardware store, but I'll be back before your shift ends. We'll continue this discussion then."

Chapter 7

In the back alley behind Ka-Bloom, Parker tested the new latch he'd attached to the dumpster. He brushed his hands together, satisfied it would work. Such things were not in his employment description, but Mrs. Nunez didn't need to hire someone when he could have a simple task done in thirty minutes. Besides, he was here anyway and he didn't have any other pressing matters. At least, not sheriff-related duties.

He sighed, hands on his hips, and eyed the back door to the shop.

Maddie was inside. At yet another job. Which he'd stumbled upon due to being sent here by The Battleaxes. Specifically, by Marie. Because he was obviously their next matchmaking target. He'd suspected their antics, of course. There were just too many coincidences as of late. After today, there was zero doubt.

Just what in the world was he supposed to do? Of all the females on God's green Earth, why Madeline Freemont?

He hated to be a hypocrite. Just last week he'd been thinking how he wouldn't mind getting in the Battleaxes' crosshairs, that being alone was growing stale and he hadn't had much luck in the ever-after department. He'd also made fun of those who'd referred to themselves as the sisters' "victims."

But, *Jesus*. Maddie? Seriously? Hell be it for him to question The Great and Powerful Battleaxes. Their matchmaking track record was something like two-hundred to none, yet he just couldn't wrap his brain around the concept. Yeah, she seemed to be much tamer these days, and yeah, she wasn't quite the snob he'd remembered, but...

Did she even like him? She didn't act like it. Sure, she'd admitted a prior crush. Except, that had been, as she'd said, over a decade ago. Plus, a crush didn't equal an interest in a relationship, nor did it make the two of them compatible.

Certifiable, maybe.

He'd planned on talking to her down the road about the things she'd said, find out what she'd meant by "unattainable," and get a better feel for her now. All his experiences with her had been as a boy and a brief stint while her father's criminal investigation had been going on. Nothing recent.

And their conversation in his car had bothered him to the point he'd been awake all night. Claims about her attention-seeking behavior from their school days, her demanding full confidentiality about her current jobs, the way she often refused to look at him like she was ashamed, and how she constantly deflected his questions with sass or distractions. She thought the whole town blamed her and didn't want her here.

His complete and utter inability to think straight in her presence didn't help.

This. *This* was the woman with whom they wanted to match him?

Before he'd left for the hardware store, he had every intention of telling her about Cupid's target on their backs and how they were being manipulated. Just lay it all out there and determine if she was as appalled as him. But she'd pulled the indignity card again by not making eye contact or completing sentences. She'd behaved like she'd wanted him to leave. So, he'd gone with instinct and had shut his trap.

Observed.

Asked questions.

His conclusion? It would be an epically disastrous and cataclysmic idea to inform her of the Battleaxes' plan. If the women thought she was "the one" for him, and Maddie was too embarrassed to show her face in town or make eye contact with him, never mind taking into account their unsettling history, then he needed to tread carefully. He wasn't even certain he would go along with this charade or if he should, but she was hitting all his curiosity triggers for him to simply let it go now.

A sigh, and he went inside. He wasn't going to get anywhere standing out in the alley.

Maddie was still at the giant table in the center of the room, a bunch of vases before her with purple and orange flowers. He didn't know jack about what they were, but the ghosts and spiders she'd made were cute. Perfect for the Halloween function. She'd also glued orange ribbons around the black vases and had stuck a gnarled black branch inside the arrangements.

He had no clue she was creative or good at this kind of stuff, but they looked really cool.

As she placed the vases in an open box and put them in a fridge, he hesitantly watched her. Seemed he'd been doing that a lot lately. Half the time, she ignored him. He would've killed for that kind of treatment in high school. How the tables had turned.

He should walk away. Just stride right past her and leave. Give her what she seemingly wanted. But something kept whispering in his ear to stick it out. A sixth sense or plain old inquisitiveness. Who knew? It refused to go away, though, and each time he encountered her, the sensation grew.

She was quite lovely. As a girl, she had been also. In a separate and different way than nowadays, however. He guessed he'd never paid attention to her beauty, what made her unique. She'd been a familiar figure for so long, he'd just stopped looking. Or, perhaps, had never seen it in the first place.

Her caramel-colored hair was up in some sort of feminine bun thingy all women had down to a science, exposing her long, regal neck. She had a small button nose and huge eyes that were a shade somewhere between cornflower and navy. Porcelain was the first term that came to mind about her skin. She had a light complexion with a bare tint of natural pink in her cheeks. Narrow face. Her lower lip was slightly larger than the upper, offsetting the balance, and yet it still managed to be a focal point due to the poutiness factor.

The inbred graceful, erect posture and her delicate hands were the only remnants of her prestigious upbringing that were apparent. One had to look hard to notice. Her jeans weren't designer, her gray sweatshirt had some wear, and she didn't have a stitch of makeup on. Even her earrings were tiny round silver studs. If he hadn't known her all their lives, she would've turned his head.

Was he attracted to her? Yes. He'd admit that much, even though the thought had been rather frightening in his car last night.

"Did you get the latch put on the dumpster?"

Yeah, her voice was interesting, too. Especially when it wasn't laced with sarcasm. Soft, articulate. He remembered it being piercing or abrasive, but that must've been an implied result of her taunting. Come to think of it, they hadn't had a lot of conversation through the years.

"Yes. All done. It should help stop any wild animal activity." He cleared his throat and walked to the table, crossing his arms.

"I know Harriet will appreciate that."

He nodded. "What are you making now?" She had at least fifteen different kinds of flowers before her, scattered in clumps.

"Ready-to-purchase bouquets for the front display."

"You're pretty good at this."

"Thanks. I enjoy it and it's relaxing." And still, she wouldn't look at him. She set one bunch in paper, rolled the flowers inside, and secured the arrangement with a Ka-Bloom sticker, then set it aside to pick up another. Rinse and repeat. "Don't you have somewhere to be? Poo-poo to examine or something?"

Maddie Translation: *Go away and leave me alone.*

Not happening.

"Funny." He rested his hip against the table. "And no. I'm off duty. Only put the badge on today because of Mrs. Nunez's report."

"Which you've completed. Civic duty done."

Maddie Translation: *Go away and leave me alone now.*

"Yep. Got the rest of the day to do what I want." He checked his watch. Her shift was over in ten minutes. "What are you doing with the rest of your afternoon? Hostile takeovers? World domination?"

"Grocery shopping."

He laughed. "I have to pick up a couple things myself. I'll go with you."

Her head whipped up so fast, he was surprised she didn't get whiplash. Round eyes met his. *Finally.* "I don't need a police escort."

"How about a friendly one?"

"I don't need one of those, either. Besides, we already established we aren't friends."

Interesting. She wasn't as intimidating as he'd once thought. Perhaps all he had to do was challenge her or knock her off-balance. "No, we established we never used to be friends, not that we couldn't be or aren't now."

"Fine. We can't be or aren't friends. There."

He grinned. "I disagree. Why don't you want to be my friend? You're going to hurt my feelings."

"I sincerely doubt that, sheriff." Swooping up the bouquets, she walked around the table to the fridge. "I only have a couple hours before I need to be at my next job. I don't have time for your games."

He wasn't playing a game. He was trying to get to know her, and she wasn't making it easy. "Perfect. I'll drive you and it'll save you having to walk." Wait a minute. The Rec Center and the school were closed on Saturdays. "What job?"

"You will not drive me, shop with me, or be my friend." She deposited the last of the bouquets in the waiting vases and closed the fridge. "I have to be at Hair Lair at six."

"They close at five."

"Exactly." She went back to the table and swept cut stem fragments into her hand, tossing them in the garbage. "I do quarterly cleaning after hours."

"You said you only had three jobs."

"No, I said I only had three regular jobs. The beauty salon is every three months for a few hours."

Did she ever do anything besides work? "You must be tired." She'd been at the center last night, the school the night before, and up early today to be at this store. "I'll drive you."

She rolled her eyes. "That'll look great, me riding in a cop car through the center of town. Let's add to the stigma."

If he had to badger her into believing it, he was going to prove that not everyone blamed her for what her father had done and that people did want her here. "You'll be in the front seat, for crying out loud."

Shaking her head, she turned and hefted a very large backpack off the counter. "I'm fine, Parker. Carry on without me." Sliding her arms through the slings, she put on the backpack and tilted to look around him. "I'm off, Harriet. See you tomorrow."

"Bye, dear. Wonderful job today."

The small, fragile smile ghosting Maddie's lips and brief closing of her eyes as if to compose herself spoke volumes. That she was grateful. That she was surprised by the compliment. And, most gutting, that she didn't hear those words very often.

Parker rubbed the pinch in his chest growing behind his breastbone and told himself he was reading too much into nothing. Even if her humbling expression said otherwise.

She pivoted and headed for the back door.

"Where are you going?"

Instead of answering, she pushed the lever and went into the alley.

He rushed to catch up. "Why are you going out the back?" His car was out front and the market was right down at the end of Main.

Again, she didn't respond.

She was starting to get on his nerves. "Are you still going shopping?"

"Yep."

Then why was she…? Never mind.

"I'll meet you there." He needed to fetch his car so they didn't have to walk a block with groceries. Because he *would* drive her home, whether she liked it or not.

She waved over her shoulder in a blasé acknowledgement.

He strode between storefronts, got in his squad, made a U-turn, and parked in the lot at the market. Just as he shut his door, he spotted Maddie along the side of the small, brick-laid building heading toward…the back. This was becoming a pattern.

What the heck was she doing? "Maddie?"

She didn't hear him. Or ignored him.

Whatever. He wasn't in the mood. He jogged toward her, gently took her arm, and guided her toward the front door.

She set her feet. "I don't go in this way."

"Through the entrance? Do you beam in? Cast member of Star Trek, are you?" He didn't allow her time to think that through. Still holding her arm, he strode right past the automatic doors. "Amazing. We made it inside without any special effects."

Jaw set, she gave him the hairy eyeball.

It was pretty quiet in the store, even for Redwood Ridge standards. Then again, most patrons did their shopping in the morning. A couple stragglers were down an aisle to the right, but that appeared to be all the current customers.

It smelled like Pine Sol. Always had. Ivory tile, florescent lighting, and six rows of shelves. Fresh produce was up front, dairy in the back. That summed up the place.

"Parker!"

Behind the sole register to their left, Mr. King waved. He had to be pushing seventy and had owned King's Market since long before Parker was born. His white hair was parted neatly on the right and a peach button-down was tucked into a brown pair of trousers that were hiked up to his chest. His appearance, as well as the stoop in his posture, hadn't changed since the Reagan administration.

"How're you doin', son? Who's that you got with ya?" He looked over the rim of his thick black glasses and squinted. "Oh, Miss Freemont." The tone in his voice went from cordial to flat, his expression following suit. "Thought you were going to pick up your order in the stockroom."

She ducked her head, hunched her shoulders, and walked up to the counter. "Yes, Mr. King. Sorry about that. What do I owe you?"

"I assume you mean today and for the groceries," he said, implication heavy on the sarcasm. "It came to thirty-seven, fifty."

She dug in her pocket and passed him some bills. "There's forty. Please keep the change and add it to the tally."

"Will do. Your items are in the back."

"Thank you, sir."

Frowning, Parker waited a beat until Maddie had disappeared through a set of double doors, then eased closer to the counter. "Why does she pick up her order?"

Mr. King shrugged. "Lots of folks call in their items. If I have the help, we accommodate."

"But she picks hers up directly in the stock room."

A nod. "Ever since she got back to town. Easier on everyone, you know?"

No, he didn't, but he was getting the picture. "And what is the tally? What did she mean by that?"

The old man grunted. "Her idea. She rounds up to the nearest dollar amount. Says it's to help reimburse me for what I invested. As if she could ever make up for what they did."

Parker tensed to the point of pain. Muscle locked around bone and joints popped. A pounding grew in his temples until he was dizzy from the pressure. Molars gnashing, he inhaled, seething at one of the town's pillars. A man Parker had known and respected for years.

"What *they* did?" he asked, calmly. He was the sheriff, and thus, he had to be objective and professional, but that didn't mean sitting idle if there was an injustice occurring.

"Yessir. That whole lyin', cheatin' family."

This was why she'd tried sneaking in the back door instead of going through the front, why she'd left the flower shop through the rear and took the alley instead of Main Street's sidewalk. She'd told him the town blamed her, that they didn't want her around. He'd figured she was exaggerating.

This was one case, one example. Perhaps he was jumping the gun. A solitary person didn't equate to a whole population. Yet the nausea in his gut suggested a different story, and he'd certainly keep his ear to the pavement from here on out.

And educate where appropriate.

"She wasn't charged with a crime, Mr. King. They didn't have any evidence on her because there wasn't any to find." Parker fisted his hand in his pocket and maintained a cool, level tone despite the irritation jacking his heart rate. "Now, if you don't like her based on other factors, then that's your business and none of mine. However, a paying customer is a paying customer. Last I checked, the motto is 'they're always right'. She's supporting your establishment every time she shops here."

He stepped away from the counter and headed toward the stock room. "Have a wonderful day, Mr. King. Good seeing you."

Shoving through the double doors, he paused and glanced around. Boxes. Shelves. Refrigerated units. A desk and filing cabinets.

No Maddie.

The damn pain-in-the-ass woman. Growling, he exited through the delivery door and scanned the side lot, adjacent street, and sidewalk. Nada. He strode around front and spotted her half a block down, heading toward the shops.

Backtracking, he got in his car, drove to where she was, and screeched to a halt by the curb. He shoved the gear in Park and got out, temper mounting. "Give me the backpack."

Wide-eyed, she looked around as if worried people might see them, and fisted the straps over her shoulders. "What are you doing?"

Her harsh whisper was louder than her speaking voice. He thought about pointing that out, but offered his hand instead.

She glanced at it and back to him, brows wrenched. "No. I need to get home to unload before my next job."

"And I'll drive you there. The backpack, Maddie. Now."

"Parker—"

"Have it your way." Moving behind her, he lifted the backpack and carefully slid it off her shoulders. "Christ. What have you got in this thing? Bricks?" She was maybe a hundred and thirty pounds soaking wet. It was a miracle she could carry it.

Popping the latch, he put the thing in his trunk and shut it. Facing her, he pointed. "In the car."

Her lips rolled back from her teeth. "You are not the boss of me. This is abuse of power."

"Nice try. Get in."

She stood there another moment, guiltily glancing around, obviously debating with herself over her options until, finally, sighing. She stepped off the curb and lifted the handle, opening the door. "You're a bully."

"Hi Pot, I'm Kettle." He climbed in and latched his seatbelt, waiting for her to do the same.

Situated, he drove her to the apartment complex in silence and got out again to retrieve her backpack from the trunk, handing it to her.

"Want help carrying it inside?"

"No, but thank you." Again, she avoided his gaze, looking everywhere but at him.

"You're welcome. I'll see you around."

And she would. He didn't know when exactly or precisely how in the past week she'd scratched under his skin again, but she was embedded there just like she'd done as a teenager. This time, he had no plans of extracting her.

He'd dated. He'd been in relationships. He'd had some messy breakups in his heyday. Once or twice, he'd even thought he'd been in love. But no one, not one single solitary female he'd been involved with from his first date at fifteen to this very moment, had the capability to rile him this way.

So, yeah. She'd be seeing him around. A lot.

Chapter 8

In a town this size, with a mere eighteen-hundred residents, the Police Station only had one deputy and one dispatcher on duty after hours. Both tended to take cat naps during slow periods. Which was often. It was all too easy to sneak in and get back at Parker.

Push her around, would he? Get her all flustered, would he? Make her remember why he'd been the focus of her teenage infatuation, would he?

Well, fine. Maddie would let him know how she felt about that.

Harmlessly, of course. Contrary to what people thought, she wasn't a mean person and she did have feelings. And, after all, she did like the guy. She just needed him to go away. And stay there. For the sake of her sanity.

Thus, as she'd left Hair Lair last evening, she'd dropped off a little prezzie at the station. Parker's stapler. In a Jell-O mold. On his desk.

Childish and petty, perhaps, but fun.

Grinning, she cut stems on the roses for the front display cases she hadn't gotten to yesterday and imagined the look on his face when he'd arrived for work this morning. She was pretty sure he'd pop into the station even if he was off duty. Regardless, he'd see her gift tomorrow if not.

"And what has you smiling so big?" Harriet raised her brows. "It wouldn't happen to be because a certain sheriff was here yesterday, would it?"

Maddie eyed her boss from across the worktable. "Nah. Just happy, I guess."

"You're never happy. At least, you don't show it. But, if you want to keep it a secret, that's fine."

Chewing it over, Maddie continued clipping. She didn't have any girlfriends to chat with about things. Any friends

71

period. Harriet had been very nice to her and she did appear interested. At this rate, what would be the harm?

"I had a crush on him in high school." She kept her gaze down, embarrassed to the point her cheeks heated. She waited for the inevitable reaction of laughter or a comeback like, *he's way outta your league.*

"By him, you mean Parker?"

The question wasn't snide or sarcastic, so Maddie released the chokehold on her tension. "Yes. I was terrible to him back then, trying silly things to get him to notice me. It never worked and he avoided me. After awhile, I played shenanigans out of spite. Stupid of me, but…" She shrugged.

"But your feelings were hurt and you acted out."

"Yeah," she said through a sigh.

The gentleness and understanding in Harriet's tone reminded Maddie of her mother. She'd been a glorified trophy wife to a narcissistic man, but a wonderful mom. When she could, she'd been there for Maddie, attending dance recitals or going on shopping excursions or baking treats for school. But several bouts of breast cancer had made her sick on and off from the time Maddie was seven until, ultimately, the disease had won right after her sixteenth birthday. She'd never gotten the opportunity to discuss her crush on Parker with her mom or get advice. Instead, Maddie had suffered with conflicting emotions of grief and heartbreak and first love alone.

She would've given everything she owned for someone, *anyone,* to show her affection. Her father hadn't been a kind man. Still wasn't. What little attention he'd sprinkled on her had been by way of dictation, criticism, or indifference. It wasn't until she'd started dating David, on her dad's insistence, and a man eight years her senior, that he'd acknowledged her at all. Even then, weekly dinners were spent talking business.

"I think that was a normal reaction considering the circumstances and your age." Harriet reached across the table and set her hand on Maddie's. "You should give yourself a break. You've grown up a lot since then."

"Thanks." Easier said than done, but she appreciated the sentiment. "Poor little rich girl, right? If only others could be so lucky and have my kind of problems." How often she'd overhead her peers or teachers or townsfolk say that very phrase.

"Having money doesn't take away your problems. In fact, it often creates more. My late husband, rest his soul, came from a well-to-do family. Pardon my language, but they were the biggest bunch of pricks this side of the Klamath."

Maddie busted out laughing, to the point her ribs ached, and she put the scissors aside before she maimed one of them. "I think that describes my family to a T." Exhaling, she sobered. "It was quite lonely, though. I don't think others realize that, just how lonely it could be."

Huge house. Huger grounds. Lots of staff and priceless, useless baubles for show. Works of art and extravagant meals. And not a soul to talk to.

"I can imagine." Harriet dropped her chin in her hand. "Parker doesn't seem to be avoiding you nowadays."

"No." He wasn't, and how odd. It's not as if she'd encouraged contact. He'd just sort of shown up. Unexpectedly. She was juggling so many balls at the moment, and though part of her wanted to soak up his attention, it was a very bad idea. "Unsure why."

"Maybe it's your second chance?"

She hummed a sound of doubt, but shrugged to pacify the question. People like her didn't get second chances. Heck, she'd never had a first one. To be brutally honest, she'd never *stood* a chance.

"Well, you shouldn't be by yourself all the time." Harriet straightened in her seat. "It's not good for you to…" The bells on the front door signaled a customer. She winked. "Be right back."

"No need to get up, ladies."

Maddie froze.

No, no, no. That very distinct male voice from the shop and footsteps headed this way did not belong to Parker Maloney. They absolutely…

Did. Damn it.

Wearing jeans and a blue tee, he leaned a shoulder against the doorframe, crossing his arms and one foot over the other like

73

he planned on sticking around awhile or had all day to hang out. His biceps bulged and tendons flexed.

That wasn't sexy. At all. Or a lot.

Gah. The lopsided grin was just a cheap shot.

"I'll give you two some breathing room." Harriet turned her back on Parker, raised her brows suggestively at Maddie, and walked into the shop.

Silence ensued where Parker smirked and Maddie stewed. Well, she tried to. It was a little difficult when her heart jacked against her ribs and her gut heated and oxygen was in short supply.

"Why are you here? *Again* today?" This was ridiculous. "Someone report a spider? Heard rumors about a mouse invasion? Go get 'em, sheriff."

The left side of his mouth caught up to the right and he completely disarmed her with a fully-loaded grin. "Jell-O, actually. Lemon Jell-O is what brings me here, Maddie. Know anything about that?"

"Nope." Quickly, she lowered her head and went back to cutting rose stems. Shoot. Snipped too much off that pink one. "Jell-O, you say? This is a flower shop. We don't sell gelatin here. Sorry. Best be on your way."

"Interesting. The prank had your name all over it."

"Wrong again. Totally don't know who put your stapler in a Jell-O mold."

His grunt sounded like a nonverbal *ah-ha*. "I don't believe I gave that much detail about the prank. Just how is it, Miss Innocent, that you knew a stapler was involved?"

Busted. Not that she'd been trying very hard to state her case. "Small town. Word travels fast. Perhaps you should've gone away the first few times I asked."

He shoved off the doorframe and strolled over, calm as you please. Every step toward her matched the errant thump of her pulse. He went around the table and right up to her, where he took the scissors from her shaking hand and set them aside. Using his foot, he swiveled her stool until she faced him, placed his hands on the table behind her to cage her in, and leaned close enough for her to count every one of his thick black eyelashes.

"What are you doing?" All right, this wasn't good. He had her so flustered she was breathily whispering. Face hot, belly quivering, she forced a swallow past her tight throat.

"Testing a hunch." He titled his head, studying her, his gaze sweeping her face in a tender, thorough exploration.

The green of his eyes had tiny gold flecks in them and he had a thin scar above his upper lip about an inch long. Things she'd never noticed because they'd not been this close before. He was all up in her business and the barest amount of oxygen remaining from when he'd arrived had vaporized the moment he'd crowded her against the table. A five o'clock shadow dusted his jaw, adding to his rugged, laid-back appeal. And when his smug grin morphed into Cheshire cat, she knew he'd caught her looking at his full mouth.

"You used to play pranks on me to get my attention in school, and now you're doing it to make me go away." His eyebrows rose as if by inquisition. "Am I understanding you correctly?"

"Yep." She fisted her hands in her lap to remind herself not to touch. He was so tempting and she wanted to know if those whiskers were soft or scratchy. Would he savor the connection or back off? Was his bite as good as his bark? "That's the gist."

A grunt of acknowledgement. A slow nod. "I didn't take your hints and listen to you as a teenager. What makes you think I'm going to start as an adult?"

Uh, well. Hmm. She wasn't sure, but she was doubting what she really wanted altogether. Want and need were such a fine line, and it was getting blurred with him in her orbit.

He smelled faintly of pine aftershave and fabric softener. A scent that was starting to become familiar. For three years, she'd been trying to do better, be better, and amend her wrongs. If he kept this up, he was bound to become her favorite mistake.

And that's what anything between them would be. A mistake.

"Know what I think, Maddie? I think you don't want me to leave you alone." He flashed another grin, quite sudden and throwing her off-guard. "Oh, yeah. Look at those huge eyes and parted lips. You're blushing, too. You don't want me to go away at all."

Panting, she stared at him, wondering when in the hell he'd gotten the upper hand.

"Took me a few encounters to realize it, but there's something here." His gaze dipped to her mouth and back up again. "Feel that? There's chemistry between us."

Shoot. She'd gotten straight A's in chemistry. It was impossible to dispute his findings. The lonely sixteen year old buried inside her cheered like a drunk sorority girl. The woman she thought she'd become was immobile with doubt and shock.

"It's three o'clock."

She cleared her throat. "What?"

"It's three o'clock, which means your shift is over. You ready to go?"

Go? "Where?"

His grin shifted from mischievous to endearing, the sneaky bastard. "Figured we'd go across the street to the café and have us a chat."

"About what?" Dang it. What rock had her brain crawled under?

"Us."

Okay, there. Finally. Synapses started reattaching and firing. "There is no *us*."

"Oh, there's definitely an us. To what extent and in what direction remains to be seen. Thus, the chat."

He wanted to talk. About him and her being an "us." Across the street at the café. A public place where… "No."

"Yes. We're gonna stand up, you're going to put on your hoodie over there, and we're going to walk across the street to Perkatory, where we will then sit down at a table, drink coffee, and speak like civilized adults."

No way. Mary Beth, owner of Perkatory, had been one of Maddie's clique friends in high school, and the first to turn her back when Maddie's father got put away. After she'd realized how dire her financial situation had been, she'd gone to Mary Beth, looking for a place to stay or to rent out the space over her café, and the woman's harsh, abrasive laugh still made Maddie cringe just thinking about it.

She shook her head, refusal on her lips, but Parker straightened.

Taking her hand, he tugged her to her feet, snatched her sweatshirt, and put it over her head. He then manipulated her arms into the sleeves, and she let him, too stunned to be uncooperative.

"See you later, Mrs. Nunez," he shouted toward the open doorway to the shop.

"Have fun, kids!"

They were out the back door and halfway down the alley before the crisp, humid breeze snapped Maddie back into reality. She dug in her heels.

He turned, brows raised. "Problem?"

"Yeah. I'm not going into the café. Especially not on a weekend."

"Worried about someone seeing you with me?"

"Actually, yes." Had he not learned his lesson from the market visit yesterday? "You're one of the most beloved patrons in this community. I'm the most despised."

"Maddie." And just like that, his entire demeanor softened. Expression, posture, his touch. Turning, he faced her, a tender smile curving his lips. "I know there are some people who harbor animosity toward your family, but—"

"Not some, Parker. All."

"*But*," he said, his tone patient, "Not everyone. I don't. Mrs. Nunez doesn't. I'm positive there are more. Hiding isn't the answer. Hold your head up high and prove to them you didn't do anything wrong."

He didn't understand. To prove her point meant stepping into the light, and she could only withstand so much hatred before she caved to the abhorrence. No, she hadn't done anything to justify their view of her, but yes, they had every right to be angry. They'd been lied to and cheated out of their hard-earned money. And by a member of their own neighborhood, right in their own backyards.

"Come with me. Please."

77

Gawd. This man. "Fine, Parker. I don't like it, but let's go."

Maybe the situation would finally click into place for him and he'd stop pushing. Of course, he might fade back into his happy bubble where he'd forgotten she existed, but at least he'd be better off.

They walked down the alley behind the storefronts, then across the two-lane road to Perkatory. He stepped in first, holding the door for her. She immediately slid to his right so he was partially blocking her from view.

The scent of ground coffee and sweet nothings hit her like a ton of doughnuts, and her belly cramped. Part hunger and part nerves. Aside from the muffins and coffee Harriet liked to bring her sometimes, it had been so very long since Maddie had indulged in these kinds of comforts.

High-glossed wood floors and cedar beams on the ceilings made for a warm, inviting hangout. Two-seater iron café tables, about half-full with customers, were to the right, and to the left was the counter. A glass display case held cookies and scones, and against the back wall were machines and canisters.

Mary Beth glanced up from behind the register and zeroed in on Parker with a pleasant smile. She held up one finger to indicate she'd be right with him and continued helping the man at the counter.

She looked the same as she had the last time Maddie had seen her three years ago. Sleek chestnut hair just past her shoulders, high cheek bones, and a willowy frame announced great genetics, and that she'd taken care of herself. Then again, she'd always been vain. She wore khaki leggings and a knee-length green sweater the same color as the pine accents around the café. Flawless makeup and red, manicured nails.

The very sight of her, of being in the same room again, made Maddie's pulse jack-hammer. They'd hung out a thousand times in their youth, countless sleepovers or cheerleading practices, and in one blinding flash, Maddie had become a leper. The friendship, the banter, idle gossip and secret admissions had ground to a halt, leaving her bereft and floundering. All the fear, all that trepidation of uncertainty she'd experienced a few years ago washed over her, through her, and she trembled.

A peek out of the corner of her eye indicated the other patrons were involved in their own company or reading, not paying attention to her. Closing her eyes, she took a deep breath to steady herself before opening them again.

"Sheriff, good to see you." Mary Beth grinned and waved him over. "How are you on this fine Sunday?"

"Great, thanks. Thought I'd have coffee with an old friend and catch up."

"Oh, I didn't see…" She tilted to look around him, and her grin fell flatter than her hair at Homecoming. She sniffed. "Didn't see *you* there."

Since the "you" was dripping with disdain and said loud enough to jerk the attention of other customers, Maddie focused on the display case. Anxiety ate at her stomach lining and bile rose up her throat. Saliva pooled in her mouth, but she didn't dare swallow for fear of vomiting.

Mary Beth straightened. "What can I get you?"

"Ah, I'll have a medium breakfast blend coffee, two sugars, and…" He swiveled to find Maddie. "What would you like?"

She said the first thing that came to mind and had no concept of what it was soon as it left her mouth.

"To go, correct?" Mary Beth blinked. Repeatedly.

Parker's jaw ticked, suggesting he'd picked up on the haze of odium suddenly infesting the small shop, but his smile didn't waver. "No, we'll sit for a bit. Oh, and a couple of those amazing blueberry scones."

She nodded. "Have a seat. I'll bring it right out."

"Perfect." He gestured to a table, and Maddie sat with her back to the counter as quick as humanly possible.

After a few tense moments, she bit her lip, gaze on the wrought iron ivy pattern on the table. "Now do you believe me?"

Chapter 9

Yeah, Parker believed her. There was definitely a lot of hostility in the café. "Weren't you and Mary Beth friends? You were always together in high school."

Gaze down, Maddie nodded.

He drummed his fingers on the table, watching her. She hadn't looked at him since they'd left the alley behind Ka-Bloom. This timid, shy person wasn't Maddie. It was as if life, someone, or a series of someones had sucked the brazen feistiness right out of her, replacing it with a hollow shell of the woman she used to be.

Full admission? Yes, she'd scared the crap out of him as a teenager. Hell, she scared the crap out of him now, too, but in an entirely different way. If he had been more observant back then or taken the time to have an actual conversation with her, perhaps things could've gone differently. But he hadn't, and here they were.

He blamed himself.

And much as it shocked him to say it, he wanted that version of her who'd taunted him in his car the other night or who fought back on every single damn thing he said. She made him think and kept him on his toes and challenged him. Being around her wasn't boring, that was for sure.

"Here you go, sheriff." Mary Beth set a coffee down in front of him, the plate of scones, and smiled. Without looking at his companion, she then set Maddie's cappuccino on the table with a little more force and without acknowledging her. "Enjoy, Parker."

Irritation crawled up his neck and made the back of his head throb. He kept it in check until the right opportunity to speak with Mary Beth alone. Confronting her would only make Maddie more uncomfortable and draw attention to them. Something she obviously didn't want.

"Thank you," he said, and waited until she returned to the counter before looking at Maddie. She hadn't moved a muscle. "When did you stop being friends?"

"I don't think we were ever truly friends." She drew a shallow breath, her exhausted and disparaged gaze on his tee. "But the sham of trying ended the day of sentencing like it did with everyone else. I thought she'd be different, thought she knew the truth." Her shoulder lifted in a barely noticeable shrug. "Guess not."

An ache grew behind his breastbone and spread. Her father and fiancé had been locked away, and she'd come home to a place that should've accepted her. Instead, it had done the opposite and shunned her. Granted, he'd only seen a few examples of bitterness, and he thoroughly believed not everyone had to feel this way, yet still.

Why had she stayed, then? She could've packed it up and gone anywhere. Started over in a clean, fresh place where no one recognized her name.

"Have you visited your dad or David?" He'd been wondering.

The trial and investigation had taken place up in Portland, and that's where both were currently incarcerated. If she didn't have a car, she'd have no means to get there. He had zero interest in seeing either one of the men, but her dad was her family.

"Not since a week after they took the plea bargain." She traced her finger around the lip of her cup, her expression pained. "I try to call Daddy sometimes. He never accepts. David and I obviously broke up."

There had to be more to that story, but he'd ask another time. "If you want to visit your father, I can take you."

Wide blue eyes met his for the briefest moment, then dipped to the table again. "No, but thank you. He made it quite clear he doesn't want to see me."

"Why?" She was his daughter. Perhaps he was embarrassed by his circumstances or didn't want her to have to see him in prison or…

"He disowned me, said I was dead to him."

Or...*that*. Not once had that possibility crossed Parker's mind. The ache in his chest became a painful stabbing. "I'm sorry. Why would he do such a thing?"

She sighed, chewing her lip. "The easy answer is because I cooperated with the Feds and he saw that as a betrayal. I thought they were innocent, that it was all a mistake. I would've been honest and given authorities whatever they asked for, regardless. I didn't realize it at the time, but a lot of what I said or handed over was damning."

Parker had no clue. He'd seen the evidence and whatnot, but hadn't known she'd been the one to turn it in. "If that's the easy answer, what's the hard one?" And did he really want to know?

"Not all families are like yours, Parker."

"What do you mean?"

She rubbed her eyes and took a sip of her cappuccino, only to wince and set it down again.

"What's wrong with it?"

"Nothing. Just hot."

A glance at the mug showed it wasn't steaming any longer. Mary Beth was looking at them with a telltale smirk, however. What had she done to it? "I'll get you another."

"No, it's fine. It'll cool off."

Not wanting to feed the problem, he let it go, but he nudged her cup aside and put the scones in front of her instead. "Not all families are like mine," he prodded.

"It doesn't matter. The past is the past."

"The past shapes who we are today. Explain. I want to know." He was desperately afraid he didn't, and he hadn't the foggiest why she was being open with him when she typically diverted or distracted, but for the sake of understanding her better, he pushed. "Go on."

"I was a disappointment from birth, being born with a vagina and not testicles."

Ah, all right. "Your dad wanted a boy."

"Yeah. He got me instead. My only redeeming quality was I followed his plan with David."

"Plan?"

"Marry David so he could take over the business. Dad hand-picked him for the company out of a lot of other candidates to be his successor. Later, when I went off to college, Dad urged me…" She squinted. "That's not exactly correct. He *insisted* I date David. After I was to graduate, we would get married and I'd be a devoted wife. I wouldn't bother with a silly career and my sole purpose was to run the household while raising offspring."

He stared at her, just outright stared while he tried and failed to wrap his head around what she'd said. There was so much wrong with that statement, he didn't know where to start. Not only had her father pimped her out for the sake of appearances, arranged a courtship as if this were the 1800s, and was sexist to the nth degree, but he'd planned on using her as a show pony example of the perfect housewife.

"I have a hard time believing you'd go along with that, to be honest."

Maddie didn't take crap from anyone. Well, not back then, anyhow. As of late, she avoided everyone like the second coming of the bubonic plague.

Again, she lowered her head as if ashamed, avoiding eye contact. "I just wanted his acceptance. I fought for it constantly. The way I saw it, if I did what he wanted, he'd finally…" She shook her head.

No need for her to finish the thought. He understood. Loud and clear. Forget pain. His entire chest cavity was in agony. "Maybe he'd finally love you?"

A nod, and she dropped her chin in her palm, turning her head to gaze out the window to her right.

Christ, how wrong could he possibly have been about her? Not only had her mother passed away when they'd barely had a driver's license, and after a long battle with cancer, but her father had never wanted her. No wonder. *No wonder* she'd acted like a spoiled little princess ruling a kingdom. She'd been acting out, using bitchery as a shield because she'd known no other way.

Her admission in the car the other night hit with full force and stole his oxygen. She'd been trying to get *his* attention. The pranks, the name-calling. And what had he done? Ignored her, just like her father and just like everyone else in Redwood Ridge was doing. If she was to be believed on that latter account. Plus, if her engagement had been an arranged one, it was plausible David had never cared about her, either.

Who'd shown or given her love? If the two men who were supposed to love her and didn't were in prison, and she truly thought the townsfolk had abandoned her, then who did she have to turn to?

His gut cranked and he wanted to puke.

Sick as the situation made him, there was still time to do something about it. He'd meant what he'd said about her showing her face around and holding her head up high. And now that he had an idea where she was coming from and her background, he knew how to handle her.

The shopping visit from yesterday came to mind. The school and Rec Center. Even Ka-Bloom and today at Perkatory. The way he'd witnessed her treatment. How she ducked in and out the rear doors like an outcast. How she took back alleys instead of front sidewalks.

His gaze flicked to the other customers, watching him and Maddie out of the corners of their eyes. To Mary Beth, not even attempting to hide her contempt or blatant show of glaring at them. For the past week, he'd barely recognized his hometown.

Maddie had been correct about one thing. He was one of the most beloved members of the community. He called it doing his job well and following in some excellent footsteps. He supposed being a decent human being and treating others with respect like his parents' had taught him helped. If things were to change, it had to start with him.

"Want to get out of here?" He smiled, hoping it conveyed his sympathy.

He didn't know where they were headed, their relationship or friendship, or if they were even compatible. But this time, he wasn't going about it or forward based on fear. Wherever they landed, together or apart, it would be because he listened with his ears *and* his eyes while keeping an open mind.

Still, she wouldn't look at him. "Sure."

"Do you have plans for tonight?" When she finally eyed him, suspicious, he smiled harder. "I was thinking we could go back to my place. Watch a movie or something. Order takeout. I can drive you back afterward." Thus therein laid the balance. Time alone *and* out in public.

"Sounds an awful lot like a date, Parker."

"Dinner and a movie? You don't say."

Another sigh, and she tilted her face toward the ceiling. "Are you a glutton for punishment?"

There was just no telling. "Hanging out with you isn't punishment." Shocker, that. "Neither is a date."

She dropped her chin, looking at him deadpan. "You haven't been on a date with me. It could be punishment."

Ha. There was some spunk coming back. "Bring it."

"I don't think it's a good idea."

"Then stop thinking."

Her lips parted, only to close again. He gave her a moment since she seemed to be mulling over his offer. Little did she realize, he wasn't offering. She might've been the aggressive one growing up, but she'd also taught him a thing or fifty.

"What movie?"

He bit the inside of his cheek to tame a grin. "I have a decent selection. You can pick."

"And what if I choose *Steel Magnolias* or *Sixteen Candles* or something equally feminine and tear-jerking?"

First, he had neither of those movies since he was born with a penis and testicles. Second, *Sixteen Candles* wasn't a tear-jerker. Paige had made him watch it umpteen times. Third, just how long had it been since she'd watched a flick that those were the two she'd suggested?

He waved his hand in nonchalance. "Man of my word. You pick."

"Okay, I guess. It's not a date, though."

"Whatever you say." He rose and scooted in his chair. "I'm going to hit the Men's Room real quick. Want to wait for me outside?"

"Sure." She stood and pulled her hood over her head, back into hiding mode.

He waited until she'd stepped out and onto the sidewalk before walking up to the counter to deal with a certain brunette. "I remember the service at Perkatory being better than today's."

Mary Beth pursed her lips, narrowing her eyes. "And I remember you having better taste. You should be more careful of the company you keep."

He gnashed his teeth to keep from saying something he couldn't take back and slowly inhaled. His temples still pounded despite the effort. "Who I choose to spend time with is none of your business. For the record, you used to keep her company, too, and it would be nice if someone had her back. It's a shame you went off rumor to form conclusions and lost a great friend as a result. She's not guilty. I would know. Consider that next time she orders a cappuccino."

Not waiting for a reply, he strode to the door and outside. He was mildly stunned Maddie had waited for him. Between storefronts, with a hood on, and trying to become one with the wall, but she'd waited.

"My car's by Ka-Bloom. You ready?"

They were halfway to his house when something dawned on him. "Uh, you're not afraid of dogs, are you?"

"Not particularly, unless they're aggressive. Why?"

"I've got a Dalmatian. He's a few years old and a bit...energetic. He's a big sissy, though, and wouldn't hurt a fly."

He should've thought of that sooner. He was willing to bet the first time Domino jumped on Maddie or wanted to play, she would get annoyed. He'd dated a few women who'd issued the ultimatum of them or the dog. Alas, his best bud remained and Parker was still single. Maddie, especially considering her prestigious upbringing, probably wouldn't appreciate an affectionate dog.

"Aren't firefighters supposed to have Dalmatians? Officers have Shepherds or Pitbulls or whatever."

"Look at you, stereotyping." He grinned. "I saw him at one of those park events and fell for the goober on the spot. He was just a pup then, maybe a handful of months old."

Actually, it had been the day of her father's sentencing that he'd stumbled upon Domino. He'd watched her walk out of the courthouse and wasn't ready to make the drive from Portland to Redwood Ridge yet. He'd strolled around the park across the street for a while and there'd been a group from the local rescue shelter. Poor little guy was cowering in the corner by a temporary fence away from his siblings.

Love at first sight. Parker had never regretted a second. Not even when Domino had chewed through five pairs of shoes in his puppy phase or had eaten an entire roasted chicken Parker had cooling on the counter. Including the bones.

"Sucker." She smiled at him, and for once, it didn't take five minutes to fully emerge like a delayed reaction. The cool shade of blue in her eyes warmed and transformed her from reserved to approachable.

"That I am." Apparently, in more ways than one.

He pulled into the driveway for his modest three-bedroom brick ranch and into the garage. While the door closed them in, they climbed out and made their way inside to the utility room.

Nails pattered on hardwood as the *clomp, clomp, clomp* of Domino barreling through the living room into the kitchen came their way. The dog was brought up short by a gate Parker had installed in the doorway.

Maddie glanced from the washer, dryer, and cabinets to the dog staring anxiously at her. "Aw, he's cute."

"He is not. Cute is for kittens. He's handsome. Aren't you, boy?"

Domino barked, and Maddie laughed at the *arrrooouuufff* howl/woof combination.

"Now," Parker said, kicking off his shoes, "Domino, this is Maddie. We are not going to jump on, lick, chew, or otherwise assault her. Do you understand?"

Arrrooouuufff.

"Excellent." He unlatched the gate and smiled at Maddie. "Might want to let me go first."

He eased through the gate into the kitchen, and that was the beginning of the end.

Domino, with free reign, hauled ass around Parker and straight toward Maddie. She got one step deep, and down she went with a squeak, flat on her back between the wall and the oak dining table, sixty-eight pounds of black and white dog on top of her.

"Son of a..." Parker quickly latched the gate and turned to grab Domino's collar. "Are you all right?"

Oblivious to his blunder, Domino gave her face a tongue bath.

This was it. Parker hadn't even gotten to the ordering dinner or choosing a movie portion of the evening, and she was going to want to go home. No making a move on her on the couch. No trying to debate if he'd kiss her goodnight. His goofy dog had just cock-blocked his first date.

Except she...*laughed.*

Parker froze a fraction of a second, then peered over the dog.

Yep. She was laughing all right. He hadn't been hallucinating. Eyes closed, hands up, nose wrinkled, she laughed. Deep, rich, from-the-gut laughter that shook her whole body.

Stunned, he didn't know what to do.

"If we're going to make out, you should at least introduce yourself." She sat up, her tongue bath pursuant, and grinned at Domino while rubbing his ears. "I don't care what he says. You are cute. However, women kinda like to be coaxed into physical activity. Slow and steady, you know? We'll work on it."

Arrrooouuufff.

Chapter 10

"I swear, he is trained. Do you want me to put him in the other room?"

From Parker's kitchen table, Maddie smiled at the dog. While waiting for a dinner delivery, they'd played with Domino in the backyard. Since sitting down to eat a few minutes ago, he'd plopped his butt next to her chair with his head in her lap.

He was adorable. Hopeful, endearing eyes and a sweet demeanor. A big baby. Well, not incredibly big. He was a medium-sized dog and about as tall as thigh-height when standing. He had lean muscle and was in great shape. Soft fur.

"Naw, he's good. Aren't you, boy?"

The half-hearted *arrrooouuufff* response was barked against her knee because he wouldn't lift his head. Or go lay down when Parker had asked. Or leave her side since their initial bonding mauling upon arrival.

Parker ducked his head under the table. "You're not giving her a very good first impression, you know."

Domino shifted his eyes to him, then up at her, never moving his head.

"Don't listen to him," she whispered. "You're a total chick magnet."

A thump, the table vibrated, and Parker straightened, rubbing his noggin. "He's not, actually. He's chased away many dates. He's gotten better about the attention-whore thing, but jumping on people when they first arrive is a work-in-progress." He picked up his fork, stabbing a bite of lasagna and pointing it at her. "This is uncanny, though. He's never this obsessed with guests. He really likes you."

"Awesome recognizes awesome." She shrugged, biting into her beef ravioli. So good. She hadn't had Italian food at Le Italy restaurant since before she'd left for college. "Thanks again for dinner."

She didn't know why she'd agreed to this date that wasn't a date. Maybe it was the appeal of a meal that didn't come from a can or the thought of a few hours inside four walls when she wasn't required to work. Nevertheless, here she was, in Parker Maloney's house. Alone, save for the dog. She was still more than a lot shocked he'd wanted to hang out after the blatant display of hostility she'd received at the café. Or at the market.

"You're very welcome." He took a drink. "Let me ask you something that's been bugging me. When you told me about your crush, you described me as unattainable. Why?"

"Because you were." Then and now.

He shook his head, expression frustrated and bewildered. "I didn't have a serious girlfriend in high school. If I had known..."

"You would've what? Transferred to another district? Ran faster in the other direction?"

"Looked at your antics in a different light."

Though he seemed sincere, she doubted him. For starters, her father never would've allowed her to date a cop's son. Blue collar was beneath them in his eyes. Second, even before the terrible thing her father had done, the town saw her as a rich bitch. She had status and quasi-respect only because of her name. Funny how that very name had become synonymous with putrescence. And third, no one liked her. Period. Not him, not their former teachers, not the Freemont Manor staff, not even the so-called friends she'd once acquired.

If anything, she would've been a laughing stock or despised much sooner had word of her crush spread. Perhaps pitied for those few who would spare her any feelings at all.

"Doesn't matter now," she said, setting her fork aside. She was about to bust. It had been eons since she'd eaten that much. "That was really good."

Grunting, he rose and collected their plates. "Don't tell my mom, but they make better lasagna than hers. Hits the spot every time."

Yeah, because she and his mom were BFFs. "Do you want some help?"

"No, you relax. I'll load the dishwasher later. Let me just put the leftovers away." He turned from the sink, bumping his chin in the direction of the living room. "Head in the other room if you like. Pick out something for us to watch. Blu-rays are in the drawer under the TV."

Rising, she pushed her chair in and strode out of the kitchen. Domino followed at her heels.

Parker had a great house. Not extravagant or posh, but cozy and inviting. It smelled like him. Pine and fabric softener. Mahogany hardwood throughout. At least, what she'd seen thus far. The kitchen cabinets were glossy and black, appliances stainless steel. The living room, though? Yes, please.

A flat screen took up nearly the entire space to the left, and sat on a low black stand that hugged the ground. His sofa was a dark burgundy sectional with the type of cushions one could sink into. Sepia-toned prints of a forest hung on ivory-colored walls. A huge red brick fireplace in the far corner went from floor to ceiling with a scarred black walnut mantel that matched his tables. There was a wall of bookshelves to the left of it, and as she moved closer, she found mostly horror or mystery titles, a few classics thrown in. Pictures with mismatched frames held photos of him with his parents and sister, lots of his niece Katie, a couple with his best friend Jason, and two of his dog.

She smiled at one of him and Domino from when he'd been a puppy. So dang adorable. Man and beast. Parker's grin could solve the energy crisis and had her ovaries crying for mercy. There was another of him holding a newborn Katie, his focus solely on the tiny infant swaddled in pink. Gah.

Footsteps tapped behind her. "I see I might have to fight for *your* attention this time."

She glanced at her feet, where the dog obediently sat, wagging his tail. "He is quite affectionate. You'd have to fight dirty."

"Not my style." He stepped beside her, gaze on the mantel. "Whatcha looking at?"

"Katie's cute as hell. You can tell she's a Maloney with those green eyes and black hair. Domino as a puppy is a close second on the aww scale. Good-looking family, Parker."

"Thanks. I'm rather fond of them." He grinned at her, winked, and headed toward the TV. "Pick out anything to watch yet?"

"No, I was too busy nosing around."

A laugh, and he squatted in front of the TV, pulling out a drawer in the stand. "Action, scary, funny?"

"Don't really care. Funny, I guess." She could use a laugh.

With him turned away, she took the opportunity to gawk at him. Lord, but the way his jeans molded to his backside. Wide shoulders, strong back. He had to work out with those guns as big as they were and the tendons in his forearms were a thing of beauty. Veins. Yum. That wasn't even accounting for his thick head of black hair. How she itched to shove her fingers in the strands.

Such a bad, terrible, no good idea being here. He'd pushed. She'd caved. But the more encounters together and the longer they spent in one another's presence was going to make it that much harder when he came to his senses. She'd be the one crying in her pillow, worse off than she'd ever been when this had simply been a girly infatuation.

Memories, though. She needed some excellent ones to carry her through the rocky times ahead. By her calculations, at the amount her paychecks currently were, it would take a minimum of five years to pay back everyone in Redwood Ridge for the money they'd invested. She'd been chipping away for two and a half years, soon as she'd settled and made camp.

Holding onto something great with him, regardless of how it would end, was selfish. But, just once, she wanted to feel good.

"Is this okay?" He looked over his shoulder, holding up a case.

She hadn't been paying attention and couldn't read the title from her position. "Works for me."

"Awesome. It's hilarious. Have you seen it?"

"No." If it had been released in the past few years, definitely not.

He loaded the movie and moved to the fireplace, switching it on. She hadn't realized it was a gas-lit. Convenient.

Daylight filtered through the window, but it was muted and fading to dusk. The room was very dim and set for a romance she wasn't positive she was ready for. Aside from a few kisses or boyfriends, David had been her sole experience in this area, barring one guy in college prior to him. And David had been as far from romantic as a human being could get.

Ramifications hit her as Parker plopped on the couch and she stood idle, suddenly nervous. All their banter and back and forth. Like he needed more reasons to run than her being out of practice.

"Come on, Maddie." He patted the cushion next to him.

Hands shaking, she walked over and sat beside him.

Oh, yes. She'd been right about how comfortable the couch would be. It was like being embraced by a cloud. With a sexy angel riding shotgun.

The title screen came on for a movie. In fact, she hadn't heard of it, but it looked funny.

Parker turned his head, pointing to the flat screen. "I had doubts when Paige brought this over, but I died laughing at a couple parts."

Sounded good to her.

Domino sat in front of her, resting his head in her lap as Parker started the movie. She absently petted the dog's ears while watching the opening credits.

As they got deeper into the film, she'd get distracted by the story and stop petting him. The dog would not-so-gently remind her with a nudge of his nose. It had been so long since she'd seen a movie or watched TV that poor Domino had to nudge her a lot.

Thirty minutes went by, and Parker leaned forward. "All right, Domino. Go lay down. Leave the woman alone."

Domino looked at her, eyes sad and pleading.

"Aww. Is he allowed on the couch?"

Parker glanced at her as if she'd lost her mind. "Yes, but he has to be invited. I wouldn't recommend it because..."

She patted the cushion next to her on the opposite side as Parker. "Come on, boy."

Domino wasted no time and hopped up, burying his face in her neck, whole body wagging instead of just his tail.

"Because that's why." Parker huffed a laugh. "He really does like you."

"Feeling is mutual." She pointed to her leg. "Lay down."

The dog promptly rested his head on one of her thighs. Parker, to be a smartass, did so on her other one. But then he didn't move.

Throwing her head back, she laughed. Who needed a movie? She had two hilarious males as floor entertainment. She petted both of them.

And Gawd, Parker's hair? So thick and soft. She threaded her fingers through it before she realized what she was doing, going from a mere petting to a full-blown come-on. Her skin heated, but she didn't stop, not even when he stilled like he was processing her sudden shift in mood.

Seconds bled into minutes, not even a twitch from him, but her respirations increased to asthmatic. Her belly clenched and a fog invaded her mind to make everything around her blurry. The movie faded to background static and the *thump, thump* of her heart grew to a thunderous *boom, boom.*

He didn't even seem to be breathing.

Finally, after she didn't know how long, he set his hand on the cushion between her and the dog and lifted his head. Up, he rose, until he was leaning over her with his face close to hers.

His gaze swept over her features, hotter than a caress. Her hair, her eyes, her mouth, and gradually back to her gaze once more. His Adam's apple bobbed and the green of his irises were almost completely swallowed by his pupils. His chest rose and fell with increased respirations to match hers.

"Maddie," he whispered, his voice coarse. "Remember that hunch I mentioned? The one about chemistry and mutual interest?"

She nodded, unable to speak.

"I think I downplayed it by a margin. Mind if I investigate?"

She shook her head, trembling from a place so deep, her core felt the vibrations.

"Good. This definitely warrants investigation." Closer he inched, his nose brushing hers and his breath fanning her jaw. His lids lowered to half-mast. "Examining all leads is important."

He sealed his mouth to hers, coaxing, a mere meeting, and held still as if testing the waters. A desperate beat passed where she didn't know whether to inhale or melt into the couch. Then he tilted his head, parting his lips, and she incinerated. His warm hand cradled the side of her face, irrevocably gentle, as he slid his tongue past her lips to touch hers.

A groan, and he stroked her tongue with his, teasing and building up the knot of need within her until her skin was on fire and breathing was a distant memory. Dizzy, she clenched her fingers in his hair while he explored.

Conquered.

Dominated.

Wider, he opened, pressing closer yet. Their chests bumped and his second groan rumbled her ribcage. His whiskers grazed her cheeks while the kiss morphed into something more frantic, fraught with desire that spurned from nowhere and exploded everywhere.

Breaths heaving, he eased away just enough to sever their mouths and still share oxygen. "That was the whole periodic table of chemistry."

Understatement. Lifting her heavy lids, she found his pinched tightly closed, as if he were trying to wrangle control. "Guess you were correct to follow the hunch."

"So glad you said that." He grabbed her hips and lifted her until she straddled him. He shoved his hands in her hair and looked in her eyes, searching. "For the record, I was an idiot."

For kissing her? Was that what he meant? She frowned. "What?"

"At fifteen. Hell, at sixteen, seventeen, and eighteen. Whenever your interest in me started and for the whole duration. I was a fucking idiot for ignoring you."

Oh, well. Dang. Okay, then. Fine, liquefy her into a boneless heap. "We all make mistakes," she breathed. Her lungs just weren't cooperating.

"This one I won't make again. I try my damnedest not to repeat my mistakes."

"That's a really good motto."

"I agree." He hauled her against him, devouring her mouth and all but swallowing her whole. His hands were everywhere. Her thighs, her hips, her waist, up her back, down again, until finally resettling in her hair. "Strawberries."

"Huh?"

"You smell like strawberries," he grated against her throat, kissing his way up to her jaw.

"Sorry?" Judging by his tone, an apology was required. She couldn't think when he was doing that tease and nip combination right over her erratic pulse.

"Don't be. It's an utter turn-on."

Holy cow and all the barnyard animals. His mouth was just too skilled for her own good. "It's my shampoo."

He lifted his head and met her gaze pointedly. "Never stop using it."

"Okay."

A mass of black and white fur shoved between their faces.

Domino licked her, then Parker.

"Damn it." He nudged the dog aside, but Domino popped back and repeated his interest in joining the party.

She laughed. "Threesomes aren't really my thing."

Chapter 11

In his car in the parking lot at Shooters, while waiting for Jason to get off work, Parker glanced at his cell. He'd texted Maddie asking her to go to the Halloween Party with him tomorrow night, knowing what her reaction was going to be.

Hell to the no.

Thumbs flying, he sent his response. *Yes. It'll make for a great second date.*

He watched the icon swirl, indicating she was replying.

Maddie: The first date wasn't a date.

Ha. She kept trying that line as if it had worked to deter him all week. After dinner and a movie at his place on Sunday, he'd shown up at the school and Rec Center Monday, Tuesday, and Wednesday to drive her home. In fact, he'd just dropped her off not ten minutes ago. She wouldn't invite him inside her apartment, only allowing him no further than the curb, but he hadn't let her climb out of the passenger seat without a goodnight kiss. Or ten.

Damn, but who knew the woman who'd once been dubbed the Ice Princess could cinder him to ash with a stroke of her tongue? He'd wondered if their flirting would equate to anything once he'd made a move or if they'd wind up without any physical magnetism. It happened sometimes. There seemed to be something interesting brewing, then bam. A kiss, and nothing.

So not the case with Maddie.

He typed his response. *Yes, it was. Dinner + Movie + Kissing = A Date.*

Maddie: Agree to disagree. Regardless, no second date. Or first.

Grinning, he shook his head. The stubborn woman. He should be irritated or pissed off, but once he'd figured her out, her deflection no longer upset him. Because she was defending herself. Plain and simple. Moreover, she was trying to protect him and his reputation. With the majority of Redwood Ridge harboring animosity toward her family, she'd been treated poorly. In her eyes, dating her would make him despised, too.

A woman with ice water running through her veins wouldn't do that or care about fallout for him.

Besides, it wasn't gonna happen. Slowly, he'd been talking with those patrons who'd said something directly to her or those whose conversations he'd overheard. Didn't mean all people would listen to him or agree, but it was a start. At the very least, it would get townsfolk debating and discussing. Since the info had come from him, it would maybe open minds a little bit.

He thumbed a reply, not giving her the option to ignore him. She'd definitely been right there in the moment with him on his couch. And her flushed cheeks, moans of pleasure, and avid response said he wasn't alone in his attraction.

I'll pick you up after your shift at the school Friday night. We'll head right to the party. He could all but hear her fuming.

Maddie: Damn it, Parker. No. I'm not going. Besides, I don't have a costume.

Boom. He had her. *I'll take care of the costume. No excuses. You can wear a mask and not be easily recognized.*

It was actually a good venue for them to attend together. A mask would ensure she'd feel anonymous and it would take townsfolk time to match the costume with her name. He wasn't going to allow her to hide any longer.

Maddie: No

Parker: Yes

Jason's truck pulled into the parking space next to Parker's. He held up his finger to let his friend know he'd be out in a second. A nod, and Jason strode into the bar.

Maddie: Not even if you slapped handcuffs on me and dragged me there.

Parker: That can be arranged. Friday. Eight o'clock. Pick you up at the school. I look forward to it.

Maddie: Parker!!!! This was followed by several angry emojis.

He sent her three angel emojis and a grinning one, then pocketed his phone and exited the car.

The place was relatively quiet, but it was a Thursday night. Familiar scents of fried food and draft beer hit him along with stale perfume and boredom. Parker found Jason at their typical corner table and pulled up a chair.

"No Ella?"

Jason held up his phone. "She just texted. They had teacher conferences tonight. She's on her way."

Awesome. Parker needed her to do something for him, if she didn't mind. "Did you eat?" He hadn't managed the task yet and his stomach was ready to eat itself.

"No." Jason waved a waitress over. "Can we get two burgers with fries? Medium-well for him. Still bleeding and mooing for me. We got someone else coming. She'll want a grilled chicken sandwich and onion rings."

"Anything else?"

"Yeah," Parker interjected. "Two of whatever you have on tap and a diet cola for her."

A nod, and the waitress headed for the kitchen.

Parker tried to pass Jason some bills, but his buddy shook his head.

"It's my turn. You got it last time." He waited until the waitress had set down their drinks before talking again, and he looked around suspiciously first. "What's this rumor about you having coffee with Madeline?"

"It's not a rumor if it's true."

Jason eyed him. "Have you lost your damn mind?"

"I have all my faculties."

"For how long?" He glared at Parker. "You spend time with her, and I'm going to be responding to an emergency dispatch about you."

"I'm sorry. Hold on." Parker unlocked his phone, glanced at the screen, and set it down again. "Nope. I don't have a drama queen translation app."

"I'm serious."

"So am I. Does the Google Play store have one? Apple says no."

Jason eyed the ceiling. "How much dip would a dipshit shit if a dipshit could shit dip?"

"I do this thing called what I want. There a problem with that?"

"Yeah, man." Jason tilted his head. "There's a problem when what you want is to hang out, *in public*, with the biggest bitch in all the land, who made your childhood miserable, whose family are criminals, and who no one likes. She's gonna eat your soul and pick her teeth with your bones."

Struggling for patience, Parker tapped his fingers on the table. He'd known the guy in front of him since before either of them could walk, and Jason was concerned about him. Parker got that. He understood. But if he couldn't get his best friend to back him up, how the hell was he supposed to get the town to do so?

"Rumors are carried by haters, spread by fools, and accepted by idiots." Parker took a sip of beer and set it down, staring at the glass. "She's not who we thought her to be. She's…different. I think we've been the idiots all along."

"How so?"

"Her mom died when we were, what? Sophomores? And she'd been sick for long before that. Her dad is an egotistical asshole who wanted nothing to do with her until she served a purpose." Parker shook his head, sick in his gut all over again. "Think about it. Rich girl, no love, and everyone at school called her a bitch. How would you respond?"

Jason's eyes narrowed, his whole demeanor deflating as if he was getting the picture. "By feeding into the perception and playing the role I was given." He swiped a hand down his face. "Jesus. So she tried to get attention any way she could, even if it was negative?"

"Exactly. Look at you, for example." Parker rubbed the condensation on his glass with his thumb, hesitant to bring up a touchy subject. "Your dad died unexpectedly when we were ten. Since then, you carried that guilt around, avoiding commitment and relationships, until Ella came along. And you have a wonderful mother you're close to and who supports your every move. Maddie didn't have that." She'd been virtually alone. Or, maybe not alone, but lonely.

"True. I get it, but how do you know she's not acting now?"

102

"Because she's doing everything in her power to go unnoticed." Parker rolled his head to loosen the muscles in his neck. "When was the last time you saw her? She's been back three years, and can you honestly say you've spotted her in town?"

"No." Jason's brows furrowed. "Maybe she's just keeping her head down."

"Or maybe everyone hated her before, and after what her father did, she's despised even more. They don't know her. The real her. None of us do." Parker sighed. "She barely looks me in the eye. She goes to work and she goes home. I had to drag her to the café kicking and screaming. And Mary Beth treated her like absolute garbage."

Jason reared. "Weren't they besties?"

"Not anymore. In fact, Maddie said she thought they never were. Get me? She's got nobody."

Up went Jason's brows. "And you want to be her somebody?"

The sarcastic doubt was back in his voice, but Parker knew Jason would eventually support him. Always had, always would. He might be a pain in the ass, but Jason was solid.

Parker shrugged. "Maybe. I'm trying. At the very least, if we don't fit as a couple, then friends."

"You want to date her?" Jason's eyes bugged from his head. He glanced around and leaned forward, lowering his tone. "Hanging out is one thing, friendship is another. But to get romantically involved?"

"She said she had a crush on me in high school."

Jason choked on his beer, coughing violently. "Come again?"

"Multiply your surprise by the number of stars in the galaxy and divide by one. That was my level of holy shit, too."

"Wow." Jason wiped his mouth on a napkin. "She had a funny way of showing it."

"Word."

"Remember that time she gave you gum that dyed your teeth blue for four days?"

"Yep. And told the Freshman body it was because I ate Smurfs."

"Smurf's *balls*. And there was that time she put itching powder in your gym shoes."

"Yep. Made the track team that year."

Jason shook his head. "She did all that *while* having a thing for you?"

"I think she did all of it *because* she had a thing for me."

"Huh." Jason sipped his draft. "Women are strange."

"No truer words."

A suspicious glare. "She play any pranks lately?"

"She put my stapler in a Jell-O mold."

Jason laughed. Hard. "So she watches *The Office*. At least she has good taste in TV shows. Does that mean she's still got a crush on you?"

"She claimed it was to make me go away and leave her alone." Parker scratched his jaw. "That's the only lie I've caught her in thus far."

A puff of his cheeks, and Jason reclined in his seat. "Okay, all that aside, starting a relationship with her might seem like a good idea, but so was getting on the Titanic, and look what happened there, man."

"I like her." Shocked as Parker was to admit it, truth was truth. "I do. I like her."

"Shit." Jason dropped his forehead on the table. "What has become of this world? Up is down and wrong is right."

"Your drama queen is showing again," Parker muttered, unamused.

"All right, all right." Jason straightened and raised his hands in surrender. "You've got a good head on your shoulders— normally—and I've always trusted your judgment—mostly—so, lay it on me. How *much* do you like her?"

"Enough to *tell you* I like her."

Bro Code: Get used to having her around.

The waitress dropped off their meals and went back to the bar just as Ella strode in and removed her jacket.

Her attention bobbed between them as she hung her coat on the back of the chair and sat. "I swear, I need to quit showing up late. I always miss something. What's going on?"

"Parker here wants to date the Devil Incarnate." Jason wrapped his hand around the back of her neck and brought her to him for a kiss. "Missed you. How were conferences?"

"Missed you, too. Conferences were an epic adventure in exhaustion. And what about the Devil?"

"That devil has a name." Parker ground his teeth.

"Sorry." Jason cleared his throat. "Parker wants to date *Madeline.*"

Ella paused, an onion ring halfway to her mouth. "Um, I thought we determined The Battleaxes weren't trying to pair you two."

"Three different times on three separate occasions I bumped into Maddie after being sent to those locations by Marie, all for phony or ridiculous reasons. Not once in three years have I run into her before last week."

"Hmm. Three might be your lucky number."

"Or unlucky," Jason drolled.

Her lips pursed as she, like Parker, ignored Jason. "I've been stalking the Pinterest boards and Twitter account. There's not been one mention."

"Yeah, about that." Parker gave Ella the long and short of the conversation he'd just had with her man. "I'm one-hundred and fifty percent certain they're match-making Maddie and I. Something tells me, because of her past, that's why they're not doing a public spectacle of the situation like they have with everyone else."

Staring at him, a wary question in her eyes, she made a point of chewing and swallowing before speaking. "Let me see if I'm following. They think Madeline is your soul mate?"

"Yep."

"Proven because they've sent you on fool's errands to run into her?"

"Yep."

"But they're not broadcasting their antics on social media this go-around because of her reputation, and that might hinder their efforts or rile the town against the scheme?"

"Yep."

She nodded slowly. "And Madeline had a crush on you as a teenager?"

"Yep." He was starting to sound like a drunk parrot, and he was only half a cup of beer in.

"But she claims she doesn't now and tells you to go away?"

"Yep."

"How do you know she's lying about not liking you?"

"Because she kissed me back."

Jason, again, choked. This time, on a French fry. "*You kissed her?!*"

"Shh!" Ella swiveled in her seat, smiling nervously at the other patrons now staring at their table. "He didn't mean me. Parker didn't kiss me. That would be silly. I'm engaged to Jason. Very happily. See?" She lifted her left hand, waving it around, neon lights reflecting off the diamond.

After a moment, she about-faced in her seat and gave Jason the stink eye.

"A little louder next time, jackass." Parker glared at his soon-to-be dead best friend. "They didn't hear you on top of the mountain."

"Sorry," Jason grated in a harsh whisper. "You might want to warn a guy first. Way to bury the lead."

Parker refocused on Ella. Female advice would be nice. Sure, he was fairly certain he knew how to handle Maddie, but he couldn't do it without help. Odds were against them and her fighting him wasn't helping. They'd barely made it to the starting gate and they'd never know if they had substance or a decent shot if he didn't do something.

"What do you think?"

She rolled her lips over her teeth. "It sure sounds like she's interested. Scared, but interested. I would just keep slowly chipping away at it. Show her that she can trust you and you won't cave to criticism."

Precisely what he thought.

"In that case, can I ask a favor?" He sighed. "She needs friends, genuine ones, who would offer support. Could you try reaching out to her? Invite her for a girl's night or something?"

He could think of no one better than Ella. She was kind, intuitive, and shy. She often felt like a wallflower that no one noticed. Maddie was outspoken, smart, and had a heart buried under all that brass. She hated attention and thought the world was out to get her. The two women would be great for each other.

"I already attempted talking to her awhile back, but I can try again."

"The trick with Maddie? Don't give her a choice. Don't ask, either. Direct the conversation. She has zero clue what to do with people who stand up to her. She's not used to it."

"I'm not very assertive." Ella's nose wrinkled. "I'll sure try, though."

"Thank you." He smiled, a semblance of relief inflating his chest. "I have a way in for you, actually. Favor number two."

For the next few minutes, he proceeded to relay his plan. By the time he was finished, she was bouncing in her seat and grinning.

"That's brilliant."

It wasn't brilliant, but it would probably work. "So, you'll help?"

"Totally. Count me in."

Parker glanced at Jason, at the concern and guarded look in his eyes. It was an expression Parker had witnessed countless times until Ella had come into the picture.

"You're going to get hurt, man." Jason shook his head. "This is a train wreck waiting to happen."

"I know you're worried, and we've always been honest with one another, so I'm not going to hit you upside the head with my police baton for speaking your mind." Parker picked up his lukewarm burger and took a bite, speaking around his food. "But trust me like you have our whole lives. If I get hurt, I get hurt. That's on me, not you."

Chapter 12

Maddie finished washing her hands in the maintence office at the school and checked the time. She'd be clocking out thirty minutes early, but she didn't think, just this once, her boss would mind. She'd whipped through her duties as fast as possible and had done everything expected of her. Normally, she played by the rules to go undetected. Tonight, she needed to be gone before Parker showed up for their so-called second date.

Part of her, a huge part, loved the attention he was doling. After all these years, it was nice to know he was interested. The rides home and not having to walk were awesome. And then there was the kissing. *Uhn*, the kissing.

But she couldn't let it continue. Her subconscious was battling to the death with her emotions on right versus wrong. Her stomach was constantly in knots. Truth was, no matter how much being with him had brought hope into her bleak existence, she cared about him too much. Even if her circumstances were different, she had absolutely nothing to offer him.

Drying her hands, she reached for her coat.

The kindergarten teacher rushed in, shutting the door behind her, and pressed her back against it. She dropped a duffle bag at her feet. Slightly out of breath, she smiled. "Hi there."

"Uh, hello." It was awfully late for someone to still be in the building. "Is everything all right, Ms. Sinclair?" She was wearing jeans and a blue sweater, her long brown strands falling around her shoulders. Nothing of notable distress. Everything seemed fine, aside from the sudden burst into the room and slightly nervous expression.

"Yes, everything's good. Please, call me Ella, though."

Uh-huh. "Can I help you with something? Did I not clean your classroom well?"

Normally, Maddie avoided all staff, but the unexpected visit at this hour and the fact Ms. Sinclair was actually a decent person kept Maddie's head up.

"Oh, no. You do a wonderful job, thank you."

Maddie nodded, and prodded the teacher with an expectant lift of her brows.

"Right, right. I should probably tell you why I barged into your office." She took a deep breath and shook out her hands as if gearing herself up for a State of the Union address. "I'm on a mission."

"From God?" Dang it. Maddie knew better than to let the first thing in her head pop out of her mouth. Why now, who knew. Perhaps she was just confused enough to lower her guard.

"From…God? Oh!" Ms. Sinclair giggled nervously. "You mean the *Blues Brothers* movie reference. *'We're on a mission from God,'*" she mimicked in low tones. "That's funny."

Unable to help it, Maddie smiled. This woman was either one heck of an actress, or she was the sweetest person on two legs. There was an innocence about her that called to Maddie, telling her to protect and befriend. Odd, that.

"No, Parker sent me on this mission."

Smile? Gone. "He what now?"

"He wanted me to come by and help you get ready for the Halloween Party. He figured you might be more comfortable going with me and meeting him there."

All right. That was it. Just who did he think he was, sending a virtual stranger to her place of work, knowing how people felt about her, and after she'd already told him no?

"I'm gonna kill him."

Ms. Sinclair pressed her lips together. "He said you'd say that."

Did he? Well… "I'm not going."

"He said you'd say that, too. And for me to tell you not to kill the messenger." The teacher put her hands up, palms out, as if seeking calm. "Please, hear me out. Look, nobody notices me. It's like I'm invisible. There are only a handful of residents who remember my name, and I grew up here. I mean, I went away, but I've been back for a few years. Being engaged to Jason kinda bumped my status a little. Not much. Anyway, you'll be less likely to be recognized with me. Plus, the costume Parker picked has a mask that will cover a lot of your face."

Maddie stared at her, not sure what to make of the woman. Sure, she seemed genuine. Maddie recalled, her first week on the job, how the teacher had tried to make nicety-nice. But Maddie hadn't survived this long by going against instinct. Problem was, her instincts were saying to listen, a complete contradiction to her ingrained fight or flight reflexes.

She opened her mouth to speak, not certain what to say, but Ms. Sinclair got a jump on her.

"I don't have many friends. I'm close with my cousin Gerta. She lives in the next county, though, and is busy with her young kids. There's Jason and Parker, of course." She met Maddie's eyes, sincerity and openness in her gaze. "I'm socially awkward. There's a long story why. I'll tell you sometime, if you like, and if we get to know one another better. But, yeah. I don't have a lot of friends. I know you don't, either. Parker told me about your family and that you're innocent. I believe him. Others may not. I do. And I'm very sorry that happened to you. Throwing two people together doesn't make them instant friends. I get that, but maybe we can try and see?"

Geez. Maddie gazed, unblinking, at the brazen honesty she so rarely witnessed. It must've taken quite a bit of courage to reveal that much and for the woman to come forward, even if Parker had requested it, and especially considering her self-proclaimed social awkwardness. Maddie saw pieces of that in the way the teacher had rambled, talking fast, and her nervous mannerisms. She had a naïve quality about her also.

Maddie found herself believing Ella. If Ms. Sinclair thought Maddie was guilty of her family's crimes, she wouldn't have come, regardless of who'd asked. Unlike most of the other teachers, Ms. Sinclair hadn't complained about Maddie to the principal or purposely left extra work for her to do that first year on the job.

Above all, Parker had sent Ms. Sinclair here, and he would never do anything to hurt Maddie. Anyone, for that matter. Not on purpose. He had a strong moral code, ethics, a huge heart, good intentions, and an untainted soul.

"The friends I used to have before all this happened have abandoned me." Maddie cleared her throat, unsure why she'd started the conversation there or why she'd opened up immediately. Perhaps it was wise to keep on that thread, though. Trust was a fragile thing, and if she was going to try giving it to another after so long without, then the woman needed to know the reason Maddie was defensive. "I wasn't a good person when I was young. I used to be one of those mean girls who thought she was better than everyone else. The people who I called friends were like that, too. Except that was the real them, and I was merely acting. Or acting out, rather. By the time I grew older and wiser, no one wanted anything to do with me."

"People can be downright cruel sometimes. They only see black and white, forgetting that the majority of us live in the shades of gray. Themselves included. And most don't readily accept change."

Maddie huffed a laugh. "Yeah."

"Especially true if their trust has been betrayed or they've been wronged. And sometimes they look for someone to blame even if that person isn't the one who hurt them in the first place."

Maddie nodded, catching on to the multiple meanings. Her father had hurt her *and* the town. The town blamed her and, thus, was hurting her in retaliation. In turn, she was hurting Parker by striking out in this vicious cycle that never seemed to end.

Too much hurt, not enough healing.

"Assuming we hit it off, I wouldn't be a wise choice in friends for you."

Ms. Sinclair smiled, gently and with sadness. "Why don't you let me be the judge?"

"You're an adult. Up to you." Maddie shrugged. "I'm an outcast. You might be hated on the association alone." She would never want to do that to another, especially someone so sweet, who'd risked a lot to attempt initiating a connection.

"If it's all the same to you, I'd rather have one great friend and be shunned by the town than have none and be accepted." The teacher's lips twisted in sympathy. "They don't know I exist, anyhow. Who cares?"

Maddie laughed. Unable to help it, she laughed. They just didn't make people like Ms. Sinclair anymore. Authentic and honest, with a green soul fresh as the morning dew, and a backbone she hid from existence, only bringing it out when necessary.

A sigh, and Maddie succumbed. Lord knew, she could use a friend herself. Not to mention, Parker had gone to all this trouble. It would be terrible of her to not attend the party. If he wanted to do this, wanted to date her and see where things led, knowing full well what the consequences were, then whatever. She'd just have to learn to deal with the guilt and meet him halfway. Besides, it didn't appear like the mule-headed man would give up until he got his way.

"What costume did he pick?"

Ms. Sinclair grinned. "A sexy cat." She bent and unzipped the duffle bag at her feet, extracting a one-piece black leotard with a tail. She held up the mask. "See, it'll cover a lot of your features."

Yes, it would. Black and sequined, with slits for eyes, it would fit above the brows, halfway up her forehead, and had long triangular sections for each of her cheeks that came to a point near her mouth.

"I brought makeup, too."

Lord, she hadn't worn cosmetics in ages. "All right, Ms. Sinclair. You won me over. Let's do this."

"Ella, please. Call me Ella, Madeline. All two of my friends do."

"Three friends now. And you can call me Maddie. All one of my friends do."

"Two friends now," Ella mimicked with a smile and looked around. "Can we use that for getting ready?"

Maddie glanced at the card table. Her boss primarily ate lunch there and that was its sole purpose. "Sure."

"Okay, have a seat."

Doing as she was told, Maddie sat on the folding chair, watching Ella lay out cosmetics, plug in a curling iron, and hang up the costume. "What are you going as?"

"Jason and I are a firefighter and a Dalmatian."

She laughed. "I hope he's the dog."

Ella straightened and pointed at her. "That's what Parker said. Too funny." She surveyed her supplies. "Hair first."

Taking charge, she moved behind Maddie and used the brush to put her strands in a high ponytail. From there, she wielded the curling iron to make ringlets, then secured them with bobby pins around the rubber band to create a loose up-do.

Maddie observed the process in the mirror over the sink the whole time, and didn't say a word. She and Mary Beth used to have slumber parties, doing each other's hair and makeup and nails, while discussing boys. It had been so long since those moments that Maddie had forgotten how fun they could be.

Next, Ella moved in front of Maddie and began applying cosmetics. Dark gray charcoal effect eye shadow. Thick mascara. Bright red lipstick. It would've been too much for everyday wear, but for the costume, it fit.

She leaned forward when Ella was finished, eying herself more closely in the mirror. "Not bad."

Ella smiled like a child being praised. "Thanks. It sounds weird, but Brent taught me how to apply makeup. I didn't know how until a few months ago."

"Brent from the vet clinic?"

"Yes. He's dating Miles, who lives across the hall from my apartment. Well, my old apartment. I moved in with Jason last month."

Yeah, Miles was Maddie's boss at the Rec Center, so she'd known that tidbit. They were a cute couple. What she'd seen of them from the shadows, anyway. She just hadn't expected Brent to teach Ella about cosmetics.

"Want some help with yours?"

"No, I'm fine, thanks. Is it okay to change in here?"

"Sure." The building was empty, save for them anyway.

She took her costume off the hanger, turned her back, and undressed. The size was slightly large for her frame, but she'd lost a lot of weight managing her meals the past few years. She knew she was too skinny, but budgeting was necessary for her situation.

When she turned again, Ella had a fitted black and white printed shirt on and was stepping into matching leggings. Thick white compression stockings adorned her legs, something Maddie

114

recognized from her mother needing to wear them during her treatments when she'd been alive.

Ella glanced up and caught Maddie looking. "The reason for my social awkwardness. I was in a fire as a young girl and have burn scars. The stockings cover them." She straightened and pulled the leggings into place around her waist. "I spent a lot of time in the hospital and rehab, not around my peers. Afterward, I was homeschooled. I tend to get nervous in big crowds and around new people."

"I'm so sorry." Maddie pressed a hand to her chest where sympathy pangs rattled her ribs. "That must've been awful."

"It was, but I got through it with the help of family." Ella sat on the chair and put on shoes. "The fire killed my parents, so I was raised by an aunt and uncle." She rose and walked to the mirror, using black eyeliner to paint her nose to look like a dog snout. "Jason's father died saving me. That's how we knew one another. Well, he hadn't connected the dots at first. When The Battleaxes set their sights on us, I was guilt-stricken about our shared past. Eventually, I told him and here we are."

Unable to move, Maddie watched as her new friend packed her things, tidied up, and set the bag on the table.

Throat tight, sinuses stinging, Maddie struggled to breathe. Once, she'd burned her hand helping the Freemont Manor cook take muffins out of a pan. A minor wound, but it had hurt like hell. But, to have her entire lower legs burned, judging by the placement of Ella's stockings, and most likely to a severe degree? Maddie couldn't fathom it. And to lose her parents, as well? Yes, her mother had passed away, and yes, Maddie missed her every day. But her mom hadn't died suddenly in a tragedy that Maddie had witnessed.

There were always those in the world who had it so much worse than herself. Things hadn't worked out well for her a good chunk of her life. Most of it had been unfair. Yet, to hear Ella's story and what she'd had to overcome made Maddie's troubles seem weak and pitiful by comparison.

Never. Never again would she feel sorry for herself.

"Ella," she breathed. "I'm at a loss. I just…" She shook her head.

Her friend walked closer and smiled, understanding in her eyes. "It all worked out okay in the end. My aunt and uncle are wonderful people, I'm very close with my cousin, and I have Jason's love." She tilted her head, smile broadening. "I'm insanely lucky."

Maddie's chest hitched. "You are incredibly strong and brave. You know that, right?"

"Thank you. That was nice of you to say." Ella studied her a moment, concentration furrowing her brow. "So are you. Don't let anyone make you think otherwise."

By sheer will, biting her tongue, and breathing heavy, Maddie battled impending tears. It was difficult, but she managed it. "If you tell Parker, I'll deny it, but I think he was onto something sending you here."

Ella laughed. "Every once in awhile, guys get it right." She glanced at the clock. "Shoot. We gotta go. The party already started."

Chapter 13

"They're late." Parker glanced around the crowded room inside the Rec Center, his heart pounding.

Sending Ella to confront Maddie was bound to go one of two ways. Either Ella would work her charming sweet magic on Maddie and win her over, or his plan would backfire and Maddie would distance herself more. After tearing him a new one.

"Women are always late." Jason, wearing his firefighter turnout gear, took a pull from his long neck bottle. "Take it as a good sign. If my girl hadn't succeeded in your mission, she'd be here by now."

True. Maybe.

Last time Parker had been this nervous was in high school. Again, Maddie being the culprit. Entirely different reason this go-around, though. He'd made some progress in regards to her. He really hoped his pushing wouldn't set them back. Having Ella in her life would do so much good for Maddie, and vice versa.

Tilting his head, he glared at the fake spider webs stretched across the wood beam rafters. Two giant, furry arachnids hung from them on opposing sides of the generous space.

No Maddie.

To his right, just past the portable bar decorated with dismembered body parts, was the main entrance to the hall. The doorway had broomsticks affixed to both sides.

No Maddie.

A fogger machine billowed white smoke clear on the other side of the room by the dance floor. Townsfolk got their *Monster Mash* on, gyrating awkwardly.

Still no Maddie.

The food table beside the dancers had snacks in witch cauldrons and small open caskets. A group of people in costumes were hovered around it.

Maddie wasn't one of them.

Round eight-seater tables covered in orange tablecloths to his left held the floral arrangements Maddie had made. Patrons sat around, laughing and talking and drinking.

Shocker. No Maddie.

"Relax, man." Jason pointed his bottle at Parker. "If she comes, she comes. If she doesn't, she doesn't. Either way, you tried."

"Promise me you'll be nice."

Jason spread his arms. "I'm always nice. Haven't you heard? Everyone thinks I'm awesome."

"Ego check." Parker shook his head. "Just…please. Be nice to her. She's going to be on edge with the majority of the adult population in the Ridge in one room. And most of them don't like her." According to her, anyway. He was staring to agree with her based on what he'd witnessed. "I need you to not be one of those people."

Jason's shoulders slumped. "Look, it's like I said. I'm not a fan of the idea of you dating her, but if she's changed, as you claim, then there's no problem. I just want to see you happy. If she does that, I'm happy."

"Thank you."

Of course, all that was dependent on her coming tonight. Parker's gut knotted, wondering if she'd show. Another visual sweep of the room indicated she wasn't here.

"Does she?"

Parker looked at his buddy, confused.

"Make you happy, I mean."

"Sometimes." Parker scratched his jaw. "She's got a quirky and sarcastic sense of humor that makes me laugh. Quick on the fly with one-liners to boot. I'm incredibly attracted to her and there's chemistry. She has this quiet, sensitive side nobody really knows about. She tries to hide it like it's a flaw. And Domino loves her."

"Domino loves everyone."

He laughed. "Yeah, but he *really* likes her. Follows her everywhere and doesn't take my commands when she's around. Totally love-struck, that idiot." He chewed the inside of his cheek, thinking. "Most of the time, though, she's frustrating. She gets under my skin and wiggles. I scratch until I bleed, but it doesn't help. Being with her takes a lot of patience because she's not very forthcoming with info, and when she does reveal something, it's typically a fact or memory that makes my chest feel like it got hit with a sledgehammer."

"Eh, I know the feeling. Ella…" Jason grinned, his focus over Parker's shoulder. "Just walked in the door."

Parker whipped his gaze in that direction, but it was difficult to make out much through the crowd.

After a beat, Ella wove around Raggedy Ann & Andy, sidling up to Jason. "Hi. You look handsome."

"Thank you. I've got a bone for the sexiest dog in the room."

She laughed.

Parker rolled his eyes, ignoring their flirting and watched the direction she'd come from. He sure hoped the dog brought the cat to play. His pulse pounded and he held his breath. Just as he was about to ask Ella if Maddie was here, she ducked under the waving arms of a group of dancers and stopped in front of them.

Releasing a long-winded exhale, she planted her hands on her hips. "Damn, it's crowded in here. I think my tail got stepped on three times."

Sweet Christ, she looked hot. Her golden hair was all curly on top of her head, the red lipstick begged to be kissed off, and there was some kind of eye shadow that blended with her mask and made the blue of her eyes a starker cornflower.

Don't even get him started on that outfit. To date, all he'd seen her wear was loose-fitting sweatshirts and jeans. He had no idea she was quite that slender, but she definitely had curves, too. Slight. In the flair of her hips. The shape of her breasts.

"You came after all." Brilliant opening, but stupid happiness was rendering him speechless.

Or the cat got his tongue.

"I did." She slid her gaze to Jason, seemingly unsure. "Hi, Jason. Nice costume."

"Madeline." He nodded. "Original being a fireman, I know. She insisted." He beamed at Ella, then refocused on Maddie, his smile slipping. "Good to see you."

"Is it?" The question came off as a challenge or defiant, but the wary hope in her expression spoke volumes.

"Straight up? I don't know." Jason slid his arm around Ella, drawing her close. "My memories of you don't jive with the woman Parker claims you are today. My mind is open. The rest is up to you."

She nodded slowly, watching him. "I don't think you'll believe anything I have to say, but for what it's worth, I'm sorry. I was a harpy back then. I was miserable and took it out on those around me."

He stared at her as if dissecting her words and rearranging them in his head to see if they fit. "Do you mean that?"

"Yes."

"Okay, I believe you."

She tilted her head, narrowing her eyes. "Just like that?"

"Yeah, just like that. I trust Parker and he trusts you. Not to mention, literal implications notwithstanding, this is the first instance we've had an actual conversation where you aren't wearing a metaphorical mask." He spread his fingers, palm up. "You owned up to your mistakes. That takes balls. I'm not giving you a free ride. Hurt him, shit will get real. But I'll give you the benefit of the doubt because everyone deserves a second chance and what Parker wants is what I want." He reared. "Usually. There was that one time in Cancun when he wanted to eat fruit from a street vendor. That was a hell no for me. He puked his guts out for two days. Ruined the whole damn trip."

Dropping her chin, her jaw following suit, she gawked at him as if trying to determine if he was for real or not.

Several beats of the music passed, thumping to the pulse in Parker's neck while he wondered how she was going to react.

Ella's head swiveled between the two, obviously as curious as him.

Finally, after the Detroit Lions won the Super Bowl and the continent of Africa solved world hunger and he won the lottery—twice—Maddie raised her hand, palm toward Jason, and gradually turned her head to look at Parker.

Eyes bugged and lips parted, she made a sound of doubt that kind of resembled *nuh-uh*. "You ate prepared fruit from a vendor? In Mexico? There are three things you never do in Mexico." She tapped them off on her fingers. "Don't drink the water. Don't reach for the hot sauce. And don't eat fruit or veggies that you can't sanitize yourself."

Jason threw his arms up in the air. "Thank you!"

Grinding his teeth, Parker stewed. "How was I supposed to know?"

"Google, man. Google is wise. Google is all powerful." Jason looked at Ella beside him. "Want anything to drink?"

"Maybe some water, please."

"You got it. Water *not* from Mexico, coming up. Madeline, come with me. We'll getcha a drink and I'll tell you all about our trip to Wyoming four years ago."

They disappeared into the crowd, and Parker sighed.

Ella laced her fingers and pressed them to her chest. "Aww, they're getting along. That's so nice, isn't it?"

"Sure." Five minutes ago he would've said yes. "More awesome if it wasn't at my expense." Whatever. "How did it go with her? Did she get defensive?"

"At first, but it didn't last long. We chatted. It was nice. I really like her, Parker."

So did he. More and more every chance he got to be with her.

Jason and Maddie made their way back, her laughing to the point her eyes were watery.

"And *that's* why he refuses to get on a horse ever again."

She waved her hand in front of her face, wheezing. "Oh, wow."

Parker glared at his friend, wishing he'd brought his gun. "Thanks for that."

"Anytime."

"Oh!" Ella clapped. "I just realized what your costumes mean." She glanced at Parker's black turtleneck, trousers, and mask covering just his eyes, then Maddie's outfit. "Cat burglar. That's clever."

"Huh." Maddie sipped her drink through a tiny straw. "That was pretty clever, actually."

Red as sin lips. Puckered around a straw.

He wanted her alone. Yesterday.

All this fuss to get her here, and he just wanted to take her home.

See how long it took to strip off that cat suit.

Figure out the spots on her body to nibble and make her purr.

"What are you drinking?" Ella leaned over and frowned at Maddie's glass. "It looks gross."

"Bloody Mary. It tastes slightly above gross." She poked her straw at something floating in her glass. "Huh. There's an eyeball in it."

"Yay, they're using them." Ella smiled. "Those were my idea. I'm on the event committee. They're reusable ice cubes."

"Well, hey. Look who's clever now." Maddie shoulder-bumped Ella. "Very cool."

As Ella preened over the praise, Parker's airway seized with a strange, sudden emotion he couldn't name.

The Maddie he'd known twelve years ago would've never complimented someone like Ella. Hell, she never would've noticed the other woman unless it was to talk behind her back or poke fun at her with her cronies. Maddie had strutted around, bitch posse by her side, looking down her nose at everyone and criticizing everything from hair to clothes to body-shaming.

A person didn't change this much even if desperate. The comments she'd made to him a few days ago about her friends from high school abandoning her and not really being true friends was reverberating in his head. Back then, with her needing love and seeking attention by any means she could, she'd probably latched onto those close to her social and economic status, not having anything of substance in common with them.

He'd thought she'd been their director. Turned out, she'd only been their best actress. Which meant, the woman he'd been spending time with as of late was the real Maddie, not the one he'd feared all these years.

Ah, and Ella. Sweet Ella. She'd been through so much in her short thirty years on Earth. She'd found everlasting love with Jason, but the display playing out before Parker's eyes right this second was factual proof that humans, as a species, weren't meant to have just one person to love. It came in all shapes and forms and titles.

Her eyes were smiling and she was chattier than he'd seen her the past couple years. Open. Comfortable. Confident. Happy.

Because Jason had broken free of his patterns and accepted her as his soul mate.

Because of Maddie. Despite being irritated with him, she'd listened to Ella and applied her honed instincts to accept someone new into her life whom she could trust.

Jason must've noticed the change in Ella also. A humble smile curved his lips as his gaze darted between the two of them, brows wrenched in a surprised kind of contentment Parker had rarely witnessed.

While the ladies carried on, Jason stepped closer to Parker and bent to speak near his ear. "I approve."

He jerked, whipping his attention to Jason, finding candidness and apology in his features.

Jason nodded and subtly pointed to Maddie with his bottle. "I approve, man. Of her. Of you. The two of you together." He shrugged. "You were absolutely right. There's no faking that kind of sincerity. We were wrong about her."

Chest tight, Parker nodded, grateful and relieved that Jason had come around. He could be observant and perceptive when he so desired. Bull-headed and a doofus all the time, but he had his moments. Like this one. It would've sucked sweaty hairy monkey balls if he hadn't been able to accept Maddie.

"Thanks."

"I should thank you. Look at her, at them. They hit it off after one hour together. Christ, did Ella need this."

So had Maddie. "Glad it worked out."

The mayor wormed her way through the crowd toward them, her two sisters in tow, and Parker tensed. Thus far, Maddie had been comfortable in her disguise. All that ended if...

"Madeline, I'm surprised to see you out and about." Marie, dressed as a hippie, folded her hands in front of her. She had a flower child headband around her short brown hair and peace sign sunglasses that made it difficult to take her seriously.

Her two sisters nodded their agreement. They, too, were hippies.

The blonde was the quietest of the three and the O'Grady boys' mother. The guys owned Animal Instincts clinic in town and all three had once been in The Battleaxes' sights. The popular veterinarians were also happily married now with offspring on the way. Shocker.

The redhead was the sassiest of the trio. She so happened to be the one who ran the town's Pinterest and Twitter accounts. Eerie how she was always able to get candid photos of the "couples" for the sites.

Maddie quickly glanced around and lowered her head. "I can leave if you prefer."

"Why would I want that? It's lovely to see you."

Suspicion lit Maddie's baby blues. "Haven't heard that line before."

"Pah, it's true. You never mind those who give you trouble. They'll get over it." Marie smiled at the others, then back to Maddie. "Making new friends, too. Our Ella here is quite creative. We love having her on the committee."

Ella, equally as shocked as Maddie, rounded her eyes. "Er, you do?"

"Of course, dear." Marie's expression shifted to a stoic one aimed at Maddie. "I have a favor. Your major was interior design in college, correct?"

"Yes, but I had to drop out. I didn't get a degree."

"No matter." Marie waved that away. "I've been looking to redecorate my office. Parker's sister, Paige, bless her heart, is the best assistant ever, but she's terribly uncreative. I tried having her rearrange furniture. It didn't work. I need a professional. Come by my office Monday morning and have a look around. Give me some ideas and we'll talk."

"Um, I think you missed the part where I said I didn't graduate."

"Oh, no. I heard you. Nine a.m., Madeline. If I like your ideas, I'll pay you a handsome fee, of course."

"But..."

They were gone. Fast as they'd arrived, the sisters had disappeared into the crowd to torment other souls to do their bidding or to pair unsuspecting couples who'd simply wanted to have a *Thriller* time.

Maddie growled and set her hands on her hips. "I mean, really. They didn't give me a chance to say no."

"They don't know the meaning of the word." Ella patted Maddie's shoulder. "We've all been there."

Chapter 14

"Okay, I admit, that wasn't so bad. Aside from the mayor and her sisters, no one recognized me. If only I could get away with wearing this cat suit all the time." Maddie pulled off her sweatshirt and set it in the backseat of Parker's car. Though chilly outside, it had been warm inside the center with all those people. She could use a cool down.

He grinned from the behind the wheel, turning down the road where her "apartment" was located. "Atta girl. Glass half-full. I would have pegged you for a half-empty personality."

"I'm just happy to have a glass."

He pulled up to the curb, put the car in Park, and looked at her as if she'd announced she was from Uranus and he needed a probe. "Odd thing to say."

She supposed it was since he didn't know the full extent of her circumstances. In response, she shrugged.

"I know things are rough right now, but people will come around, Maddie. They only need to hear the truth and see you the way I do." He glanced out the windshield, gaze solemn. "You won over Jason and Ella tonight. More will follow." He pointed forward, then out the driver's window, the passenger's, and stuck his thumb toward the back. "This place? It's so beautiful. It's our home. These people? They're family. Why do I feel like I need to tell you that?"

That may be the case for him, but it hadn't been for her. Perhaps he was right. People would come around if they knew and accepted the truth. As of the past three years—heck, her whole childhood—that hadn't happened. She was doomed to forever be the spoiled rich princess or the convict's daughter who "got away with it."

She smiled, unsure of what else to say. "Thanks for the invite and the drive home."

Ugh, she was tired and still had to hike up to her tent. And she had to be at Ka-Bloom early tomorrow. Harriet was going out of town to visit her niece in the morning, leaving Maddie at the shop alone for the first time. She didn't think that was a great idea, but Harriet was the boss.

"You're welcome for our *second date* and the lift." He offered her a wicked side-glance.

He'd taken off his mask before leaving the party, but his hair was askew where the fabric had been tied around his head. Scruff dusted his jaw bracketing his smiling mouth. The low light under a streetlamp made his eyes a darker green.

He was so dang attractive her girly bits clenched. The ball of heat in her belly whenever she was in his presence began to expand. Anticipation skated along her nerve-endings. This was the point where he always kissed her. They'd make out for a few glorious minutes, and the high would carry her up the mountain to her real home.

"Gonna invite me inside this time, Maddie?"

"Nope." If she actually had an apartment, yes. Alas, she didn't. And she didn't think he'd appreciate where she really laid her head at night. In fact, he'd probably lose his mind and flip out. She conjured a good excuse, which stemmed from the truth. "I have to get up early tomorrow for work. It's already past my bedtime."

Reaching up, he grazed the back of his finger across her cheek, his gaze tracking the move. "Bedtime, huh? I could get behind that. Except you won't let me in."

Dang, he made it hard to breathe. "I told you. I have to get up early tomorrow for work. Besides, my place isn't fit for company."

"All right. Then let's do dinner at my place this week." Sexy grin. "We'll go to bed early like responsible adults."

Implication? Implied. He wanted to take this beyond dates, flirting, and kissing to the next level. Her body got onboard and danced a waltz. Her mind threatened mutiny with all the warning signals. The cage around her heart unlocked.

Just for clarification… "You want to sleep with me?" Because, geez. Even David hadn't seemed like he'd wanted to when they'd been together.

"Sleep would come afterward." Parker's gaze swept her face, his smile impish and his eyes heavy-lidded. "But, yes. I want to sleep with you." He leaned over the center console and brought his lips within a whisper of hers. "Know what? You want it, too. No sense in denying it."

"I'm not in denial." Actually, she might be the only one of them living in reality.

"Good. My place. You and me. This week."

"Okay," she breathed, but that was all he let her say.

Closing the millimeter of distance, he sealed his lips to hers and groaned. Gentle, warm fingers gripped the back of her neck, cupped her cheek, yet his kiss was anything but timid.

He tilted his head and went deep, stroking her tongue with a fevered urgency that had her bones melting. She sank into him, into the drugging pull of longing she hadn't experienced in so long, if ever. He had this charismatic, endearing way about him while intimate that contradicted the humorous, sometimes dominating aspects of his personality. Like his goal was to ruffle her feathers and smooth them in the same beat.

He took control, yet gave her the reins.

He touched her, held her as if she were precious to him.

He kissed like he wanted no one but her and had to have her now.

Sweet mercy. He tasted like peppermint and coffee, smelled like pine and fabric softener, and who knew that would be an aphrodisiac of epic proportions?

And then, just as her body was about to wave a white flag because it couldn't keep up with her heart rate, he slowly pulled away just as he typically had the past week. In no hurry. Calm as you please. Lingering over her lips as if reluctant to move or savoring the sensation.

"Have a wonderful night, Maddie." A flutter of his lashes, and he lazily lifted his lids. His gaze darted between hers. He smiled against her mouth. "By the way, that costume? It should be against the law."

"You picked it."

He grunted a sound of agreement. "And my punishment was watching you wear it all night and having to keep my hands to myself since we were in polite company."

"Well, I had a good time. So, thank you. See you later?"

"Yes, you will." He straightened in his seat. "I've got dinner with my folks tomorrow. You okay walking from Ka-Bloom?"

Every job she had, he'd shown up to drive her home at the end of her shift. It was considerate and gave them opportunities to talk. "Yes, I'll be fine. Goodnight."

He nodded, and as always, he watched her until she ducked inside the apartment building's lobby.

She waited until he pulled away, gave it another minute in case, then headed out the rear exit.

It took forever to fall asleep due to giddy happiness, but once she had, she zonked out cold. Daylight crept upon her without her being aware.

Prying her lids apart, panic struck her chest while she reached for her phone, then eased when she realized it was only seven. Internal alarm clock, she guessed.

While she had her cell unlocked, she checked the weather app. This pocket of their region rarely got below freezing overnight, and almost never in autumn. December through February were the coldest months. Once or twice the past few years she'd had to sneak in and sleep at the center due to extreme conditions. She had a battery-powered heated blanket to tuck inside her thermo sleeping bag for when it got really cold. Habit had her checking temps to see if she needed to bring it with her to work to charge.

Alas, it would be mild in the forties the next few nights and in the fifties during the day. Humidity would make it seem warmer. Sometime later in the week, though, she needed to make time to pull out the winter gear from her totes. The extra cover for her tent to retain heat, along with the floor padding and her snowsuit to sleep in. She had a decent amount of firewood, but she should get more.

She got ready for work, and by the time she arrived, Harriet already had things rolling. The sign had been flipped to Open, lights were on, and the coffeepot perking.

Maddie set her stuff on a chair in the back room. "Anxious for your trip?"

"More like excited. It's been almost a year since I've seen my niece. She just had a baby last month. I just love babies."

Maddie smiled, tamping down her own anxiety. Harriet had everything planned and prepared for the shop while she was to be gone. She'd even contacted clients who'd placed advance orders so they knew someone else would be minding the shop when they picked up their flowers. It was a job Maddie could do well on her own, but she hadn't dealt with customers. Her choice, but still. People might wander in, see her, and storm out. She was scared to death Harriet was going to lose half her clientele by her return date.

"Everything will be all right." Harriet smiled as if reading Maddie's mind, and donned her coat. "It's only a couple of days. I have total faith in you."

"I still think you should've closed."

"No need." Harriet sobered and reached for her purse on the counter. "One of these days, I'm going to retire. I can think of no one else I'd like to pass my legacy to than you. This will be good for you, being on your own."

She'd told Maddie variations of this story before, but it rendered her mute, regardless. Hope and pride and unadulterated fear filled her head and heart, causing her throat to swell, then promptly clamp shut.

Harriet's niece was her only family, and she didn't live in Redwood Ridge, nor have an interest in taking over Ka-Bloom. More than once, Harriet had hinted at remaining the owner, but having Maddie work full-time and being responsible for all duties. Or that Harriet might pass the torch to Maddie altogether and sign over the shop. The woman had flip-flopped on which she'd prefer come that time.

Maddie hadn't taken the discussion all that seriously until right at this moment. Somehow, it didn't seem rhetorical any longer. Harriet refusing to close the store while she went away felt like a test for Maddie. After all she'd been through, it would be a dream to run a business. Plus, she was rather good with numbers and she loved designing. Even the mayor had asked for her services, which she'd been avoiding. And putting off. Hard.

But with the majority of townsfolk harboring a grudge against her, any adventure was bound to tank. No one would buy her product. No one would even walk through the doors, and if they did, it would most likely be to laugh at or taunt her.

"You'll do a great job, just like always." Harriet smiled as if by way of reassurance. "You have my number. Call anytime."

Maddie nodded and watched her leave.

After a few deep breaths, she checked the advance order list. A few of those could wait until midday, but the rest couldn't. The front door had a bell to let her know when customers arrived, so she'd work in the back until a ding came.

She was ten deep in arrangements for the notary club when the door chimed. Gut sinking, she wiped her hands and headed into the shop.

One of the girls she'd gone to school with was examining the arrangements in the refrigerator display. Darlene Dancourt had been a pudgy, shy mouse who Maddie used to pick on. She'd called the girl horrible names and made her feel bad about herself. Maddie had caught glimpses of her around town, but hadn't spoken to her. She'd lost a lot of weight since high school and had gotten engaged last spring to one of the Wildlife Rescue personnel.

"May I help you?" Maddie wrung her hands, ordering her stomach to settle.

"Yes, I..." Darlene blinked repeatedly. She must've realized who Maddie was because her jaw clenched. "What are you doing here?"

"I'm minding the shop for Harriet while she's out of town."

Darlene, obviously torn, stared at Maddie, the display, then back again. Her expression was wrought with nervous tension and she was clearly debating whether she should leave. She ran her hands through her short brown wavy strands, tapping her foot and biting her lip, the movements desperate in nature.

After a tense stare down, she turned for the door. "Forget it."

"Darlene." Maddie rolled her lips over her teeth, struggling for the right words. "I'm sorry for how I treated you in school. It was mean and you didn't deserve that. I'm not the same person anymore. You can go if you prefer, but you seem unsettled about something. Maybe I can help?"

A turn of her head, and Darlene looked at the refrigerator again. "None of these will work."

"I can make a special arrangement if you like. What's it for?"

Darlene blew out a breath and closed her eyes. "Keith's parents are coming in from Seattle tonight." Her lids popped open, anxiety in her stare. "We've been there to visit, but this is the first time they've come to our house. We just got engaged. I wanted everything to be perfect. His mom is kind of picky, you know? I'm a great cook, and we cleaned the house top to bottom, but I was thinking flowers for the dining room table might be a good touch."

"Will they be staying in a guest room?"

"Yes."

"Any hobbies of theirs?"

"He does what she says. She likes to crotchet, I suppose."

"Do they have any floral allergies that you know about?"

"No." Darlene laughed. "She has arrangements all over her house and intricate gardens in the backyard."

"Do you have about twenty minutes to spare?" Maddie pointed to the back room. "I can whip up something real quick." Since Darlene appeared skeptical, Maddie held out her hands. "Tell you what. If you don't like my arrangement, you're no worse off than when you came in. Twenty minutes?"

"Okay, sure. Why not?" A sigh, and Darlene took a seat in one of the awaiting chairs.

"Be right back."

Maddie hurried into the workshop and pulled one of the extra pumpkins from the fridge, along with an array of colorful mums. Getting to work, she carved the top off the pumpkin and hallowed it out. Then she set a wide bowl inside, halfway full with water. Cutting the purple, yellow, red, and orange mums, she arranged them in the pumpkin.

That done, she snatched a narrow, tall wicker basket and affixed two crotchet hooks on the front with some wire, then connected the hooks with a strand of pink yarn. Luckily, Harriet had a lot of craft stock lying around for personal touches just like this one. Maddie set another tall vase inside the basket and cut irises, white roses, ferns, and a couple tall swirling sticks for extra oomph.

Satisfied, she carried them into the shop and set them on the counter near the register. "Okay, Darlene. The pumpkin is for your dining table. This should last you about five to seven days if kept inside. The basket is for your guest room. Both arrangements will need more water when you get home, but for transportation purposes, I only filled them a bit."

Darlene rose from the chair and slowly walked over. Brows wrinkled, she examined the arrangements. "You did all that in fifteen minutes?"

"Well, you seemed frazzled, so I didn't want you to have to wait. In-laws can be scary. I hope these help."

"Wow." Darlene straightened, wide eyes on Maddie. "These are really great. Thank you!" She dug in her purse. "What do I owe you?"

"Nothing. They're on the house this time." The pumpkin and mums were overstock. The rest Maddie would pay back to Harriet. "I just ask that you accept my apology for my behavior growing up. You look amazing, so obviously nothing I said was accurate."

Darlene stared at Maddie for several ticks of the clock before finally clearing her throat. "I ate my feelings as a girl." She shrugged. "It was the only thing I could control. Food. But thank you for saying that, and I accept your apology." She pointed to the flowers. "Are you sure you won't take anything for these?"

"I'm sure. Just come see us again soon. Maybe for the wedding arrangements. Congratulations, by the way."

"Thank you." Darlene lifted the flowers and headed for the door. She paused and turned. "Harriet should hire you full-time. You're very talented."

Maddie smiled, warmth filling her chest. "Thanks."

Chapter 15

"What do you mean, she doesn't live here?" Parker fisted the sweatshirt Maddie had left in the backseat of his car last night and glared at Miles. He figured he'd swing by and bring it to her after dinner with his folks, perhaps sneak in a make-out session since he sorely needed a fix, but the Rec Center director was claiming she didn't live in the complex where he'd dropped her off countless times.

A shrug and helpless expression was all Miles offered. "Sorry, sheriff. She doesn't, nor has she ever resided here."

Parker glanced at the two other buildings, then the three across the street. Maybe her apartment was in one of those? But, no. She'd gone into *this* complex when he'd driven her home. "You're her boss at the center. Did she put an address on her application?"

"When she first applied, she listed the former Freemont Mansion. I remember because I had to have her update it for our records last year. She has a P.O. Box on file now."

That was of zero help. Parker ran his fingers through his hair, clenching the strands. Just what in the hell was going on?

"All right. My mistake. Thank you."

Miles nodded and headed toward his car at the curb.

Drumming his fingers on his thigh, Parker tried to think. It made no sense for her to tell him this was her apartment if she didn't actually live here. He wasn't a threat, so she wouldn't have given him a phony location. Would she? And she didn't have a car. Thus, her real residence had to be within walking distance from here.

He pulled his phone from his pocket and typed her a message. *Just got finished with dinner at my folks' place. What are you up to?*

The icon swirled. *Getting ready for bed. Long day tomorrow.*

He thought about asking where this bed was precisely situated, but rousing suspicion wouldn't aid his cause. If she suspected he was checking up on her, the fragile trust they'd built would crash and she'd shut down.

Ok. Hope you have a great night. Sweet dreams.
Maddie: You too.

Whatever. He'd pick her up at Ka-Bloom tomorrow after her shift and drop her off. From there, he'd watch and see what she did. Not ideal, but it would do.

He headed home and let Domino outside, tossing the ball for a few minutes. Mindless TV couldn't get his mind off the situation. He spent half the night tossing and turning, wondering where she was sleeping or why she'd lied about it.

By the time he got in his car Sunday afternoon to fetch her, he was crawling out of his skin. Stupid, asinine theories had embedded themselves in his brain.

To steady himself, and since he had a moment to waste, he popped by the station to check on things. Nodding to his deputies, he strode into his office and stopped short.

The hell? Aluminum foil. Everywhere. Nearly his entire office was covered in it. Monitor, keyboard, a lamp, filing cabinet, *the desk*. It looked like a 70s sci-fi studio set.

One of his officers, Kevin, leaned back in his chair at his cubicle. His goatee twitched with a grin and his shaved head gleaned from the fluorescent lights. "Got yourself a prankster, boss."

"No kidding." Laughing, Parker swiped a hand over his face. Scratched his jaw. Shook his head.

This had Maddie all over it. Other people sent flowers or thinking-of-you texts. Not her. Oh, no. She wrapped his office in foil. Or set his stapler in a Jell-O mold. Why be normal?

Mercy. She made his eye twitch and gave him a headache and frustrated him to the moon and back. But, damn, did he want her.

Smiling, he backtracked to his vehicle and drove down Main. Again, her living situation pressed against his skull. She acted no different when she got in the car, of course. Thanking him for the ride, blah-blahing about her flower orders. He asked a

138

couple mundane questions to appear interested. Yet, all he could focus on was the lie.

Parking at the curb outside the apartments, he craned in his seat to face her. He typically tried to get her to invite him in, but this afternoon, he needed the opposite in order to investigate. She'd always left it up to him to make a move, too.

She stared at him, her face an attractive blank page. Those eyes, though. Oh, those baby blues. They held a world of uncertainty.

Alrighty. He'd nudge her. "You gonna kiss me or not?"

Up went her brows. She didn't take the bait, however.

"Come on, Maddie. I dare you. Kiss me."

And, *yessss*. She still couldn't resist a dare.

Off went her belt. Over the console, she leaned. One hand braced on the back of his seat, the other on the wheel, she brought her face close to his. He got the briefest blip of cornflower blue in her irises before her lids drifted shut and her lips met his.

Shit, her mouth could decimate a kingdom. He tried to go at her slow, ease into it like the times he'd kissed her prior, but she wasn't having it. He couldn't tell if he should weep or rejoice.

Perhaps both.

At the same time.

She'd managed to fuse their lips in a vacuum seal that required the need for air and yet no desire to actually acquire it. The tension in her neck as he wrapped his fingers around her nape and her insistent moans of pleasure indicated her sense of urgency and sheer impatience. The gentle sweep of her tongue and cajoling languid swirls told an opposing story. Always a contradiction, his Maddie.

Hold it, hold it. *His* Maddie? As in, possessive?

He paused mid-kiss, fingers deep in her hair. He tried to think through the pounding of his heart, heat of his skin, and the way his pants had shrunk, but it was rather difficult.

Screw it. Thinking was stupid.

Except she must've noted the change because she carefully drew her head back, lifting her lids. "Everything okay?"

"Hell yeah. Would rather be doing this horizontally, though."

Her grin flashed, unbidden, and lit up the whole vehicle. "Tomorrow night? Are we still on for dinner at your place after my shift?"

"Barring a major catastrophic event, yes. And by catastrophic, I mean my death."

That earned a laugh. "Goodnight."

"Sweet dreams, Maddie."

She exited and walked up the sidewalk to the lobby. He waited a few seconds and drove up the cul-de-sac, turned around, and parked a few doors down. Cutting the engine and lights, he waited.

From his vantage point, he could make out part of the park to his right, the side of the apartment building, and the road stretched before him. Dusk rolled in, heavy with fog and humidity. Stars threatened to poke through the darkening sky as streetlamps kicked on.

Five minutes passed, then ten. All the while, he kept his gaze locked on the light-colored brick exterior of her complex. Her *supposed* complex.

A blur caught his eye from the corner of the building. Squinting, he trained his gaze on the form retreating from the rear door and heading deeper into the park. Jeans, black sweatshirt hood poking out from the top of a purple coat, backpack, and long blonde hair.

Yep. Maddie.

He shook his head, watching her as his gut clenched. What in the hell was she up to? And where was she going? There was nothing in that direction except the rocky bluffs overlooking the Pacific or the public nature trails.

When she was a good distance away, he silenced his phone, climbed out, and followed her.

She bypassed the lookout to the bluffs and made her way past the parking lot for the nature hike reserve. From there, she veered left and took the trail that had the steepest incline.

Immediately, he was swallowed in cypress and redwoods, the canopy overhead masking the sky. Small creatures scurried, but the thick bed of pine needles absorbed the sound of his shoes. He held back a good ways so she wouldn't notice a tail, and his gut cranked the farther up the range she went. Beyond this point, she'd be getting into dangerous activity for predators. In fact, to the right, the overlook was where the county had posted signs not to tread past the markers.

As if to assuage his erratic heartbeat, she went left and off the trail. Frowning, he followed. A few yards in, and she slowed to a stop. He couldn't see what she was looking at, foliage blocked the view, but he put his hand on the butt of his Glock in the holster on his belt and listened.

Nothing. No snapping twigs. No patter of feet. Not even an owl.

He waited, watching her, his heart thundering so hard it cracked ribs.

After a couple beats that lasted a couple years, she kept going. Rounding a particularly large redwood, he came to an abrupt halt.

She stood outside a tent, using the light from her phone to peek inside. Seemingly satisfied, she crawled inside and zipped the enclosure behind her.

Dumbstruck, he stared, unmoving, waiting for what she'd do next. But she never reemerged. A muted glow came from inside the tent moments later, and he nearly died on his feet.

Please, for the love of God and all the angels in the heavens, tell him this wasn't home for her. That she was merely camping or playing yet another prank on him.

He glanced at his surroundings, taking stock. Railroad spikes were in the ground encasing the perimeter, barbed wire wrapped around them for a crude fence. He stepped closer, mindful to keep quiet and still maintaining distance. A hole dug in the earth in front of the tent's opening was lined with rock, firewood arranged on top. Over the tent, secured to trees, was a large nylon tarp to, he assumed, provide additional cover.

No. She wasn't playing a prank at all. This was too elaborate a setup for a night of camping, too. And she'd been here awhile. Charred firewood that hadn't completely burned was in two piles on the far side of her base, nearly as tall as him. A black garbage bag hung from a tree branch next to it.

He was going to be sick. Placing a hand over his abdomen, he struggled to inhale and quiet the nausea. Worry and anger and fear crippled him, until standing became difficult.

How long had she been out here? Since her return to Redwood Ridge? Shit. That had been, what, three years? Or had it been a result of circumstances? Perhaps just something she'd done over the summer? It was November now, though. Getting colder. Too chilly to be camping.

And, Jesus. Why? Why the hell was she living in the damn woods in a damn tent a quarter of the way up the damn mountain? There were apartments available. Houses for rent. Even some of the storefronts had lofts or studios over them. She had three jobs. Worked here and there at who knew how many others. How the actual fuck had she wound up...

He choked, his sinuses stinging. Claws shredded a path from his gut to his esophagus.

Homeless. His Maddie was homeless.

He thought about how much weight she'd lost since their teenage years, the way she chronically kept her head down or the things he'd heard townsfolk mutter about her. To her face and behind her back. How she always struggled when someone had been nice to her or had issued a compliment.

This town, the very place he loved and had sworn to protect, where they'd both been raised and called home, had abandoned her. Had epically failed her. Had shunned her and rendered her an outcast. And *this*? He looked at the now darkened tent. This was the result. This was what happened when the patrons used their powers for evil instead of good, when they followed crowd mentality without knowing all the facts.

He pulled his phone from his pocket with shaking hands, resisting the urge to stomp over and drag her back to his house like a Neanderthal. *Asleep yet?*

A ping resounded from inside the tent. *Almost. I guess you're not, lol.*

No. He didn't think he'd sleep until they found Amelia Earhart's body. Or until he knew Maddie had a safe place to land, preferably in bed beside him.

Tilting his head, he dissected that errant thought. She'd never go for it, would know or suspect the offer to stay with him would be out of pity. She accepted kindness, but he had a feeling she'd refuse charity.

Thing was, that's exactly what he wanted. Her, in his house, playing with his dog and eating dinner at his table and sleeping in his bed. Absurd, considering they had just begun a relationship they'd yet to even consummate. But, there he had it. What he wanted was all-in with her.

How many dates or girlfriends over how many years, and Maddie Freemont was the one who'd penetrated skin and bone to root in his soul. If he were being honest, he'd seen this coming the second he'd run into her in a janitor's uniform at his niece's school.

Maddie didn't give him the warm fuzzies. She set him ablaze.

She didn't offer a sense of comfort or security like settling would imply. She locked his heart in a cage, only to be released or handled by her.

She wasn't an itch. She scratched all of his.

She didn't pacify his moods or mind. She stirred it into chaos so all he could think about or feel was her.

She didn't sit idle or let him do the same. She was action, the emotional adventure he'd been seeking. A challenge and riddle he'd never solve, but would die trying.

He stared at his phone. All his adult life, he'd craved what his parents had. The kind of relationship born from love and trust. A connection and meeting of the minds with mutual respect. They still slow-danced in the kitchen in front of the fridge and held hands watching TV on the couch.

Parker had been looking, not finding his match. Refusing to settle. He simply assumed he'd know when he found her. Of all the women in the world, though, it figured the one who seemed to be perfect for him was the very female who he'd avoided all these years.

Ran from instead of toward.

Ignored instead of embraced.

Maybe a part of him had known all along, but hadn't been truly ready. What an epic dolt he'd been.

Regardless, he wasn't scared now and thumbed a text. *Can't sleep. Keep thinking about you.*

Maddie: Good or bad thoughts? The aluminum foil was just a joke. Not that it was me or anything. Because it wasn't.

Grinning, he typed a reply. *It was probably Jason needing attention. He feels left out I'm spending free time with you.*

Maddie: No doubt. You should definitely slap cuffs on him.

His skin heated and his pulse thumped. *Would rather put you in my cuffs. And you wouldn't have the right to remain silent.*

A sultry laugh came from her tent. *Rawr. Go to sleep, Parker. Tomorrow you can frisk me.*

He bit his tongue in order not to laugh and alert her to his position. *All right. I look forward to it. Sweet dreams.*

A glance at her tent, and he couldn't do it. He couldn't walk back to his car, get in, and drive home. Couldn't cozy up in his bed when she didn't have one. Couldn't leave her out here on the side of a mountain. Didn't matter if she'd probably been living under these circumstances for quite some time. Didn't matter if she seemed resolved to her situation. This was the last night she spent out here. He wasn't okay with it, and come tomorrow, he was going to fix it.

Without her knowing, of course.

He moved a few yards away and plopped on his ass, his back against an oak. He'd sit sentinel until he could gather more intel in the morning. His back was going to be pissed, but he'd deal.

Prepping for a long night, he zipped his coat, pocketed his cell, and settled in.

And, yeah. Come daylight, after intermittent sleep, his back screamed. So did his legs and neck. With a megaphone.

Standing, he stretched, found a tree to relieve himself, and stretched again. He wondered when she planned on heading into town or if he'd have to wait half the day until her shift at the school.

Just as he was debating leaving to check on the station and come back later, she emerged from the tent. Easing behind a tree, he watched as she went out of her makeshift gate and into the woods. A handful of minutes later, she returned, only to duck in the tent and out again, this time with her backpack.

She seemed a tad sluggish as she walked toward the hiking trails, head down and dragging her feet. Maybe she hadn't slept much either or wasn't a morning person.

When he no longer heard her footsteps, he gave it a good five minutes and strode over to her camp.

Push and pull dragged at his conscience. What he should do, instead of invading her privacy, was just flat out ask her what was going on. Why she was living off the land and not under a roof. But he knew her. Stubborn and independent. Strong as she was vulnerable. Not only would it embarrass her if he acknowledged the situation, she might dig in her heels and put a halt to their relationship.

In time, she'd accept that he cared and would allow him to help. Yet, she wasn't at that point. Saddest part, and it gutted him, was she didn't trust that people were genuinely concerned or wanted what was best. And truthfully, not many in town had helped her mindset. They only saw her as the action her father had taken, not the person behind the sass.

It was a viscous circle. Another thing he was determined to fix.

A sigh, and he dragged the tab on the zipper, crawling inside the tent. On his knees, he surveyed the circumstances.

There was padding under the framework, which meant she'd insulated the tent for elements and comfort. The sleeping bag was thermo and designed for frigid conditions. She had a blanket folded on top and a battery-powered lantern beside it. Four very tattered paperbacks lay by a pillow. To his right were two large totes, and after peeking inside, he found more winter gear. To the left were more totes containing canned food, clothes, toiletries, and ledger notebooks. She also had a flare gun, taser, and stacks of bottled water.

The fragile bit of hope he'd been harboring shattered. This was, in fact, home for her. Judging by the amount of items and the organization involved, she'd been at it a long time. When was the last occurrence where she'd had real food not from a can? Slept in a bed? Heck, how and where did she shower?

Focusing on the notebooks, he opened the top one. Acid ate at his stomach while he glanced at accounting notes. How she nickeled and dimed every purchase. Flipping pages, he went to the last entry, wanting to weep. The first page had been dated two and a half years ago.

Snatching another ledger, he pried the lid, not sure he was prepared for what he'd discover. And, shit. He was right. He completely wasn't prepared. Not even if someone had told him ahead of time and had tattooed it on his arm.

Names. Pages and pages and pages of names. Two columns were beside them. A dollar amount and checkmarks. Some people had them, others didn't. And he recognized every one. Not because they were residents of town, but because they were victims of her father's scheme.

He stared at his sister's name and the exact percentage she'd given. Paige didn't have a checkmark.

Opening the accounting book again, he scrolled to the date of a person with a mark, then verified Maddie had deducted the withdrawal from her average. He scanned another, and another, and yet another. All the names checked off had deductions.

Shaking, he closed both notebooks and replaced them. His chest constricted to the point of pain and he fisted his jacket, struggling to breathe.

She worked three jobs. She lived in a tent. She ate canned food and slept in unfathomable conditions. She had no car or other amenities besides a cell phone, which probably was a necessity for her employers to contact her. And all so she could…

Holy shit. Holy, holy shit.

And all so she could reimburse those townsfolk who had been wronged, despite the fact she hadn't been the person to wrong them in the first place. Poverty, barely scraping by, and every red cent that wasn't to sustain life was being repaid to others in a debt that wasn't hers.

He closed his eyes, burning with frustration and unshed tears. The majority of town treated her like refuse. Aside from a handful of patrons, the rest ignored her. Said ugly things. Spouted insults. Until he and she had crossed paths again because of The Battleaxes, she hadn't a friend to turn to. He'd gotten Jason and Ella on her side, and there was Miles and Harriet who seemed to appreciate her, but that was a very sad number considering there were eighteen hundred residents in Redwood Ridge.

This couldn't go on. Her living conditions or their treatment. It had to end.

Chapter 16

Bent over a child-size toilet, Maddie set her hands on her knees and fought a wave of dizziness. Her third one in an hour. Her muscles cramped, her bones ached, and the fever she woke up with this morning was making a comeback.

Exactly what she didn't need.

And she was supposed to be going over to Parker's tonight.

She could cry. Nothing went her way. Ever. She wasn't one to pull the poor-me routine or give in to emotion. Really, there just wasn't much point and it solved zilch. But, dang it, anyway. She could seriously break down and cry right now.

Throat tight, eyes burning, she shook her head and straightened. She'd just have to cancel. She'd been looking so forward to a night alone with him. Dinner. Talking. *More.* Ah, the more. She was unequivocally ready for more.

But there was that bitch Karma again, rearing her head. *What's this I hear? Maddie Freemont seems happy? Excited? Finding a bit of good luck? I must put a stop to it immediately.*

Boom. The flu.

To boot, it was forecasted to be rather chilly tonight. After midnight, the temp was supposed to drop to twenty degrees. Pretty cold for these parts. She was working inside a heated school, and she couldn't get warm. Her tent would be unbearable, despite thermo gear.

Such was life. Such was *her* life.

Snatching her phone from her cleaning cart, she thumbed a text to Parker. Maybe she could catch him before he left to pick her up. *Gonna have to reschedule tonight. Not feeling well. Sorry.*

No sooner had she put her phone down, and his reply came in. *I'll pick you up at the usual time. You can rest at my place, get a good night's sleep while someone takes care of you.*

Shocked to her marrow, she stared at the screen and his words. Nowhere in the history of ever had someone taken care of her. Or wanted to. Her mother, though wonderful, had been sick on and off all Maddie's life. Her father provided servants and clothes, an education and shelter, but he'd never been compassionate. David had been as tender and sympathetic as a fish. And just as cold. Their relationship had been an arranged one with little affection involved.

But, Parker? Geez, good ole Parker Maloney. Funny, sweet, and endearing. He had excellent intentions with his offer, but it seemed early in the game to be showing one another their worst side. Nothing screamed slam-on-the-brakes in a budding romance faster than being in the same space as someone with the flu.

I'm probably contagious. Not a great idea. Thanks, though. Another time.

She pushed the cart into the maintenance office and checked her mail slot. Empty. From there, she filled her reusable bottle with water from the cooler and shoved it in her backpack. Clocking out, she donned her coat, hat, gloves, and slid her backpack over her shoulders.

It was going to be a long walk home. Once she got there, she'd start a fire, take some pain relievers, and sleep. Yes. Sleep sounded so amazing.

Since no one was around, she gave in to the urge to whimper and headed for the front of the building, legs like lead. Letting the door close behind her, she descended the cement steps, face down and bracing against the wind, and walked right into...

Parker. Of course. When had he ever listened?

He cupped her jaw, staring down at her with a deep wrinkle between his brows. "Jesus, you're hot."

Kinda like the polar calling the grizzly a bear, wasn't he? "Why, thank you. I'm not even wearing makeup today. How kind of you to say."

His jaw ticked. "Why didn't you call in sick if you have a fever?"

She shrugged, too tired to argue. He wouldn't understand that every little infraction would give them grounds to fire her.

My, he was a sight for sore eyes, though. Sore everything. His midnight strands caught the wind and tumbled into disarray. Piercing green eyes darted back and forth between hers, concern in their depths. His full, unsmiling mouth was framed by a day's worth of scruff. He smelled good, too. Pine and fabric softener and yum.

"Come on, honey. Let's get you home."

She didn't know what to reel at first, the home comment or the term of endearment. He always called her by name, typically with exasperation in his tone.

Allowing him to guide her, she slumped in the passenger seat of his Charger. He buckled her in, shut the door, and rounded the hood. From there, he cranked the vent dial to full blast, turned on the heated seat function, and drove out of the lot.

"I'll getcha there fast. You can take a hot bubble bath and climb in bed. Sound good?"

It sounded amazing, but she didn't have a bed or a tub. It had been since before her father's incarceration that she'd relaxed in a bubble bath.

Unbidden, hot tears trekked her cheeks. She swiped at them, confused, staring at the wetness on her glove.

"Maddie?" Parker looked at her, the road, and back again. His expression dialed straight to oh-shit. "Hey, it'll be all right. You'll feel better soon enough. My mom's making some of her famous chicken soup and bringing it by. I swear, it's a cure for everything. They should've had it during the plague. Would have had a lot less casualties, that's for sure."

How she found the energy, she hadn't a clue, but she laughed. Then moaned because the act made her bones hurt more.

Hold on. He'd called his mom for reinforcements? Because Maddie was sick? And his mother was willing and able to do a kind gesture for the most hated woman in town?

"She, um…" Maddie cleared her throat. "She doesn't have to go to the trouble." Heck, she had no way to reheat soup unless she took it with her to work tomorrow.

"It's no trouble. Trust me, she loves cooking. She'd like to meet you one of these days. Her words were 'very soon.' Both my folks. When you're better, of course."

Of course. Since that was normal. For other people.

"I met your dad during my father's investigation. He was there when the Feds talked to me also."

"He remembers." Parker scratched his jaw. "We talked about it last night at dinner, actually. They weren't surprised we were together. Dad never thought you had any part in the scheme. In fact, he reiterated that to the FBI many times."

"What?" She whipped her attention to him, getting a terrible case of dizzying whiplash for the effort. She pressed her hand to her forehead.

"Not everyone is out to get you. Though, I was relieved my parents weren't against the idea of us. I'm close with them and they mean the world to me. Alas, they're happy if I'm happy."

Was he happy? He'd implied it.

Her fever must be worse than she thought, delusions of grandeur a side-effect.

And he just drove past her street. Well, the street her "apartments" were on.

Their conversation clicked into place, slowly because of the flu. He'd said his mom was running soup over. To his place. Duh.

Know what? Maddie didn't care. If he was ready and wanting to take her to his home, then fine. She'd let him. She felt like something scraped off of a five-year-old's shoe and sleeping in a bed would be heaven, not accounting for the bath. She'd take it. Moreover, she needed it. He might regret it later, but that was his problem. Besides, she was too exhausted to argue.

A few minutes later, he turned into his driveway and pulled into the garage. Cutting the engine, he faced her. "Give me a sec to put Domino away. He can maul you another time when you're not dead on your feet."

Eyes closed, she huffed a laugh. "Okay."

He disappeared into the house, only to come back in what seemed like seconds. Opening her car door, he held out his hand. "Let's get you situated."

She hadn't a clue what that meant, but she followed him inside.

He headed straight for the hallway while she waited in the living room. Cabinets banged. Water ran. Finally, he poked his head around the corner. "Come on."

Again, she followed him, this time, into the bathroom. A pile of clothes were on the toilet lid and the tub was a quarter of

152

the way full. Bubbles, too. Steam plumed in the small space decorated a navy blue with a sailing theme. The towel rack was an anchor and a lighthouse figurine sat next to a soap dispenser on the vanity.

"Those are my sweats and a tee. They'll be too big, but should be comfortable. Water's pretty hot. Might want to check it first. The bubble bath is my niece's for when she's over. Unfortunately, it's cherry-scented. Sorry. Need anything else?"

"Uh, no." She tried to swallow and couldn't manage. Damn if he wasn't trying to take care of her, after all. "Thank you."

He smiled and pressed a kiss to her forehead. "There's ibuprofen in that drawer if you need some. Towels are in the cabinet under the sink. I'll be around when you're done. Take your time."

Just like that, he stepped out, closing the door behind him. She stared at it, the wood grain, half-expecting him to come back in and say, *just kidding. I'll drive you home.*

A sigh, and she tested the water temperature with her hand. It wasn't scalding, so she fished in the drawer for pain reliever. Swallowing two, she stripped and climbed in the tub.

Ah, God. *Yesssssssss.*

Hot water engulfed her lower half, chasing away her chills and relaxing her muscles. Before she got too comfortable, she used the liquid kid soap and shampoo combination to wash her body and hair.

Twisting the knob, she shut off the water and leaned back, soaking. It had been so long, so very long since she'd had the luxury of a bubble bath. She'd almost forgotten how much she loved them. As a teen, she had a routine every evening of taking a swim in the mansion's indoor pool, then rinsing off in the shower and a hot bath afterward. Sometimes, she'd read until she fell asleep or just let the water work its magic. Often, she'd envision her troubles going down the drain, too.

If only.

She kept an eye on the clock, careful not to take advantage of his generosity. Twenty glorious minutes, and she pulled the plug.

Once dry, she eyed his clothes, which smelled like him. The gray sweats had to be rolled twice at the waist to fit, and that was while tightening the drawstring. The black tee came down to her knees. So comfortable, though.

She tossed the towel in the hamper, rinsed the tub, and yanked the curtain closed. On her way out, she turned the light off and the exhaust fan on. She found him in the kitchen, putting Tupperware in the fridge. He'd changed into a pair of green and black flannel pants and a white shirt. Barefoot, though. Sexy.

"Hey. Thought you'd be longer. Feel better?"

Actually, she did and nodded. "Thank you."

He smiled. "Got some soup for you. Mom came and went."

When she didn't move, he gestured at the table. "I already had some." He pulled out a chair for her.

Stunned, she sat while he claimed a spot across from her. "You were serious about the taking care of me bit. I'm not used to that."

He said nothing, just watched her through those unfathomable mossy eyes. Sincerity, concern, and affection radiated in his stare.

She wasn't used to that, either, so she picked up a spoon and took a bite. It was good. Really good. It had been eons since she'd had homemade soup. Shredded chicken with diced carrots, celery, and onions in a hearty broth with fine noodles. Heavy on the noodles. Her favorite.

"Thank your mom for me, please. This is very yummy."

That earned a half-smile. "She'll be pleased to hear that." His throat worked a swallow, his eyes penetrating. "Why has no one taken care of you?"

She paused, spoon halfway to her mouth. "I can take care of myself."

"Admirable quality, but everyone needs pampering once in awhile."

She wouldn't recognize the notion or concept if it latched onto her face and wiggled. Shrugging, she chewed and swallowed. "I'm not exactly surrounded by people wanting to help. Besides, I told you, my father didn't dole attention."

His eyes narrowed, jaw ticking. "So you've had no one since your mother passed away?"

"There were some people who gave a damn. Or, well, pretended to, I guess. And don't go feeling sorry for me. I deserve what I got. I was a harpy as a girl who was only happy making others as miserable as I was. By the time I realized what I was doing and who I'd hurt, it was too late. Throw in what my father did, and it wasn't worth the effort to try and amend matters."

He offered a slight shake of his head, more involuntary than argumentative. "Are you punishing yourself, then? Is that what slunking in the shadows is for? Your attempts at invisibility? Sentenced to a life of solitude for seeking attention? You were a kid, Maddie. I may not have realized the reasons for your behavior back then, but I'm a fully functioning adult now. I'm here. Others will come around, too."

She stared at her half-eaten soup. "You sound so sure of yourself."

"I am." Forearms on the table, he leaned into them. "You aren't your father's mistakes and they weren't your crimes. Quit punishing yourself. You owned up to the mean girl act. Apologize to those you hurt. I'll bet more than half of those people will forgive you. If you continue to act guilty, they'll treat you that way."

She thought about his best friend, Jason, and how he'd reacted, about her former classmate, Darlene, when the woman had come into the flower shop. Both had been wary, but ultimately had accepted Maddie's apology.

Perhaps Parker was onto something. Except there was a huge difference between I'm-sorrying her way through townsfolk whom she'd said awful things to as a petty child and her attempting to pay back those residents who'd been scammed by her family. In their eyes, she was no better than her dad.

Sins of the father.

"What about David?"

Setting her spoon aside, she blinked at Parker. "What about him?" He was ancient history.

155

"You were engaged for a couple years, right? Dating beforehand? Surely, he'd taken care of you when you were sick or having a bad day."

Apparently, that was the norm for couples. To boost morale and support one another. A shoulder to cry on and arms which held. It hadn't been her reality.

Unable to look Parker in the eye, she examined a carrot floating in the soup's broth. "Dad picked him, remember?"

"Yeah, but there was love, correct? In some form?"

"No." Agony clutched her chest, and she grew weary of struggling to stay above water.

Her mother notwithstanding, Maddie had never been loved. It was a terrible, eviscerating admission. Even to herself, she'd made excuses for everyone's reactions or treatment when, truly, she'd played no part in their conduct. Because she was a non-entity. She'd been so invisible and unimportant that she hadn't left her imprint anywhere. Like she'd not existed in the first place.

She'd been trying to change that by letting Parker in, making nice with his friends, helping those she could, and disappearing from view when warranted. It hadn't mattered, though. There wasn't a trace of her to be had in Redwood Ridge.

"His mistake." Up went Parker's brows, his gaze determined. "He was too stupid to recognize a good thing when he had it in his hands. His mistake, my gain. I'm not him. On so many levels, I'm not him."

While she reeled, he swiped a hand down his face and tilted his head to glare at the ceiling. Eternities passed, her heart separating ribs, with her wondering if he'd meant the line he'd just fed her. His posture and mannerisms indicated he was frustrated or pissed off at himself. Or her.

Perhaps both.

"I don't have a crystal ball and I can't read tarot cards." He lowered his head and closed his eyes. "We could be wasting our time or setting ourselves up for failure by attempting to be together." He waved his hand in a clear I-don't-know gesture and met her gaze again. "But we'd be idiots not to give it a go. There's something here between you and me. No way in hell would you have let things go this far if you weren't feeling it also. So, here's the deal, Maddie. You be you. I'll be me. We'll meet somewhere in the middle. And in the mean time, get used to being taken care of. That's how I roll. Be independent. Move mountains if you want. It's a rather attractive trait. But I will be there at the end of the day to catch you. That's what relationships are about, being strong when the other can't and caring enough to let them."

He stood, setting his palms on the table and leaned forward. "I care about you. Get used to that, too. Because I'm not them. I won't ignore you, use you, or cast you aside. Doesn't matter how this plays out, that won't change. You deserved so much better than those before me. And, honey, you're about to get it."

She couldn't breathe. Blink, swallow, move, or breathe. She blamed it on the flu because about halfway through his sexy, holy-crap, her-heart-just-melted rant, she nearly face-planted into a bowl of chicken noodle soup.

Flu, indeed.

"You done?"

Yep. Stick a fork in her.

He pointed to the soup. "Are you done?"

Lamely, she looked at the bowl. "Uh-huh."

A nod, and he took the dish to the sink. Then...

Well, she knew she was delirious *then*. The entire night was one long fever-induced dream from which she never wanted to wake.

He scooted her chair back, placed an arm under her legs, the other behind her back, and picked her up as if she weighed nothing. Through the kitchen, living room, and down the hallway, he went.

She got the briefest glimpse of a king-size bed, gray walls, and sage-colored curtains that matched the bedspread before he set her on the mattress. He proceeded to tuck her in and pressed his lips to her forehead, speaking against her skin.

"Be right back. I'm gonna let Domino out real quick."

The bedroom door closed. Nails pattered on hardwood. Hinges squeaked in the other room.

Moments passed.

Squeaky hinges. Dog nails on flooring. Parker muttering softly. His bedroom door opened, he came in, and he closed it behind him. He shut the drapes, walked to the nightstand, switched off the lamp, and climbed in bed beside her.

"Come here."

She didn't move. Couldn't, rather.

"Come here, honey." Rolling on his side, he wrapped an arm around her and tucked her against him. He fidgeted with the blankets so they were both covered and resettled. "In case you missed the memo, this is also the taking care of you part."

Her arms were trapped between them and her face was pressed against his collarbone. Warmth encased her from his embrace and the bedding. The mattress was so soft and he smelled good and her lids were heavy and her mind in a fog. He could've told her he was Batman and she was Catwoman for all she comprehended.

Safe, damn it. He'd instilled a sense of safety she'd never known simply by being himself.

She rode the current, too sore and tired to battle the waves. "Thanks, Parker."

"You're welcome." His chest rumbled as he spoke. "By the way, I turn into a sniveling, whining two-year-old when I'm sick. Be prepared."

She huffed a laugh and closed her eyes. "I can handle it."

"I think you can handle anything, Maddie."

Chapter 17

At the stove in his kitchen, Parker flipped scrambled eggs while waiting for Maddie to finish showering. He'd already changed the sheets and fed Domino. Not that his dog realized the fact by the way he'd wolfed down his food or stood sentinel while Parker cooked.

He shook his head as the faint sound of a hair dryer shut off down the hall. When he'd picked Maddie up from work last night, she'd been hotter than the surface of the sun and barely standing upright. He'd taken for granted normal comforts while ill. A bed. Blankets. Soup and a microwave to heat it. A bathtub. What in the hell would she have done if he hadn't made her come home with him? How had she coped in the past? The thought of her alone in a tent on the side of the mountain, feverish, shivering, made his gut ache.

All through the night, he'd held her while she'd whimpered in her sleep. He'd rubbed her back, smoothed her hair, tucked the blankets tighter. She'd woken up drenched from sweating off her fever, but feeling much better. Thankfully.

Hurray for her. His concern had yet to fade.

He'd already made a call to Harriet Nunez at Ka-Bloom the second Maddie had gotten in the shower. The flower shop owner had no idea Maddie was homeless. No one did. It wasn't a tidbit he planned on sharing around, but Harriet cared about Maddie and was more than willing to help.

At least he'd accomplished something productive.

Maddie strode into the kitchen wearing yet another pair of his sweats and a tee he'd laid out, pausing in the doorway. Her hair was up in a messy knot, a few loose caramel strands framing her face. The clothes hung on her, making her appear even more fragile. She had her color back, though, and she seemed less foggy than the night before.

"Have a seat. I made us breakfast." He dished the eggs onto two plates and served them with blueberry muffins he had leftover.

She sat, saying nothing.

She ate, saying more nothing.

She drank her juice, saying nothing so loud, his ears popped.

Afterward, she stared at him like she finally wanted to spit out some words, but he had a feeling he wasn't going to care for whatever sentence she spouted.

"Anything wrong?" Stupid question on his part, but worth asking. Perhaps it would get her started. He was at a loss and had been from the second they'd awoken this morning. Something had shifted for him in the wee hours, and he had zero clue if that was a two-way street.

Ever since she'd popped back into his life again, his world had been in a tailspin. One blow after another, a series of shocking revelations about her, and emotions he wasn't sure what to do with kept assaulting him from every angle.

And last night? The knockout. Because as he'd held her, he realized their situation wasn't merely his give-a-shit gene activating to take care of someone in need or him wanting to do the humane thing in regards to her. Nope.

She'd shivered, and he'd been cold.

She'd moaned from pain, and he'd hurt, too.

She'd nuzzled closer, seeking comfort, and he'd never wanted to let go.

He was nose-diving way past in like with her and headed straight toward Faceplantville. She had an amazing work ethic, plus a sense of honor despite her circumstances. Though the debts weren't hers, she was willing to pay back what townsfolk had invested because she viewed it as the right thing, no matter how much it would cost her to follow through. She was gorgeous and funny, strong and kind. That last bit had been a lot to swallow, but she *was* erringly sweet by nature. The quality was hidden under a blanket of sass, yet there nonetheless. And for a woman who hadn't been shown a lot of affection, she was sure quick to offer it when warranted.

Mercy, and the chemistry. One couldn't formulate or fake the sparks between them. He wanted her every second they were together and thought about her each instance they weren't.

Just what in the hell was he supposed to do? Beg? Plead? Roll over and act stupid? If he waited for her to decide, she'd be playing pranks on him in a nursing home from the room beside his forty years from now.

Domino set his head in her lap, and she smiled at the dog, petting his black and white fur. Her guard was down, shields disabled, and her tender side slipped past her walls to pummel Parker yet again. He wondered if she knew she smiled from her eyes when she was like this. Her irises transformed into a deeper cornflower.

Christ, even Parker's dog was fucking infatuated with her.

And she'd never answered his question.

His pulse pounded and his gut heated and his skin grew tight. "Are you feeling better?"

She nodded.

"Fever gone?"

Another nod.

"Got your strength back?"

Nod, nod, nodding.

Excellent. He didn't want to talk, anyway.

Rising, he rounded the table, nudged the dog aside, scooted out her chair, set his hands on the arms, and leaned over her until all she could see, hear, or smell was him.

Tit for tat.

He stared into her wide eyes, past her flushed cheeks, to her perfect pink mouth. "Calling in your rain check."

Her forehead wrinkled. "What?"

"Yesterday you tried to cancel because you were sick. You're better now. Rain check."

Realization warmed her complexion. Anxiety stirred in her eyes to contrast her first reaction. Always a contradiction, his Maddie.

She cleared her throat. "It's not raining."

And forever arguing. Even that was cute as hell.

No, it wasn't raining. The skies were clear without a cloud in sight. He took it as a sign and eased closer, hovering a millimeter from her lips. "Are you going to discuss the weather or kiss me?"

"I was just stating a fact. It's not raining."

"I'm noting barometric pressure regardless."

She flashed a grin. "Low front or high?"

"Definitely low." Below the belt, for sure. He was crawling out of his skin with the want of her. "Kiss me, Maddie." Before he imploded.

Her grin morphed into a sly half-smile that scattered his synapses in all directions. "Where?"

Ah, hell. He was done playing.

"Everywhere." Sliding his hands under her thighs, he lifted her and pivoted.

She wrapped her legs around his waist as he walked out of the kitchen, through the living room, and down the hallway, the dog on his heels.

"Domino, stay." Parker kicked the bedroom door shut and set Maddie on her feet. He shoved his hands in her hair, dislodging her bun, and met her gaze. "You stay, too."

He left her side long enough to shut the drapes and toe off his shoes, then returned to find doubt in her eyes. Again. He studied her a long beat, wondering what had happened in the past five seconds.

Chewing her lower lip, she stared at his chest. "I haven't done this in a long time. I'm not very experienced, either."

Judging by the crimson in her cheeks and avoidance of eye contact, that had taken a lot of courage for her to admit. To him, it only proved she trusted him and was letting him in. Finally.

"We'll have to practice. Often."

Her gaze darted to his and dipped to his grin. Slowly, doubt faded from her expression and was replaced with humor. Only when heat won the battle did he erase the distance between them.

"I want you. I don't care how few or many came before me." He almost blurted he wanted to be her last, but got himself in check and fisted the hem of her shirt instead. "Do we need protection?" He was safe. Per her, and he believed her, she hadn't had a lover in awhile, but birth control was another matter.

"Up to you. I get the shot every month."

Perfect. He was done chatting.

Tugging the tee over her head, he paused to look at her while removing his own. She had small breasts with pert pink nipples, erect and demanding attention. He was only more than happy to oblige. Hands on her narrow waist, he ducked and drew a bud into his mouth.

Her gasp made his blood pump faster. Ferocious need coursed through his veins, creating its own current, and he had to know what other sexy little sounds she made when aroused. Moving to her other nipple, he swirled his tongue, earning a moan, and that was it. He was so hard he could hammer nails.

Mouth drifting north, across her collarbone, over her neck, he moved his hand south, under her waistband to her perfect round ass. She gripped his shoulders, head back, and arched into him. The room tilted, and he laid her sideways on the bed, standing over her.

Watching her, he unbuttoned and unzipped his jeans, shucking them and his boxers while she looked her fill. Breathing labored, she explored him with her gaze while he rid her of the last barrier between them, tossing her sweats over his shoulder.

"You're beautiful." And she was. He straddled her, palms braced on the mattress. She had a waifish figure that could perhaps stand more protein in her diet, but considering her circumstances, that was to be expected. Slender or not, she was amazing just as she was. Long strawberry-scented hair spread over his navy sheets. Peaches and cream skin. Flare of hips. And white-blonde curls between the juncture of her thighs. She about took his breath away. "Beautiful, Maddie."

A trace of a smile ghosted her lips like she didn't quite believe him, yet she was willing to accept the compliment. "Thank you. You're pretty amazing yourself."

He kissed her brow, her cheeks, her mouth, and she immediately opened for him. Lips parted, she swept her tongue against his in a slow dance that didn't match the erratic beat of his heart. Still, it was right.

Him.

Her.

Them.

Their vast and plentiful contradictions that seemed to make up the whole of their relationship. As if there was only balance because of the offset. What a strange, interesting pair they made.

She went lax under him the deeper he sank into her kiss, and whatever tension she'd been harboring seemed to evaporate. With her sweet scent infusing him, he shifted and worked his way down her body, reveling in her soft, warm skin. When he spread her thighs, he glanced up at her, adoring her heavy lids and the way she was unabashedly staring at him. He kissed one thigh, then the other, and she trembled.

Feisty, stubborn Maddie Freemont. In his bed. Putty in his hands. Who knew?

Gently, he parted her folds, ran a fingertip through her slickness. Her hips rose as she silently begged for more. He'd give her that more and then some. Hell, he'd give her anything at this point. There wasn't an atom encompassed in his DNA that wasn't acutely attuned to her every sigh and nuance and response.

Palming her backside, he buried his face in her curls, nibbling her nub, swirling his tongue. She bowed, breasts aimed at the ceiling, and heels digging into his shoulders. Her reaction had him grinding his shaft against the sheets, needing relief from the pressure, but unwilling to stop her pleasure. She was amazing, utterly freaking amazing.

Only when she fisted the blankets over her head and started to fall apart did he crawl back up and settle between her legs. This first time, when she came, she'd do it with him inside her. He'd spend the rest of the night, the week, the month finding inventive ways for her to orgasm. But today, right now, they were teetering together.

Weight on one forearm, he gazed in her baby blues as he aligned himself. She didn't look away or close her eyes. She gazed right back, and he swore, he never had a connection to another woman like he did with Maddie right then. Everything else but the two of them melted into background static and became nonexistent.

The trust and affection in her depths told him a story, the way she viewed him, and it ripped the ground out from under him. Shook him to his core. Tightened his airway.

No doubt whatsoever, she could save herself, had for years, but she was silently asking for him to help. She could fight her own battles, defend herself, yet she passed him her sword just this once. To her, he appeared to be a hero. *Her* hero. The sentiment radiated in her tender, vulnerable gaze. Not from his brute muscle or sheer will, but because he knew her capabilities and chose to stand beside her anyway. He saw her, the real woman as a whole, and had stayed. Based on their bond in this fragment of time, she'd recognized those things and had succumbed as a result.

That didn't make him heroic. It meant he was human. And a smart one at that. He'd take Wonder Woman over Barbie every day of the week and twice on Sundays.

He got the horrible sensation no one had ever bestowed her that honor, had acknowledged her strengths while offering support. It was the people like her who needed it the most and received it the least.

Sliding his arms between the graceful arch of her spine and the mattress, he wrapped her against him. Held her as he entered her slowly and with care. Cherished the hot, tight connection and the way she seemed to grip every part of him.

When he was fully inside her, he paused and rested his forehead to hers, completely unprepared for what the moment would mean. He'd had sex. He'd made love. He'd even fucked a time or two. But, this? With Maddie? There wasn't a term to describe it. They'd barely begun, and he couldn't wrangle his emotions.

Relief, concern, bliss, pride, and shame coagulated into a messy knot, encased with the sheerest form of happiness he'd yet to encounter. He blew out an uneven breath and closed his eyes.

As if understanding his state, she slid her warm, soft hands up his back and held his face. His whiskers rasped against her palms in the quiet of his bedroom. She kissed each of his lids, then sought his mouth.

What else could he do but surrender? It's all he'd managed since they'd reconnected a couple weeks ago. Surrendered. Over and over. To the Battleaxes. To the situation. To her. He'd be a liar if he said he regretted it.

Taking the kiss deeper, he withdrew from her body, the effort agonizing, and plunged into her again. Her lips parted wider. Her gasp sucked the air from his lungs and into hers. She shoved her fingers in his hair, clenching the strands, and grabbed his shoulder from behind with the other as if needing to brace herself or to hold him against her.

Like he was going anywhere.

He opened his eyes, finding hers, and rocked inside her. Their breaths mingled. Their bodies danced. And in the muted light of day, while in the throes, she was the most gorgeous creature. Brows wrenched, baby blues saturated with lust, and cheeks pink, she moved under him. With him. Around him. As much inside him as he was her.

There was no learning curve, no point where he wondered what she wanted or how. She told him all he needed to know with her touch, with her sounds and sighs of pleasure. He'd always considered her eyes or her face a tell for her moods. She could be so expressive and it was often in opposition to whatever her mouth spouted.

Dolt that he was, he should've been watching her body. A mistake he wouldn't make again.

Have mercy, she was tight. Supple, giving, and tight. Dots spotted his peripheral while he pumped harder, faster, rolling his hips to ensure he ground against her where she needed it most.

Panting, he broke away from the kiss and opened his mouth over the thumping pulse in her neck. He'd been known for his patience, but stamina was a thin tether with her. The way they fit, her hands everywhere, her scent blending with his... He could barely find the strands of control, never mind grab them.

He moved one hand to her hip, down her thigh and behind her knee to spread her wider and thrust at a slightly different angle. Her moan ended in a purr and nearly did him in. The vibrations rumbled his chest and his shaft until he had to groan also or perish. He adjusted his other hand from behind her to cradle the back of her head, intent on being gentle, but he wound up fisting her strands with urgency instead. Which earned a louder, longer moan.

She'd be the death of him. So be it. He could think of worse ways to go out and none better.

"Parker..." A breathy, desperate exhalation followed his name, but she needn't say anything more. Her body grew taut and her teeth sunk into her pouty lower lip. She flung her arm above her head.

He pressed his palm to hers, lacing their fingers, and drove into her for all he was worth. Her hard little nipples grazed his chest as her breasts were crushed between them, the friction astoundingly extraordinary and sending his nerves into a riot of sensitivity. Lightning crackled along the path and sizzled heat to every square inch of skin he owned.

"That's it, honey. I've got you." Except someone needed to catch him.

Hips grinding, she accepted his thrusts as she fought for release. He was right there, lower back tingling in warning. He was this close to begging when her walls gripped his shaft in a vise. Her fingers fisted around his and she convulsed under him.

A sharp cry, and he followed her, chasing his own orgasm. His muscles locked and his bones fractured. Light so white it shimmered blue blasted behind his lids. His release lasted an eternity with her seizing him in a state somewhere between ecstasy and pandemonium.

Sucking oxygen, he slowed his thrusts, still quaking, and muttered incoherently against her throat. Eyes pinched shut, he collapsed on top of her, hoping he wasn't too heavy because moving was impossible.

Blessed silence ensued, just the sound of their ragged breathing and a whippoorwill outside the window.

Damn. When could they do that again?

That was, if he was still alive.

Briefly, he took stock. Thundering heart. Satiated muscles. Euphoric state of mind. Check, check, check.

Yeah, they were absolutely doing that again. As many times as his body or hers would allow.

Speaking of… He rolled to his side, taking her with him, and lazily covered them with a corner of the blanket. Her limbs like a bandage around him, she snuggled against him.

He kissed the top of her head and smoothed his hand over her back. He'd been wondering if their chemistry would translate to the bedroom. Often, he'd been interested in a woman he'd been dating, but they'd wound up lacking that oomph factor between the sheets. Sometimes, no matter how one flipped the pieces, they didn't fit. Wrong mould.

This wasn't his first rodeo. He'd had great sex. He'd been interested in other women before Maddie. What he hadn't had was her. The sync. A connection. Invested awareness with his heart and his mind.

Funny, all the toiling in seeking his right match had boiled down to finding the one female who didn't require any effort.

Relationships took work, yes. But not in the areas that mattered. Wanting to spend all his time with her. Missing her when apart. Someone to rouse his wit, heartbeat, and mood, yet still be the balm. Easy conversation on basic or difficult topics. Similar interests with enough differences to keep a balance. Comfortable silence. Compatibility in bed and out. Unforced attraction. Similar goals. Character and morals. Those things couldn't be fabricated. They were there or they weren't.

Well, shit. There he had it. His answer.

That made the Battleaxes like, what? Four-hundred and twenty-six to zero in stats? Uncanny.

Maddie stirred against him, nuzzling his chest.

His Maddie. His one. His only.

Jason was going to laugh his balls off when Parker told him.

A contented sigh, and she tilted her head to look at him. A small, secretive smile curved her lips. "What are you thinking about?"

How crazy her pranks were going to get when he dropped the L-bomb on her. How hard he was going to have to convince her she was worth loving and needed to get onboard with the idea. How stupid he'd been in his youth when she'd been in his face the whole time.

He tucked a strand of hair behind her ear, letting his fingers linger in her strands that smelled like strawberries. "Irony. I was thinking about irony."

Chapter 18

Maddie slowly opened her eyes, attempting to orientate herself. It had been three years since she'd slept in a bed with a roof over her head. The night before last, Parker had demanded she come home with him. Thankfully, her bug had only been a twenty-four hour thing, but the comfort of his home and his arms had made being sick not so bad.

Gah, he'd been amazing.

Their lovemaking had been even more amazing. David had been her only true experience in that area, aside from her first boyfriend Freshman year of college. Neither guy had been particularly spectacular. Parker? Holy crap. He'd set her on fire, and she hadn't cared an iota about the burns.

Moreover, he'd been tender and sweet with a side of naughty. He'd taken her to work at the school and had picked her up again after her shift, not even giving her the option to go home. They'd come right back to his house for a late dinner he'd cooked—le sigh—and had made love twice more. Triple le sigh.

What was she going to do about him? He was easy to talk to and be around. He had integrity and a great family. Was nice to her and cared about people. Defended her when necessary. Steady job. Great in bed. Sexy as sin.

But he was still the sheriff of Redwood Ridge and she was the most hated woman in town. He might say he didn't care now, yet there would come a time the animosity would get to him. Living in a constant state of guard duty was no way to exist. It was possible he'd lose the respect and trust of the townsfolk he was sworn to protect.

Guilt clawed at her stomach lining and ripped its way to her esophagus. She adored him. So damn much. Always had, if she were being honest. Even before her family had done their damage, she wasn't deserving of a man like him. She'd treated people poorly in her juvenile attempts to seek attention. Him, most of all. She feared no amount of apologizing or payback would ever win them over. A few had seen past her façade to what had really been the root of her behavior, but she could count those people on one hand.

Letting out a quiet breath, she looked at Parker, still asleep on his side, facing her and lightly snoring. Half of his handsome profile was squished into his pillow. Thick black lashes fanned his cheeks and scruff dusted his jaw. His midnight strands were in disarray and begging for her fingers. He had one arm braced on her waist like he was concerned she'd sneak out, and the other bent under his head.

Lordy, his biceps alone could dampen her panties. If she were wearing any. Which she wasn't because they hadn't bothered to dress before falling asleep. He smelled like snow and spice, and she wanted to lick him from head to toe. Touch him as they'd done last night. Watch his face twist in the pain/pleasure combination as he came, knowing she'd been able to give him that release.

Arg. Guilt, though.

They talked about everything. She could trust him and never doubted that. But she had yet to mention her current living arrangements or why she was in that position. Yes, it was by her own choosing. It would be selfish to spend most of her paychecks on rent or utilities when her family had taken money from good citizens for the sake of ego. Parker would go ballistic if he ever found out she was residing in a tent at the foothills of the Klamath. He might understand, but he wouldn't ever accept it. Or allow it.

And then she'd never achieve her goal of making amends. Never be able to move on with her life and start a future.

"I can hear you thinking, honey." His quiet, hoarse voice was but a rumble in the room. Yet he was louder than an AC/DC concert with Megadeth as an opening act. "What's on your mind?"

Everything. Nothing.

She didn't answer, though. Wasn't sure how.

Eyes still shut, he squeezed her side, then rubbed his thumb tenderly across the spot as if by encouragement. "Talk to me."

Fine. They needed to have a where-were-they-going relationship convo, anyway. "Do you want kids?"

He peeked one eye open, then the other as if in afterthought. He blinked. Twice. "Worried the birth control didn't work?"

"No." She routinely got the shot, and prior to that, habitually took the pill. Mostly, she did it for regulation. Obviously, she hadn't had a partner in ages. Not until a few days ago, anyhow. "Just wondering."

He propped his head in his hand and stared at her, his expression a blank mask. "We've come to that dating point where we need to discuss the future to decide if we break up or make a run of it. Am I right? You're having a mental freak out?"

She sighed and rolled to her back. Men. Stupid, intuitive men. She'd laugh if she weren't so frustrated.

"All right, Maddie. I'll bite. Yes, I want kids. A whole litter of them, but I'll settle for two. I want a family. Always have. Don't you?"

"Family doesn't have the same meaning for me as it does for you."

"And blood doesn't always equate to family. Love and bonds therein come in all shapes and forms. You aren't your relatives. You're better than your father and nothing like him. You can form your own family if you so desire."

He had a point. He wasn't wrong, either. However, there were other factors he was blatantly ignoring.

"I wished for a brother or sister growing up. Siblings, sure, but like what you and Paige have. Someone to talk to and play with, who always had my back. In hindsight, it's probably a good thing my parents didn't have more children."

"I can't imagine my life without Paige in it. I'd do anything for her." He swallowed, eyes narrowing a margin. "You may not have gotten your wish as a girl, but you're not alone. I have your back, you know."

Be still her heart. And he wasn't getting her indirect message. "Thank you, but you do understand that may hurt you in the end."

"Don't care. No one dictates who I love."

Love, huh? It wasn't an admission. He'd sure implied it, though. Then again, they were discussing numerous forms of love, as he'd said himself. His statement could've been hypothetical. Regardless, the giddy girl inside her who refused to shut up clapped like a lunatic.

"I wanted kids once upon a time. Two or three. A boy first, then a girl, so she'd have an older brother to look out for her like you did with Paige." Like no one in existence had ever done for her. "I know that's an archaic way of putting it." She shrugged. "It's just what I used to think. I'd still love to have children of my own someday, but I don't feel like it's a good idea considering the stigma behind my name. Others might take out their aversion to me or my father on them."

"Let me lay it out how I see it. Theoretically, if we were to admit our love, get married, and have children, they and you would have my name. Time and proof would erase the lingering animosity from townsfolk. We've talked about this before. Stand up to them. Show them who you really are and they'll grow to like you as much as I do."

Hand on her waist, he rolled and slid her under him until he hovered over her. Arms braced on either side of her head, he settled between her thighs and stared down at her. Affection warmed his emerald eyes.

And he was hard.

In point three seconds, she was wet.

He rocked against her, gliding his thickness between her folds. Heat blasted from her core, sending vibrations throughout her whole system. She ran her fingers over his hard pecs, down the ridges of his abs and around to his firm backside.

Such an incredible specimen of a man. Skin tone slightly darker than hers and hinting at a fading tan. A scattering of hair as black as the strands on his head dusted his chest and left a trail to his good parts. Biceps that bulged. Hands that were as huge as they were gentle. Veins and tendons and yum.

Leaning in, he brushed his lips over hers. "I care about you. If nothing else penetrates that stubborn, witty mind of yours, remember that much. The person you pretended to be all those years ago doesn't exist. The real you, the woman who makes my pulse jack and plays practical jokes and gives my dog attention and who rose from the ashes to become a self-sufficient, intelligent member of society? I care about that version of you, about all the aspects of you."

He offered a light kiss, his lids drifting shut. "So much, I don't know up from down and can't see straight. Let me do that, Maddie. Don't fight me or us. You've had enough battles. We're not one of them. Give in and let me care about you."

Chest tight, sinuses stinging, she opened her mouth to tell him yes.

But he tilted his head and took the kiss deeper. A shift of his hips, and he entered her in one smooth, swift thrust.

Bombarded with sentiment and sensory overload, she moaned and wrapped her arms around him. Like they had in previous lovemaking, the muscles in his back rippled as if he was a caged beast ready to break free.

Burying his face in her neck, he withdrew and thrust again. And again. Slow, steady, and with such intimacy, she thought they'd merged into one person. His pelvis ground against her clit and there wasn't a square inch of her skin that wasn't in direct contact with him. Legs tangled. Arms banded. Chests pressed together.

She never knew it could be like this. Sex had been neither a chore nor particularly pleasurable. It was an act between two people and a form of release. Parker had changed all that, had shown her how wonderful it could be with a partner who recognized her needs and understood her on a molecular level.

Over and over, he said her name. A coarse, desperate grunt of mutterings against her neck. His motions grew more frantic, his frame tense, and she melted into him. Let go. Admitted defeat, waved a white flag, and gave in to the insane pleasure he offered.

Close, so close he brought her to the edge that she feared she'd never stop falling once she jumped.

Her body decided for her. She clenched around him, vibrating, as unimaginable heat wracked her body and she convulsed from the inside out. Breath trapped in her lungs, she rode out the aftershocks, clinging to him.

Taut, quaking, he followed. He grunted, pumped twice more, and went rigid as he found his own release.

Moments passed as he panted and went lax on top of her. She cherished the weight and warmth of him, holding him to her and stroking his hair.

He shifted the slightest bit, moving to her side, arm across her middle and face on her breast. His ragged breath skated across her already sensitive nipple. It seemed as if he wanted to say something by the way his jaw ticked, so she kept mum, letting him work it out. Her chest was tight and her throat too raw to speak, anyway.

Gah, why did she feel like crying? There went her eyes again, growing hot. She'd never, not once, been one of those sappy females who'd wept after sex.

"Maddie, I—"

A piercing, screeching siren blasted through the room, jerking her heart from behind her ribs and lodging it in her esophagus. A red light blasted from his cell on the nightstand.

"Shit," he muttered and untangled from the sheets, stumbling to his feet.

Covering her ears, she watched as he snatched his phone, his thumbs flying. "What is that?"

"Amber Alert," he said, but he wasn't paying much attention to anything but his screen. The siren and lights stopped, and he rubbed a hand over his face. "We have a missing teenager. That's all I—"

His cell rang, the music of his tone breaking the blessed few seconds of silence. Another phone, she assumed his landline, rang from down the hall.

He swiped the screen. "What's the situation?"

She sat up, concern flipping her stomach, and adjusted the sheets to cover herself.

Three seconds passed, and then he was a flurry of motion. Cell to his ear, he opened a dresser drawer and stepped into a pair of boxers. Another drawer, this time jeans. He yanked the phone away from his head long enough to put on a tee. The bed dipped as he donned socks.

"Last seen?"

The sharp bark of his tone startled her. She jumped, and for a millimeter of a second, he looked over his shoulder at her like he'd forgotten she was there.

"I'm on my way." He slid his feet into shoes and rose, reaching for a belt on a nearby chair. "The Miller's daughter was on a field trip with the fifth grade science class and got separated from the group. They're not sure how long she's been on her own, but they looked for two hours before heading to the bus and calling for help."

He looked at her, expression wrought. "I'm sorry. I have to handle this." He glanced around helplessly as if unsure how to handle the sudden alteration in plans.

Of course, he did. He was the sheriff.

"Go." She rose from the bed, searching for her clothes. "I'll feed Domino and let him out. I can lock up and get home by myself."

He opened his mouth, only to snap his shut again. Lips a thin line, he shook his head. "Maddie…"

She shoved her head in a shirt. "Parker, go. A child is missing. I understand. Don't worry about things here. I got it handled."

A harsh sigh, and he strode toward her. Hands holding her face, he kissed her forehead and ducked to look in her eyes. "I'll call you later. We need to talk."

The four worst words in the English language.

Skilling her expression blank in order not to add to his load, she nodded. "Be careful."

"Always."

She stood in the center of his bedroom after he'd left, orientating to the vast disruption and how quickly the morning had turned sour.

She didn't know the Millers. If memory served, Dane Miller had been quite a few years ahead of her in school. Six? Eight, maybe? She couldn't picture his wife or their daughter, but hoped like hell everything was all right. They must be out of their minds with worry.

Once she'd made Parker's bed and righted his room, she fed the dog, let him outside, and threw the ball for him a couple times. From there, she locked up behind her, then walked toward the park, checking her phone for the Amber Alert.

Delia Miller was twelve years old with shoulder-length blonde hair, blue eyes, and an adorable scattering of freckles on her nose. She was about five feet, two inches tall with a curvy body shape, last seen wearing jeans, a red sweatshirt, and black sneakers. Her class had been on the hiking trails just north of the park, cataloguing fauna for science when they realized she was no longer with them. Maddie stored the information to memory in case she happened to spot the girl.

The town was in chaos as she made her way past the shops. Everyone had closed their businesses, were rushing around, or standing about discussing the situation. Maddie kept her head down through the park and took an alternate, longer route up the mountain since police, the fire department, and search parties would, no doubt, have the parking lot at the base of the hiking trails flooded. Her presence would only distract them or add to the commotion. It was more important they focus on their efforts.

The back way to her home base was more of an incline and not as safe. There were no steady trails mapped out and the terrain was rocky. The only reason she knew where she was going was because, a time or two, she'd explored the area when bored.

Redwood Ridge was pocketed between the Pacific Ocean and the Klamath Mountains. There was no direct access to the water since the elevation was high and rocky bluffs led to a sheer drop. The town had put up guard rails at the edge of the western part of the park, but they ended where the forest began.

The foliage grew thick the deeper she went since she had come from that direction. Rain tinged the air and a blanket of fog covered the ground. Immediately, she was swallowed by maples, oaks, cypress, and redwoods. Some trunks of the latter were wider than she was tall. A cloud cover ensured no extra warmth from the sun, but filtered daylight helped her in the trek.

A brisk, salty breeze blew from the bluffs, and she pulled her hood up to block the wind. Forty degrees felt more like thirty, and she sure hoped that missing girl was wearing more than the afore-mentioned sweatshirt. Though midday, it would only get colder as dusk descended. That wasn't even accounting for the danger of animal activity.

Poor thing must be scared out of her mind. Maddie remembered coming out here her first night, cold, frightened, and utterly alone. And she'd been a full-grown adult at the time.

Halfway to her tent, a rustling came from her left. She paused, hand on the strap of her backpack. She had her taser and BB gun in there, but couldn't recall if they were under her clothes or in the side pocket. She should've paid better attention as her heart thundered and she struggled to listen over the blood whooshing past her eardrums.

It would be surprising if the search parties had made it this far yet. She had no clue where, exactly, the girl had gotten separated from her class, but Maddie suspected this was too wayward a path for teachers to allow kids to venture. Then again, Delia had been missing for at least three hours. Or...

Maddie swallowed, her stomach in knots. *Or* a lynx, mountain lion, or bear was nearby. The rustling sounded way too loud for a squirrel or birds. Frozen, she darted her gaze everywhere, not spotting anything through the fog.

It came again, closer, louder, and Maddie frantically removed her pack, setting it on the ground. As she dug through, shoving aside clothes, a whimper rent the air. The snap of a branch cracked, then nothing.

Panting, struggling for air, she tilted her head as if that would help her figure out what it was or the direction of the noise. Several pulse-tripping moments passed. Just as she was about to root through her backpack again, the sound of a desperate, feminine whimper carried on the breeze. A helpless cry followed.

Maddie straightened. "Hello?"

A gasp, and all was quiet.

Heavy breathing. Not hers. To her right? Straight ahead?

"Hello? Anyone there?"

The breathing changed to a wheeze and had definitely come from her right. Not far away, either.

"Delia, is that you?" Gosh, she sure hoped so, if for no other reason than she was in a very isolated location.

Maddie slowly walked forward, rounding trees. She caught a flash of red and stepped over a large, fallen tree. Hunkered down was a girl, back to a trunk and hands over her head like she was dodging gunfire. Blonde strands peeked out from a hoodie. She conformed into a tighter ball, shaking.

Pausing, not wanting to frighten her, Maddie set her bag aside and held out her palms. "Delia? My name is Maddie. I live in Redwood Ridge, too. Everyone is looking for you, sweetie. I won't hurt you. Can I come closer?"

The girl jerked her head up and around. Dirt streaked her face and a thin trickle of blood dripped from her hairline to just above her eyebrow. It was almost dry, implying her injury had happened awhile ago.

Red-rimmed blue eyes stared back at Maddie, wide and panicked. "Am I in trouble?"

"No, sweetie. Everyone's just worried, that's all."

A sob, and Delia covered her face. "I didn't mean to get lost. I found some really cool mushrooms and was looking at them. Then I couldn't find anybody."

Maddie knelt in front of the girl. "You're okay now. We'll get you home in no time. I know the area pretty well. Can I look at your head first? You have a little blood right there." It didn't seem bad, just a scratch, but Maddie wanted to make sure before she started taking Delia back down the mountain.

She nodded, and Maddie got a little closer. It was, in fact, just a superficial cut, no longer than half an inch. It didn't appear deep enough for stitches.

"Nothing major." She smiled to hopefully ease the girl's mind.

"I bumped it on a branch."

"It happens. I'm quite the klutz myself." She smiled when Delia laughed, and took off her sweatshirt. "Here. Put this on. You're shivering. It's getting chilly out."

"Thank you. What was your name again?"

"Maddie." She kept it at that in case Delia recognized Maddie's last name. No sense in making her more frightened than she already was. "How about we get you home? Your parents will be happy to see you."

Chapter 19

Parker was being pulled in about fifty different directions at once, and they still hadn't found the Millers' daughter. Considering how often they'd done search and rescue for idiot tourists who thought they could handle the terrain and see all the pretty scenery, rescue personnel should have this down to a science by now.

But every case was unique, and this was a missing girl. One of their own. Added to the drama was the problem of where Delia had wandered off. None of the students seemed to recall when they'd last seen her and the two teachers chaperoning the trip hadn't done a head count since they'd gotten off the bus at arrival.

Parker was at the Millers' small brick ranch home down the road from his with Kevin, his best deputy, leading the hunt from a walkie-talkie and in constant contact with his dispatcher, Sherry. Their mayor, Marie, was stationed at Town Hall with the resident volunteers, coordinating efforts on that front. Jason was at the firehouse, directing his firefighters and the Wildlife Team, who were on the mountain, hopefully in the general area where the girl had disappeared.

Weather had been on their side. The temperature was mild, no rain or snow was forecasted, but that didn't mean squat when it came to the Pacific Northwest. Anything could happen at any time. Not to mention, if Delia had wandered north or east, had gone outside the safe parameters or markings, there was no accounting for animal activity.

Rendering her helpless. A scared, alone, innocent twelve-year-old.

Parker thought about Maddie again for the umpteenth time. How she'd been sleeping at a makeshift camp for who knew how long. She'd obviously taken precautions, had seemed to be doing well, but that didn't erase all the what-ifs.

Yesterday, while she'd been at work, he'd paid a visit to Harriet Nunez after speaking with her by phone. Above Ka-Bloom, the flower shop had a studio apartment she'd been using as storage space. All he'd had to do was tell the woman Maddie's situation, and Harriet had spent the day with two friends cleaning out the apartment. Harriet had felt terrible, but he'd reassured the woman no one had known Maddie's circumstances. It's how she'd wanted it.

Parker had furniture on the way, set to be delivered today. Harriet claimed Maddie had never been upstairs, so she wouldn't suspect the changes.

The plan? Harriet was going to ask Maddie to move in above the shop under the pretense of it being part of her new role as manager of Ka-Bloom. Free rent and included in her salary. It would get her out of a tent and under a roof. She could still work toward paying back the residents, but it wouldn't leave her homeless in the process.

And she'd never be the wiser that Parker had set up the whole thing. She could hold on to her pride.

His walkie crackled to life and Jason's voice emitted from the speaker. "You there, man?"

"Yep. Go ahead."

Parker glanced at the Millers on the other side of the well-worn oak table that matched outdated cabinets in the cozy kitchen, a map spread out between them on the surface. Red boxes outlined quadrants that were numbered. Three of the ten were blocked out, having already been searched to no avail. The couple were clinging to hope and sanity by a thin thread.

"Five, six, and seven are a no. Rick said there's no sign anyone's been there."

Rick being the head of the Wildlife Commission. His crew often aided in searches and handled animal activity.

Damn it. Parker pinched the bridge of his nose, frustrated. "Thanks."

Mrs. Miller choked a sob and began pacing anew. Her short salt and pepper strands were standing up on end from the number of times she'd fisted them and mascara smudges under her eyes had left raccoon marks hours ago.

Kevin offered Parker a pained smile and got on his radio to check the status at Town Hall.

Marie's voice pierced the speaker. "There's a camp set up in quadrant four. Empty, though. Volunteers are moving on to eight."

Kevin muttered a "thanks" and shrugged at Parker.

The camp was Maddie's. Parker hadn't been fond of the idea of volunteers searching that area, but a girl was missing. If Maddie wasn't there, where was she? Still at his place? Working? Perhaps she'd heard the commotion and had gone to hide?

He'd been on the cusp of telling her he loved her this morning when the Amber Alert had gone off, interrupting everything. Christ knew, he'd mulled over the words, how to say them, or even if he should, but she needed to know how he felt. Love was something that should never go unsaid. She may not be ready to hear it or feel the same way, yet he couldn't give a good damn.

There were instances, fragile moments, where he could've sworn she was right there with him, up to her eyeballs in ever-after. Ready to plunge or already sunk. But then she'd have periods where she'd shut down, armor in place, needing to protect herself because love had not been an emotion she could trust.

Again, he didn't give a shit. He'd say it until he turned blue and she went deaf. His whole adult life, he'd been idly seeking his other half, the person he wanted to go home to and spend forever beside. Fear and an obstinate gorgeous woman weren't going to stop him now that he'd found her.

Pulling his cell from his pocket, he got ready to text her to check in, but the front door banged the wall in the foyer. The *smack* reverberated down the hall and into the kitchen.

"Mom? Dad?"

Mrs. Miller let out a wail and rushed from the room, her husband on her heels. Kevin followed, allowing Parker to precede him.

In the few seconds it had taken him to walk across the hardwood floor to the front of the house, Delia was already sandwiched in a hug between her folks, nothing visible but the top of her blonde head.

"Oh, my God. Are you all right? What happened? Where were you?" Mrs. Miller held her daughter at arm's length, hands on her shoulders. "You scared us into the grave."

"I'm okay, Mom. I'm so sorry. I got lost."

"It's okay. You're home now." Another fierce hug caused the poor girl to grunt.

"Thanks to Maddie. She brought me back." Delia wiped at her tear-streaked face, soiled from the elements. "I didn't know what to do. She helped me."

Maddie? She was here?

Parker glanced past the family to the woman standing alone on the front porch. She had her head down, hair blocking her face, no coat, and shoulders braced against the wind. His heart turned over in his chest.

He walked closer and held open the screen door. "You found her?"

"Yeah." She stepped into the doorway, but didn't cross the threshold. "I was walking near the bluffs just inside the northwestern flatiron base when I spotted her. I think she's all right. A little scared, but all right."

"Maddie who?" Mrs. Miller, arm around her daughter's shoulders, turned toward the door. She sized up Maddie in one fell swoop. The relief and gratitude in the mother's expression flat-lined straight to contempt with a side of derision faster than a downshift. "Madeline Freemont," she ground through her teeth. "What did you do to my baby?" She looked at Delia, her gaze landing on a cut on her daughter's forehead. "Did she hurt you?"

"No, Mom." Delia pressed her hand to her head. "I bumped it on a branch. Maddie found me and brought me home. She didn't do anything wrong, I swear."

"Get out." Mr. Miller, silent most of the day until now, pulled his shoulders back until his spine resembled rigor mortis. "Get away from our daughter and out of this house."

"Dad, no! She helped me!"

"I'll leave." Maddie, head down, shoulders sunk, peeked over her nose at Delia. "I'm so glad everything worked out and

184

you're safe." She released an uneven breath, addressing the couple, but not making eye contact. "You have a very sweet daughter."

"Hold it." Parker, divided between duty and Maddie, held up a finger. He focused on the couple. "Maddie found Delia and brought her home. Nothing nefarious happened and your daughter is safe, thanks to her. Instead of yelling at her, how about some gratitude?"

Mr. Miller said nothing, jaw tight and posture rigid.

His wife, however, appeared confused and torn.

"It's okay, Parker. It doesn't matter." Maddie pivoted the porch.

The fuck it didn't matter.

"I'll be right back. Kevin, make sure no one moves." Parker chased after her, catching her on the sidewalk by the curb. He gently stopped her retreat with a hand on her arm. "Are you okay?"

"I'm fine." She stared at his chest in that submissive stance of avoidance he'd grown to despise. "The important thing is that Delia's safe and sound."

"Thanks to you."

She shrugged. "Right place at the right time." A swallow worked her delicate throat. "I don't think her head wound is serious, but they may want to have a doctor look at it. I'll see you later."

She started to walk away, but got nowhere since he was still holding her arm.

"Yes, you *will* see me later. Let me get the rescue crew updated and things calmed down here. Then we'll talk."

For the longest few seconds of his life, she stood, gazing at the horizon.

Finally, she shook her head. "There's nothing to talk about, Parker. I never should've allowed us to get this far. Tonight only proved me right." She chewed her lower lip. "We're done. These people? The town? They hate me. They're going to start hating you. Being together is going to kill the career you love."

185

"I can love you both." Shit. Okay. He probably shouldn't have blurted it out for the first time like that, but whatever. "I can love you and the job. In fact, I do."

For that, she looked at him. With awe. With regret. Then quickly shut it down as if the emotions had never been there at all. And he nearly died where he stood.

He knew her, knew every nuance and quirk and expression. And the one she was giving him now said there would be no getting through to her. Reason and emotion and all the rationalizations in the world were not going to get her to listen to him.

Worst part? The most gutting? She was telling him goodbye, ending the wonderful relationship they'd built because of him. She cared enough about him that she was willing to give up a good thing for the sake of his happiness.

The stubborn, blasted woman didn't realize *she* was what made him happy.

She cleared her throat, watery gaze drifting somewhere over his shoulder. Away. Already gone.

And there it was, punching him in the face even though it was his abdomen that felt the blow. Maddie didn't cry. She didn't open up and expose her tender side to just anyone. If there were tears in her eyes, those amazing baby blues, then he'd gotten under her skin, past muscle and tissue, around her ribcage, and had her heart in his hands.

"I love you, too." Her voice cracked, and her lids drifted closed. When she lifted them, her gaze was at her feet. Resolved. Determined. "Thank you for being kind to me and for trying. I wish you well, Parker."

She stepped off the curb. Walked away. Never looked back.

And he let her. For now. Because while she'd been trying to collect herself and say goodbye, he was planning. Scheming. Turning gears and figuring out the best form of attack.

He raised the walkie talkie to his mouth. "Stand down, everyone. Delia Miller has been found unharmed. She's home with her family. Thank you for all your efforts. Hang tight for orders from the mayor."

Pulling his cell from his pocket, he texted Marie. *Spread word. I'm issuing a town meeting in one hour. It is advised that all residents who are able should attend.*

The icon on his screen whirled, and a second later, the mayor replied. *You got it, sheriff.*

Her voice emitted from his radio speaker announcing the meeting as a press conference, but he shut off his unit and went back inside. Finding Kevin, he gave orders to take a statement from Delia and then head to the meeting.

An hour later, Parker stood a few feet from a podium in the Town Hall, next to Jason at the front of the long, rectangular room that was packed to the gills with townsfolk. Marie and her sisters were chatting on the other side of the stage and Kevin was behind them, beefy arms crossed and stance wide. Folding chairs in neat rows in the center of the hall were occupied, and standing room in the back and sides had people shoulder-to-shoulder. They only used this space for official business or committee meetings, but Parker had never seen it this full.

There were roughly eighteen-hundred residents in Redwood Ridge, and he'd say about half were in attendance. A good number and a decent start. Once he'd had his say, word would spread. One couldn't scratch their ass in this place without everyone knowing about it.

The one soul he didn't see? Maddie. Which was probably for the best.

Jason rubbed his jaw. "You know this capacity is against fire code, right?"

"Arrest me."

His buddy laughed. "With the cuffs you've got on you? People might get the wrong idea. Ella will probably take offense, too."

Frowning, Parker glanced at his utility belt. Next to his gun in a holster and his badge was his set of PD-issued handcuffs. Also attached were a pair of pink, fuzzy cuffs.

Christ. He couldn't help it. Despite all the pandemonium and what he was about to do, he laughed. Tilted his head back and laughed. Damn Maddie and her pranks, anyway. Mercy, did he love her. Most likely, she'd snuck those on his belt last night, unaware of the emergency that would unfold later.

"Didn't know you were that kinky, man."

Marie walked up to them and leaned close. "You ready to start?"

Parker nodded. Moreover, he was ready to finish.

The mayor gave a brief welcome to the crowd and announced Parker as if no one knew who the hell he was and this was a presidential press conference. Going with it, he smiled and stepped up to the podium.

Now or never. "Thanks to the effort of volunteers, the police department, the fire station, and Wildlife Rescue, I'm pleased to report Delia Miller is home with her family." He waited for the applause to die down. "The biggest thanks needs to go to someone else, though. Despite search parties doing their best, it was one citizen above all who found Delia and got her back safely. Madeline Freemont happened to be hiking at the time and came across Delia. She was scared and a little banged up, and who knows what could've happened if Maddie hadn't found her."

There was point-five seconds of deafening silence, and then the room erupted. Shouts and accusations were hurled into the air, making Parker even more determined and pissed off.

Temples throbbing, he put up his hand to quiet the room. "I'm the third generation of Maloneys in Redwood Ridge to serve this great town of ours as an officer. I'm a member of this community. And until recently, I've never been more proud to call this place home."

Well, that shut them up.

He glanced at his best friend since the age of diapers beside him. Jason nodded for Parker to keep going, an all-knowing grin twisting his lips like he'd caught on to Parker's plan.

Gripping the podium, he looked at all the recognizable faces, his parents among them in the front row. "We're not without our faults. Pinterest and Twitter serve as news and give us updates before the Ridge Gazette can go to print. There is no sense of privacy because we're the reason clichés exist. Everyone knows everybody's business and gossip spreads faster than wildfire. There's fog and overcast more often than sunshine. We're often judgmental and hold tight to old fashioned morals and values instead of updating with the times. We don't have chain super markets and fast food and mega stores dotting our landscape."

He sighed, nodding. "But those things are also the reason why we're so wonderful, why we choose to stay here amidst all the other places we could live. It's what makes us unique. We get to wake up each day with a view of the mountains to our east and the ocean to our west. There's community events for holidays. We can walk down the street and know the people we pass. If one of us goes down, there's hundreds of hands prepared to help us up again. We support one another. It truly does take a village, and you all raised me, as I hope one day you'll raise my kids."

A shake of his head, and he glanced at the wood grain of the podium before him. "Lately, I've been witness to a side of us that I didn't know existed. An ugly side that makes me ashamed. Madeline Freemont is a part of this town."

"The hell she is!"

"She's a liar and a cheat!"

"Put her in jail with her old man!"

Parker ground his teeth. "And that's exactly what I mean!" His shout rose above the others and echoed back to him. "Crowd mentality without the facts."

As the room grew quiet once again, he drew a calming breath. "Her father, Nicholas Freemont, and her ex-fiancé, David Weaver, did a terrible thing. They took advantage of us, scammed us out of our hard-earned dollars, and broke the law, never mind our trust. They will spend a very long time in prison for that. But Maddie wasn't a part of their crimes."

"Of course, you say that! You're sleeping with her!"

Several yells of confirmation rang through the room.

Parker threw his hands in the air and shrugged. "Yes, I am. I'm also in love with her."

Crickets chirped. Jaws dropped.

Jason barked a laugh. "I knew it."

Brows arched, Parker met their gazes, addressed them directly. "I'd like to say who I date or sleep with is none of your

189

business, but let's face it, that's not true. At least, you don't think so. Small town. Gossip. Rumors. Whatever label we slap on it doesn't matter. We make everything our business. Here's the thing you need to remember, though. I'm in love with her, yes, but I've never lied to you and would never get involved with someone who could do those things. I hold my position as sheriff because you put me here. You elected me. I do my job very well. So hear me when I tell you Madeline Freemont had no knowledge of her father's dealings and committed no crimes. If you have a hard time believing me, then ask our former sheriff. Dad?"

His father rose from his seat and turned to face the room. Parker had gotten his dark hair, height, and green eyes from him. What he inherited most was his dad's sense of integrity and honor. That's what Parker hoped made his old man proud of him, what Parker strove to achieve every second of the day. To stand up for what was right.

"It was me who initiated the first stage of the Freemont investigation and who eventually took it to the FBI. I was there for the entire duration." His dad shoved his hands in the pockets of his khakis and rocked on his heels. "Miss Freemont isn't guilty of anything except for romantic interest my son. I kind of feel sorry for her."

The crowd laughed.

"And for the record, I'm not sleeping with her."

More hoots and laughter.

"I also approve of their relationship."

Heads turned from him to Parker.

"Thanks, Dad." While his father reclaimed his seat, Parker sought the faces of those on Maddie's list. "She did nothing wrong, yet she's been repaying those of you who invested. You know who you are and many of you are in this room. It's going to take her a good long while, and she's doing it not because she's guilty, but because she thinks it's the right thing. Think about that, about what kind of person does something so noble. It comes at the expense of herself and her own well-being. She's working three jobs and a dozen side ones all so you can get your money back."

He looked at Marie, tilting his head for her to join him. He waited until she was by his side before nailing his coffin shut.

"We bolster one another. We help each other. But the person who needs it most is Maddie, and she hasn't received it. So, yeah, I'm ashamed of you, of us." He unclipped his badge and handed it to a wide-eyed Marie as gasps rent the air. "If the woman I choose to love and be with is making you lose faith in me as a sheriff, then I'll resign. If you don't believe in her innocence or character after all I said, then I'll quit right here, right now."

While the crowd muttered among themselves, Jason unclipped his fireman Captain's badge and passed it to the mayor, earning more gasps.

He leaned toward the microphone. "I've known this fool since before we could talk. Like you, I was skeptical of Madeline's supposed transformation. I remembered her as a rich bitch, and a mean one at that. But then I got to know her. If we all judge ourselves based on our pasts, then we're in big trouble. Before Ella, I was an unsettled hellion. Love and time changed me, made me a better man. Where Parker goes, I go. He resigns, I resign."

"Um, well." Marie set the badges on the podium and clasped her hands. "This is unexpected."

Jason grunted. "Like all the couples you matched through the years? You and your sisters?"

The crowd laughed.

"I guess we should discuss the matter on the table." Marie smoothed her shoulder-length brown bob as if suddenly nervous. "I, for one, would hate to see either of these great men quit their positions."

Parker shrugged. "The choice is yours, Redwood Ridge. Either you trust and believe me, or you don't."

Chapter 20

When Harriet had called Maddie yesterday and asked her to stop by the flower shop, she'd almost said no. She'd broken things off with Parker, had been yelled at and ordered to leave the house of a couple whose daughter she'd tried to help, and she wanted to crawl under a rock to die.

How quickly things had changed. Just a day before, she'd woken up in Parker's arms, secure in the knowledge they could possibly have a future. Then, bam. Bye-bye joy. Karma had the last word again.

Much as it killed her and she missed him, she'd done the right thing. He was the town hero and everybody loved him. Her included. He deserved nothing but happiness and a woman who wouldn't put a hitch in his career. When she'd walked away from him, she'd made the decision to stay in the Ridge one more year, pay off the last of the victims, then find another town where she could start fresh.

She just...couldn't do this anymore. Living in a tent, counting pennies, and afraid to show her face in public. Working her knuckles to the bone and receiving no appreciation for the effort. Parker had been correct about one thing. She hadn't done anything wrong. Residents of Redwood would never see it that way, though, and so she'd move on. Start over somewhere else.

One year. Three-hundred and sixty-five days until her liberation.

But then Harriet had called as Maddie had entered the park. She didn't know why, but she'd about-faced and headed to Ka-Bloom instead of up the mountain. Harriet had been good to Maddie and she couldn't make herself say no.

Shock would be an understatement and putting it mildly after Harriet's offer. She wanted Maddie to work full-time days at the shop as a manager, taking over all duties, and a perk to the position was free rent and board in the studio apartment over the store. She was already making more an hour at Ka-Bloom than her other two positions.

Honestly, she'd thought Harriet had jumped onboard the hate train and was playing a trick on Maddie. But, no. Here she was, in her very own place.

Safety.

Security.

Four walls and a roof.

Heat and air-conditioning.

Running water.

A refrigerator and a toilet.

Standing in the middle of the wide open space, she wanted to cry. It was even fully furnished.

There was hardwood throughout, except in the small bathroom, which had checkered tile. The walls were painted light beige and made the apartment seem even bigger. A nice bay window in the living room section looked out onto Main Street, sheers as curtains. A black sectional was situated in the middle of the area and served as a divider of sorts for the room. The plain black coffee table in front of it matched the simplistic TV stand housing a twenty-inch flat screen. No cable connection, but there was a Blu-ray player. Perhaps she'd celebrate later by borrowing a couple movies from the library.

The tiny kitchenette was separated by an island. White cabinets and countertops. Appliances, too. A two-burner stove resided next to a fridge. Eventually, she'd have to buy dishes and utensils. There was a private entrance via stairs in the alley behind the building, and the door to come and go was in the kitchen.

The bedroom was off to the right. Since it was a studio, there were no walls enclosing the area, but she could maybe buy a folding screen or something. No one would see her, anyway, so she guessed it didn't matter. The bed was a full size, also white, with a tall matching dresser and nightstand on either side. No sheets yet, but she'd get some.

Heaven. It was utter heaven.

Once she'd accepted Harriet's offer, Maddie had spent all night bringing her gear from camp up to the apartment. *Her* apartment. All hers. She'd unpacked her clothes, cosmetics, and had put her canned goods in the cabinet. Her notebooks she'd set in the nightstand drawer and would look at nightly like she'd been doing. Crunch numbers and pay back victims.

She hadn't slept a wink, and didn't care. This morning, she'd turned in her two-week notice at the school. She hated that job and working full-time at Ka-Bloom more than made up for the pay. She'd keep the position at the Rec Center a couple nights a week. Miles had been good to her and she liked cooking.

Her smile died on her lips as a wave of grief hit her square in the belly. She missed Parker. He'd never been inside her fake other apartment, but she wanted to invite him over to her real one. Cook them an intimate dinner for two and make love afterward. Maybe watch a movie and cuddle. This accomplishment seemed so hollow without being able to share it with him.

He'd texted this morning, saying congratulations on her new position. He'd texted late last night, too, claiming he missed her and they weren't over. He'd said he would give her time, but then they would talk.

There really wasn't anything to talk about. As long as the town harbored animosity toward her, his career would be at stake. Sheriff duties aside, no way could she stomach him being treated the way she had most of her life.

Still, she wanted to reply to his many 'I love you' messages. Alas, she hadn't the courage to respond.

A knock came from the door and she frowned. Harriet, perhaps? Striding over, she turned the knob to find...

"Darlene?" Maddie hadn't seen her former classmate since she'd come into the flower shop all flustered about her in-laws visit.

"Hello." Darlene smiled. "Sorry to bother you. I know moving can be so hectic, but can I come in for a second?"

"Uh, sure." Maddie stepped aside, granting the woman entry. "How are you?"

"Great, thanks. My mother-in-law loved those flower arrangements, by the way. I can't thank you enough. I brought you a house-warming gift. Sorry, but I didn't have time to wrap it." She held out a large plastic bag.

"Oh, wow. Thank you. That is totally unnecessary. You didn't have to do that." How had she known Maddie had a new apartment?

"Eh, it's just a small token. Have a look."

Maddie dug into the bag and pulled out a set of peach sheets, the exact size for her bed. Also a white comforter with pretty black dandelions on it.

"Oh, I needed sheets. Thank you so much." Suspicion mounted, but Maddie shrugged it off for the sake of politeness.

"You're very welcome. Now, the bedspread is a hand-me-down, but the sheets are new. I decided the design didn't fit in my guest room, so it's all yours." Just like that, Darlene turned and opened the door. "Sorry to cut and run, but I've got errands. Let's do coffee soon?"

"Uh, yes. Okay. That would be lovely."

And the woman was gone, leaving Maddie to stare after her.

Alrighty, then. How nice, though.

Smiling, she unwrapped the sheets and set them on the bed, preparing to make it, when another knock sounded. Figuring Darlene had forgotten something, Maddie headed across the living room to the kitchen, only to find Ella and Jason standing on her threshold.

"We don't mean to intrude." Ella grinned, flipping her long, cocoa locks over her shoulder. "I know you're busy, but we figured we'd bring by some bath towels. Jason and I combined households and these just don't match his décor. You know how it is. Maybe you could use them since you just moved? They're a nice pale yellow. There's a shower curtain in here, too." She passed Maddie a box.

"Uh, okay." She glanced at the box, then Parker's friends. "Thank you so much."

"Oh, anytime." Ella waved her hand in a whatever gesture. "We can't stay. I have grocery shopping to do, but I hope you like them."

Jason, charmer that he was, grinned. "I expect an invite for drinks soon. It's not home until someone gets drunk and passes out on your floor."

Unable to help it, Maddie laughed. "I suppose not. How's next week Friday?"

"Works for us. Happy new apartment."

"Thank you. And thanks for these. They'll be very helpful."

As she closed the door, she narrowed her eyes. Something was amiss here. How had Darlene known Maddie needed sheets and how had Jason or Ella known she'd needed towels? Sure, those were basic items and easy housewarming presents, but still. That was more conversation and friendly faces than she'd seen...well, ever.

She'd no sooner put the box in the bathroom, and yet another knock sounded. This time, the Battleaxes whooshed inside after she answered.

"Hello, my dear." Marie clasped her hands, her sisters on either side of her, each holding a bag. "We come bearing gifts. Every new place needs a set of dishes, silverware, and glasses."

All right. That was it. Not that Maddie wasn't grateful, but what in the heck was going on? Three different sets of visitors in under thirty minutes was just plain weird. And not a coincidence.

"I can see you're speechless. No worries. I apologize for not getting here sooner, but duties held me up." Marie smoothed the lapels of her pink power suit while her sisters set the bags on the floor. "We cannot thank you enough for helping little Delia yesterday. Everyone is talking about how great it was and how lucky she is you found her. Well, we're off. Ta-ta."

Jaw near her knees, Maddie stood frozen.

Was that what was happening? The town was thankful she'd helped Delia? The girl's parents sure hadn't seemed to think so last night. Then again, it only took one person to know she'd moved. In less than twenty minutes, the whole vicinity would be aware. Plus, the Battleaxes were a force to be reckoned with, and if they'd spread word about Maddie's role in bringing Delia home, then that could account for all the sudden positive attention. If the women had told the residents to show support, anyhow.

But, would it last? A few people weren't the whole population.

Another knock. Overwhelmed, Maddie almost didn't answer.

The three O'Grady brothers, who ran Animal Instincts Veterinary Clinic, and their wives smiled, waving at her. She'd gone to school with all three guys and two of the gals. It was the middle brother, Flynn's wife, Gabby, who came inside first, leading the pack.

"So glad to see you again." Gabby's long blonde ponytail slapped Maddie in the face as she hugged her. "We are all kid-free right now and thought we'd say hello while we had a babysitter."

She used sign language while she spoke, something Maddie recalled her doing because Flynn was deaf. Even as children, he and Gabby were inseparable best friends. It made sense they'd wound up together.

"It's, uh, good to see you, too?" Maddie probably shouldn't have phrased it like a question, but she hadn't really traveled in their social circles.

Cade's wife extended her arm. "We haven't chatted before. I'll just shake your hand until we know each other better. I'm Avery."

"Yes, hi. I'm Maddie. Nice to meet you."

The woman had a very soft, comforting way about her that radiated calm and take charge simultaneously. And it was very obvious why every female in the Ridge needed antidepressants when she'd fallen for Cade. Not only was he a reformed playboy and sexy as sin, but he obviously adored his wife. It was apparent by the way he smiled affectionately at her and smoothed her wavy light brown strands.

Actually, in honesty, all three men were attractive. Cade with sandy blond locks and blue eyes, Flynn a strawberry blond with hazel, and Drake with chestnut, almost black hair and deep brown eyes. Anyone could tell they were brothers by the high cheek bones and angular faces, plus the full mouths that screamed sensuality. Tall, lean, and with athletic frames.

Zoe, Drake's wife, nodded, her droll expression not as welcoming. "Madeline." She twisted her lips, running her tongue over her teeth. "You still a megawatt bitch?"

She was the one Maddie remembered most from her school days. The woman was a badass. Tiny, but mighty. She said exactly what she thought and filleted souls in her path. Maddie had been a little afraid of her. For years, Zoe had dyed her hair crazy, bright colors. No one knew why. Blue, pink, green, orange, red. Now, though, her short brown hair was natural and cut pixie short. It suited her pretty face and waifish body type. She also sported a very large baby bump. Like, ready-to-pop kind of bump.

"No." Maddie cleared her throat. "If I have to be, I guess, but no. I'm not that person anymore. I was acting out and trying to make others as miserable as me. Sorry for anything I might've said or done to you."

"Oh, no one does anything to me. You're good there." Zoe skimmed her gaze up and down Maddie as if sizing her up. A beat passed, and she nodded as if satisfied. "Awesome. We shall be friends. In that token, we come with a peace offering." Her eyes narrowed. "Are you allergic to cats?"

What? "No."

Drake opened the door, reached down, and brought in a small animal carrier. "We checked with Harriet first. She said pets are allowed. This sweetheart is eight weeks old and the only survivor of her litter. She's had all her vaccinations, is spayed, and has taken well to litter box training."

Before Maddie could sputter words, Cade opened the door and brought in a large tote.

"Supplies. Give me a sec." He strode through the kitchen toward the bathroom.

Ah, geez. Um… "I don't know how to take care of a cat."

"Totally simple." Gabby waved her hand, dismissing Maddie's concern. "They're pretty independent. Food and water daily. Scoop the litter. Come in for check-ups once a year. Dole attention. You're friends with Ella Sinclair, right? Jason's fiancé? She's great with cats. Drop her a call if you have questions. Or we're always around."

199

If she said so. Maddie always did want a puppy or kitten. Something to cuddle with who would love her unconditionally.

Cade returned, set the tote on the floor, and took the carrier from Drake, disappearing again. Moments later, he rejoined them. From the tote, he took out two small dishes and a mat, arranging them on the floor in the kitchen along the wall. He filled one with water and one with food, put a bag of food on the counter, then tossed a couple small fuzzy pink balls around her living room.

"All set. Her litter box is in the bathroom. She's actually using it now. You'll want to show her where her food is when she's done. The balls will keep her busy and give her something to play with so she doesn't get into trouble. All you have to do is name her."

"Wow. I, uh…don't know what to say." Adopting a pet was not on her list of to-do's. Admittedly, she was excited and curious. "Thank you."

"Well, we'll let you get settled." Gabby hugged Maddie again. Tighter. "I'm very glad we got to reconnect. Let's do a girl's night out soon. It'll be fun."

Zoe rolled her eyes and pointed to her belly. "Designated driver here."

A laugh, and Maddie ran her fingers through her hair, beside herself. "That sounds great. Thank you again. This was…wonderful." She glanced at the six of them, a content family and noticeably very happy. They'd found love thanks to a trio of matchmaking Battleaxes. She couldn't help but be jealous. "Come by anytime."

Flynn signed something she couldn't interpret.

Gabby watched him and grinned, lighting her cherubic face. "He says you might regret that and asked if you want to have a drink at Shooters on Saturday night."

Dang. Just…dang it. "Count me in."

Over the next two hours, she had a steady stream of visitors, proving her earlier doubts wrong about a couple people being nice not translating to the whole population. And presents. All of them brought presents.

Miles and Brent with lamps. The ladies from the hair salon with three framed photos of nature for her walls. The owner of Le Italy Restaurant with a pan of lasagna. Frank from the hardware store with a plunger, batteries, and extra light bulbs. Emma Jane from Shooters with bottles for mixed drinks and a bartending book. Sharon from Sweetums Bakery with cupcakes. Jessica from the nursery with two potted ferns.

Mr. King from the market had been most surprising. He'd brought her fresh groceries. Inside a bag next to milk was a note that said, *Your debt is paid. No more rounding up your purchases. Please use the front entrance from now on.*

Beside herself, Maddie sat on the edge of the bed, throat clamped, eyes wet, and chest aching. She petted the brown and black fur of her new calico kitten as she held her in her lap, listening to the quiet hum of her purr and wondering how this had happened.

Her head spun just thinking about her good fortune. Maybe, just maybe, her luck was changing? People were realizing she wasn't the monster her father was and she hadn't hurt them?

Blowing out a breath, she looked at the kitten. She was insanely cute and affectionate. Maddie was in love already. "You need a name."

A squeak served as a half-hearted meow.

"Squeaky? No," she said immediately, not liking it. "Hope?" Not bad, especially considering Maddie's new found sense of hope blooming. It didn't seem to fit, though.

Her cell pinged an incoming text.

"We'll discuss a name and find one we both can agree on." Rising, she set the kitten on the floor and found her phone on the island.

Parker. He'd been the incoming text. Her belly somersaulted and promptly sank. Hesitating, she unlocked her screen.

Please look out your front window.

Confused, she moved to the pane. And gasped.

No. No way.

Easily, a hundred people stood on the street, staring up at her window. She scanned the faces, and none of them seemed to be her visitors from today. Pressing a hand to her chest, she struggled to breathe.

Just as she thought perhaps the hoard had come with torches and pitchforks, Parker stepped forward to the front of the group, a bouquet of cheerful flowers in his hand. He glanced at his phone, thumb moving over the screen.

Open the window.

She stared at his message, struck stupid.

Please, honey?

Snapping to, she unlocked the latch and lifted the pane, sticking her head out. "Parker? What's going on?"

He held out his arms, grinning. "Thought I'd bring a few friends over."

A few? Half of them wouldn't fit inside her tiny studio. And none of these residents had been particularly friendly to her in the past.

"To clarify, they're your friends *and* mine. That's what we do here in Redwood Ridge. We show support and help one another. We're odd, but you'll get used to it. I'm the sheriff here in these parts, and this is the welcoming committee."

Oh, sweet Baby Jesus in the Manger. It was him. Today had been all his doing. The visitors, the presents, the smiling faces. All Parker. She knew it.

To the left, someone lifted a white poster board and flipped it over, exposing a word. Others in a line followed until each individual sign spelled out, *Welcome To Redwood Ridge.*

She slapped a hand over her mouth, swallowing a sob. Her sinuses stung and her eyes watered until she could barely make out their forms. Her chest cracked wide open.

Another text came through. She had to wipe her eyes to read it. He'd sent a link, and after clicking on it, her knees gave out.

It was the town's Pinterest account. Specifically, a board titled "Parker & Madeline." There were a couple pictures of them as children, taken in their various classrooms. First grade and fourth? Another was of him at bat in high school, her in the background in a cheerleader costume. A recent, candid shot of them from the café was there, along with two of them in costumes at the Halloween Party.

And, smack her with the stupid stick. How in Hades had she not connected those dots sooner? All the unexpected pop-ins at her jobs? The way he'd just kept showing up wherever she'd been? For three years, they'd never crossed paths. Until a couple weeks ago.

They'd been on the Battleaxes radar. Matched and set up without her knowing it. Each couple they'd paired had their own board. And there was hers and Parker's.

Her phone pinged with a second link. This one was to a tweet from the @RedwoodRidge account. *Huge thank you to Madeline Freemont for helping to bring our dear Delia home. We are forever grateful.*

More texts to more tweets came through.

These spooky and cool flowers for the Halloween Party were made by the awesome Madeline from Ka-Bloom. Attached was a picture of the arrangement she'd made.

It was hard saying goodbye to our lovely librarian, Fern, but these gorgeous and personal arrangements made by Madeline at the flower shop sure were a great tribute.

Ruh-roh, Redwood-ians. We spot a new couple in town. Check out our sheriff and his girl. We think they are adorbs. That tweet had a picture of her and Parker walking down the street outside the café.

All the responses were positive ones, complimenting her arrangements or saying she and Parker looked good together.

What had he done? In twenty-four hours, he'd managed to sway a good portion of the population in her favor. How? How on Earth…?

Can I come up?

Shaking, she typed a reply. *Yes.*

Waving her hands in front of her face, she took several deep breaths to compose herself. Regardless, she wasn't ready when Parker strode in, shutting the door behind him.

Her stomach flopped and her skin heated.

Gah. So handsome. Jeans and a blue tee. Scruff and wind-blown black hair. Purposeful stride and…

He tossed the bouquet on the sofa on his way to her. "Those are for you, but first, I need to say something."

Arm around her waist, hand in her hair, he hauled her halfway up his body and sealed his lips to hers. A firm, unyielding kiss that stole the oxygen from the room and left her dizzy. She grabbed his shoulders for balance, but he opened his mouth, tilted his head, and stroked his tongue with hers, rendering her incapacitated to anything but him.

Pulse pounding, heart tripping, she moaned.

He eased away and rested his forehead to hers. "Do I make myself clear or do I need to repeat myself?"

"Huh?"

"Repeat myself it is."

Again, he went at her, devouring her in a kiss that left her a pile of goo.

"That's what I think of your goodbye. We're not over. We're not even just beginning. This has been in the cards since you first stole my ball cap at recess and ran away with it in kindergarten. You might have realized the potential, but it took me a little longer." He smiled, brushing his nose against hers. "Sorry for the delay. I'm here now."

"Okay," she whispered. Shock wouldn't allow her to say more.

"And I hate to say I-told-you-so, but, well. I told you so. They've come around, our beautiful town, and have accepted you. Forgiveness was a mere matter of time and they realize you aren't to blame for your father's mistakes. Some may hold grudges, but they will see reason soon, as well."

He wasn't giving up on them? And he'd swayed the residents he served toward her side? It had to be him. There was no other explanation or a soul who cared about her enough to try the feat. Helping Delia wouldn't have produced an outcome to this degree.

It wasn't real. None of it. Was it?

"You orchestrated all this, didn't you? The apartment, the job offer, the gifts people brought, and them believing the truth. This was all your doing."

"No, honey. Your work ethic and creativity got you the job and its perks. The presents were from residents wanting to do something nice. And the truth was there all along. You proved it to them by helping to bring a scared, lost girl home. By repaying debts that weren't yours. By being you."

Biting her lip, she stared at him, her eyes hot and her heart full. "What about you?"

"Me?" He swallowed, smiling as his gaze swept her face in a tender caress. "You had me all along. I love you. Your giving nature and your spine of steel. How you challenge me on everything. Your sassy mouth. The way you can handle anything life throws and still come out stronger for it. The adorable pranks." He reared. "By the way, nice one with the pink handcuffs. I thought Jason was going to die laughing as I stood in front of Town Hall with those things on my belt."

She rolled her lips over her teeth. "Sorry."

"No, you're not."

"Yeah, I'm not." Wait. "Town Hall? For what?"

"Nothing you need to worry about. Just updated the townsfolk on a few facts." He grinned, green eyes alight. "I wasn't done. Quit interrupting. I love the way you are with Domino. Your beauty inside and out. I love how you make me feel. *You* are what I've always wanted."

"You're what I needed." She closed her eyes a moment, cupping his cheeks. How had she gotten so lucky after a lifetime of none? When she looked back at him, it was all she could do not to cry. "I love you, too."

"Good. Guess I won't need to use the handcuffs, after all."

"I think you should."

He laughed, vibrating her ribcage. "All right. Remember it was your idea." Carefully, he set her on her feet, arms still tight around her. "I have ideas of my own."

She just bet he did. In question, she raised her brows. "Pray tell, sheriff."

"Well," he drolled, face tilted toward the ceiling. "It involves you in a white dress and me in a tux sometime soon. Shortly after that, perhaps in a couple years, there will be little humans with tiny feet running through our house. Domino will help babysit and wrangle them, of course."

She was not going to cry again. *She wasn't.* "Of course."

"And it involves get-togethers with friends, where we'll tolerate Jason's company because we really want to see Ella."

"That's a given."

"And side-by-side rocking chairs as we grow old and watch fading sunsets. Family and home and happy endings. That sort of thing."

"I see." Solemnly, she nodded, when she wanted to squeal at the heavens. "They aren't bad ideas. There's one flaw to your plan, though."

His brow wrinkled. "What?"

She jerked her chin at the small furball squeaking a meow by their feet. "Her."

He blinked at the kitten. "Where did she come from?" He shook his head. "Never mind. Rocking chairs, fading sunsets, happy endings, and a cat in the window. Deal?"

"Deal." A contented sigh, and she rested her cheek on his pec. She didn't know what she did to deserve this or him, but whatever. She'd accept, with open arms, this overflowing amount of joy and never take it for granted. "It sounds perfect."

Check out more books in the Redwood Ridge series, including an excerpt from the first chapter of *Residual Burn*, below…

Fall in love one laugh at a time…

Redwood Ridge series by bestseller Kelly Moran
www.AuthorKellyMoran.com

www.AuthorKellyMoran.com
Enchanting ever-afters…

Residual Burn
Redwood Ridge 4
© 2019 by Kelly Moran

Chapter 1

"You cannot be serious." Hands on his hips, Jason Burkwell glanced up and shook his head, then looked around, expecting to be *Punk'd*. Maybe they were reincarnating the show just for his benefit.

No cameras. No laughing crowds of hyenas as if he were the butt of an infamous joke.

Sunlight filtered through the budding trees onto the sidewalk and adjacent asphalt street. A soft spring breeze drifted, bringing a hint of snow and pine from the Klamath Mountains in the distance. Other than a couple guys from his unit, there were a few stragglers coming out of their homes to catch the action. All in all, though, it was same ole, same ole in their quaint little postage stamp town.

"I'm always serious." Lou crossed his beefy arms above his paunch, gray mustache twitching. The rustle of his tan and yellow turnout gear crackled over that of the rig's dying siren as he faced Jason. "A call's a call."

Uh, yeah. Ten years as a firefighter at Redwood Ridge's sole station, three of those being a lieutenant, countless emergencies from wildfires to pedestrians in trapped cars, but not once had Jason responded to...

"That's a cat in a tree, Lou." He peeked up at the white ball of fur cowering on a branch. The thing was tiny and maybe a few weeks old. How the hell did it get up there? "This is so cliché, it's a crime."

The two other jugheads in full gear laughed from their positions against the truck.

"Well, aren't you going to get it down?" Mrs. Fieldstone, two-hundred years young if she was a day, frowned at him through coke-bottle glasses. "Quit pussy-footing around."

The jugheads laughed harder at her unintentional quip.

He whipped them a shut-it-or-die glare and faced his former elementary school principal. All four-feet, ninety pounds of her was just as frightening now as she'd been when he'd sat in her office as a boy countless times for whatever he'd done wrong. "Of course. One of us will get right on it."

"It's your turn," Lou grumbled. "I took the last call."

Jason pinched the bridge of his nose. "Oh, come on. Name any occasion where we've responded to a 911 dispatch about..." He waved his hand at one of the many maples lining the suburban street, barely biting back the retort he would've rather said had scary Mrs. Fieldstone not been standing beside him. "An animal in need."

"Last week." Lou sniffed. "The Sundry's cocker spaniel dug up Gertrude Miller's prize-winning rose bushes. Again. I had to listen to her yammer for thirty minutes. I repeat, it's your turn."

Okay, fine. Yes, most of his job involved non-emergent cases. Fifteen-hundred residents in idealistic small town Oregon, it wasn't like he expected to diffuse bombs. Half the time, he spent his shift playing poker at the station or putting out kitchen fires gone awry. But, dude. A cat in a tree? This was embarrassing.

Parker Maloney pulled up in a PD-issued blue Charger and climbed out of the vehicle. As the sheriff, he didn't wear a custom uniform. Instead, he had on a white tee, open leather jacket, and jeans. Habit put his hand on the holster at his waist while he stepped onto the curb beside Jason.

"What's going on?" Parker removed his sunglasses, exposing green eyes that rarely missed a thing, and shoved his fingers through his black hair. "Everybody okay?"

Jason snorted and bumped his chin toward the branch above their heads.

Up went Parker's brows, lips twitching. "If that's not the most cliché thing I've seen, I'll eat my handcuffs." He leaned closer to whisper out the side of his mouth. "There's a pussy joke in here somewhere."

What a comedian. Jason narrowed his eyes on his best friend since the age of potty training, not surprised he'd thought the same thing moments ago. "Wayne, fetch me the short ladder, would you? Let's get this done." He had a beer with his name on it at Shooters. Hopefully, with a hot woman as a chaser.

"Sure thing, boss."

"Mrs. Fieldstone, you're looking pretty as always." Parker leaned around Jason and winked.

"Pah." She waved her hand and blushed. "Such a sweet boy. Why you still hang around with this hellion is beyond me." She jerked a thumb at Jason and scowled. "Trouble with a capital T."

"That he is, ma'am. I've got an eye on him."

"Keep it up, and I'll tell her who really stole the mascot costume and strung it up the flagpole in seventh grade." Jason ran his tongue over his teeth and accepted the ladder from Wayne.

Positioning it against the tree, he climbed several rungs until he was at shoulder-height with the branch. The white furball trembled and stared at him through big blue saucers. All right. It was kinda cute. He went to reach for it, but it cowered and scooted farther away.

Mew.

"I don't know what you're complaining about. You're not the one losing his man card and self-respect in front of an audience." Unbuttoning his outer gear, he slipped the coat from his shoulders and dropped it on the ground.

A catcall whistled from across the street. "Take it all off, Jason!"

"See?" he murmured to the furball and turned his head. "Now, now, Mrs. Rutherland. What would your husband say?"

Mew.

"I'm comin', I'm comin'." He stretched his arm across the branch, then held his hand still for the cat to sniff. After a beat, the furball eased closer and rubbed against his fingers. "There you go." Gently, he plucked the thing from where it had its claws dug into the bark and set it against his chest. It burrowed into his tee and kneaded, promptly falling asleep. "You're welcome."

As he climbed down, cradling the purring kitten, cheers rang out like he'd saved a group of children from a nitroglycerin factory or something. He rolled his eyes and took a bow while Wayne secured the ladder to the truck.

"That's all, folks." Lou lumbered behind the wheel of the rig, the jugheads jumping in back. "Have a good weekend," Lou called out the window.

"Hold it." Jason ground his jaw. "Where do you think you're going? You're not leaving me here."

"It's officially," Lou glanced at his wrist, where no watch was present, "off-duty o'clock. That fuzzball's not getting in my truck. Parker will drive you back to the station after you figure out where to go with your new girlfriend."

Seething, Jason watched the rig disappear around the corner, then glared at the cat. "Don't get too attached. I don't do relationships." Neighbors began to disperse into their homes and he faced Mrs. Fieldstone. "Here you go. One rescued kitten."

"That's not mine." She lifted her cane in a move Luke Skywalker would've been proud of and shook her head. "You think because I'm an old woman and live alone I have a hoard of felines skulking around? Well, I don't. I hate cats." She looked at Parker. "Arrest him for stereotyping." With that, she did an about-face and hobbled up her front walk.

Jason stood a good five seconds after her door slammed, staring. "Doesn't matter how old I get, she's still a scary broad."

Parker chuckled, the jerk. "You have the right to remain silent. Not sure stereotyping is an actual crime, though. I'll have to check ordinances."

"Yeah, yeah. Laugh it up." Jason sighed and glanced down. Furball had made itself right at home between his pecs and was vibrating his ribcage. "Now what?"

"Come on. I'll drive you over to the Animal Instincts clinic. The O'Grady boys will know what to do." Parker snatched Jason's coat from the ground and strode to the car. He tossed the jacket in the backseat and held the rear door open for Jason. "Offenders sit in the back."

Narrowing his eyes, Jason dropped in the front seat and finagled the belt. "Explain why I put up with you again," he said as Parker got behind the wheel.

"To wheedle out of speeding tickets?"

Good point.

They were silent as they drove out of the subdivision and onto Main Street. Passing lampposts and storefronts with awnings, Parker slowed to a snail's pace in case one of the many townsfolk crossed without paying attention--a common occurrence. A dense pocket of fog hovered in the distance, near the cliffs hugging the Pacific, and brine hung heavy in the air. Spring fever ran rampant and pastel eggs hung from oak trees lining the cobblestone road.

Jason would've rather slept through the season, if it was all the same to him. Easter baskets and jellybeans reminded him of the day his dad died, forever left an itch under his skin and an ache in his chest. Going on twenty years, and it still felt like yesterday Lou had shown up on his mom's doorstep, covered in soot and a haunted look in his eyes.

Maybe it was time to take a weekend trip. Jason was due for another one of his adventures from reality.

Parker turned into the veterinary clinic's lot and cut the engine. Though Jason knew the three O'Grady brothers and their wives, had grown up with them, he hadn't been in the office since he was a boy and their father had run the place.

Together, he and Parker exited the car and headed inside. Animal fur and Lysol blended for an interesting mix of scents. To the left, the waiting room was empty and decorated with a cheerful mural of dogs and cats doing human things. To the right was the front desk, where two women were bent over a chart. A large cage containing a cockatoo sat off to the side and a cat glared balefully from atop the printer.

Avery, Cade's wife, glanced up and smiled. "Hey, guys. We were just closing, but come in." She brushed her wavy brown strands from her face and rocked an infant seat on the counter with her other hand. "What brings you by?"

"Jason got himself a new pet." Parker leaned across the desk and grinned at the newborn sleeping in the carrier. "He's gotten bigger in the couple weeks since I've seen him. May I?"

Since babies made him twitchy, Jason stayed put. Parker was a natural with kids and the family thing, despite not having a wife and little ones of his own. Jason, not so much. He'd rather gnaw off his dominant arm than settle down.

"Oh, sure." She unclasped the harness fit for mountain climbing and passed the bundle to Parker. "Watch it, though. Ovaries will clench all over the Ridge if they see you holding a baby."

A laugh, and Parker shook his head. "I'll risk it. Handsome guy. Good thing he takes after you and not Cade."

"I heard that." Wearing blue scrubs, the youngest O'Grady came out of the back room and kissed his wife's cheek. "Can't disagree, however."

Gabby, Flynn's ball and chain, flicked her blonde ponytail off her shoulder and dropped her gaze to Jason's chest. "Is this the cat you rescued from the tree?"

"Damn. It's been, what? Twenty minutes?" Gossip pretending to be news traveled fast in these parts, but even that was record speed. Jason stroked the kitten's head. "It didn't have any tags."

"Let's take a peek." She came around the desk, rubbing her very pregnant belly. She attempted to take the furball from him, but it let out an angry mewl and clung to his tee, so she withdrew. "Aw, she's already attached. Definitely a girl. Why don't you follow me? Flynn can do a quick exam. He'll be glad to get out of a meeting with the Battleaxes, anyway."

Jason froze. "They're here? As we speak?"

Terror struck his midsection. The Battleaxes, as Cade had once named his mother and two aunts, were meddling busybodies who ruled the town with an iron fist, oatmeal cookies, and a side of matchmaking. They'd set up countless couples over the years and didn't compute the meaning of the word no. Jason had done his level best to stay off their radar.

"Yep." Gabby smiled, turning her head as another brunette entered the room.

Ah, Zoe. He'd always had a soft spot for her. They'd grown up together and their formal communication had primarily been flirtation, even though they'd never hooked up. There were very few women he liked too much to sleep with, and Zoe was numero uno. Besides, she was married to Drake now, the oldest vet brother.

"You can't be that desperate for some action." She grinned and erased the distance, offering an awkward hug with the furball between them. "This chick's not even your species." She petted the kitten.

"Zoe, baby, are you jealous?" He drew her to his side with his free arm and... Hold the phone. Was that a baby bump she was sporting? Had to be. With her waifish body type, it was hard to miss. "Man, not you, too. Is there something in the water? When are you due?"

"September." She pulled a sonogram image from her scrubs pocket. "Meet the newest O'Grady fetus."

"Hell," he grumbled, smiling at the black and white blob. "Grats to you both. But if you were interested in being knocked up, why not call me first?" Not that he was serious. No way, no how. He'd spoil the crap out of Parker's offspring instead if his best buddy ever found his mate.

"Next time."

"I've got an event committee meeting." Avery slung a purse over her shoulder and faced Parker. "Just pass the baby off to Cade when you're tired of holding him." She kissed her husband and the infant's cheek, then rushed out the door.

Speaking of. If the Battleaxes were in the building, Jason needed to bolt also. "Gabby, want to take the furball so I can leave?"

"If Flynn's going to examine her, you'll have to stay and take her home afterward."

"Uh, the cat's not mine. Can't you guys find her a family? You do that, don't you?" His apartment didn't allow pets, even if he did suddenly want the responsibility. Which he didn't.

"Our boarding room is full." She shrugged in a sorry-not-sorry gesture.

Well, crap. He opened his mouth, but quickly shut it again when Drake and Flynn emerged, followed by a middle-aged blonde, brunette, and redhead. The breath stalled in Jason's lungs while his brain screamed *abort*.

"Parker, Jason, lovely to see you." Marie, town mayor and eldest Battleaxe, puffed her brown bob and clasped her hands.

"Jason, how convenient we should bump into you. I was about to head to the station to ask you a favor."

He shot a panicked look at Zoe, but her *I-dunno* expression was of no help.

If they wanted a favor, one of two things were about to happen. Either they were going to swallow his soul, leaving him indebted to them, or they were attempting to set him up with whoever they thought was his perfect match. There went his ten-year streak of avoiding them. It had been a good run, he supposed.

"Oh, don't look so afraid." Rosa, middle Battleaxe and unnatural redhead, smoothed her cheetah-printed shirt. "It's just a teensy-weensy little thing."

He doubted it and focused on Parker, handing the newborn to Cade, while he thought of an exit strategy. Screaming and running probably wouldn't work. They'd chase him. Or would get their flying monkeys to do it. Flynn was flipping through a chart, and Drake, after covering the bird's cage, picked up the cat off the printer and was halfway down the hall. The guys were of zero assistance.

"We appreciate all you do for our town." Gayle, youngest Battleaxe and the boys' mom, smiled serenely at Jason. Her champagne hair was two shades lighter than Cade's and less strawberry than Flynn's. She was the calmest of the three, but shouldn't be discredited as part of the Cupid Cult, angelic appearance aside. "We thank you for doing your part in keeping us all safe."

Parker coughed, grinning behind his fist.

Again, Jason opened his mouth, but Rosa had her phone aimed at him. "What are you doing?"

"Documenting your harrowing rescue, of course." Several clicks filled the room before her thumbs flew over the screen faster than a hummingbird's wings. "And...done." She nodded. "Nice, we have ten @ responses on Twitter already."

He sighed and glanced at the kitten, oblivious to his torment. "What's the favor?" He was going to regret asking, but any longer in their presence and his head might explode.

"Bye, Mom." Cade, infant carrier in tow, kissed Gayle's cheek and strode out.

Drake came out of the back room, wrapped an arm around Zoe's waist, and headed for the door. "Lock up, kid, would you please?"

"You got it." Gabby went behind the desk by Flynn, where Parker had successfully put himself out of the line of fire.

Abandoned, Jason tentatively eyed Marie. "Lay it on me." At this rate, he'd agree to selling Girl Scout cookies if it meant ending this day. "The favor?"

Marie adjusted her pink power suit. "As you know, the annual Firefighter's Charity Ball is next weekend. We'd like your help."

Uh-huh. "I signed up for the raffle tickets at the donation table." Actually, he was big behind the scenes, too. It was his way of honoring his dad while getting more funding for the station. There were only five paid employees at the house, him being one of them, but the rest were volunteers. Donations raised went into updating equipment, rig maintenance, and other things so they didn't drain the town's resources. "Do you need me for a longer shift?"

"No, we think you'd be better in a different capacity. The auction, in particular."

Oh. His shoulders sagged in utter relief. No matchmaking, no soul-sucking errand. Just transferring his services during the venue. "Not a problem. I can do that."

"Excellent." Marie nodded, and the posse moved to the exit. "We'll send someone by with the details sometime this weekend. We're off to a committee meeting."

"Okay," he muttered, but they were already gone. He frowned, wondering why they'd made such a big deal of the situation. Until he looked at the others behind the desk and did a double-take at their raised brows and stupid grins. "What?"

"Uh." Parker rolled his lips over his teeth. "You know, the thing you just agreed to is a Bachelor Auction. As in, women will bid on you. For an exclusive date."

ABOUT THE AUTHOR:

Kelly Moran is a best-selling & award-winning romance author of enchanting ever-afters. She is a Catherine Award-Winner, RITA Finalist, RONE Award-Winner, Readers' Choice Finalist, Holt Medallion Finalist, and a 2014 Award of Excellence Finalist through RWA. She's also landed on the "10 Best Reads" and "Must Read" lists from USA TODAY's blog.

Kelly's been known to say she gets her ideas from everyone and everything around her and there's always a book playing out in her head. No one who knows her bats an eyelash when she talks to herself. Her interests include: sappy movies, MLB, NFL, driving others insane, and sleeping when she can. She is a closet coffee junkie and chocoholic, but don't tell anyone. She's originally from Wisconsin, but she resides in South Carolina with her three sons, a cat, and her two dogs. She loves connecting with her readers.

www.AuthorKellyMoran.com